There was a time—not so long ago—when the people of America came together with a common purpose; when those who were not fighting on foreign soil were united at home by victory gardens, ration books, production lines; when a year could pass with no holidays, no vacations, and often no time off; when personal sacrifice was the theme.

Forty years later, the concept of such a national effort must seem overwhelming and, indeed, outside the experience of many readers; but for some of us it is a very real memory—not a bad one, at that! A job had to be done, and with the work, the privations and restrictions came also laughter and joy.

SWING SHIFT

Building the
Liberty Ships

Joseph Fabry

Strawberry Hill Press

Strawberry Hill Press
2594 15th Avenue
San Francisco, California 94127

Manufactured in the United States of America

Edited and typeset by Jane Leith Cormack
Book design by nina
Cover design by nina
Drawings by David Healy

Library of Congress Cataloging in Publication Data

Fabry, Joseph B.
  Swing Shift.

  1. World War, 1939-1945--Fiction. I. Title.
PS3556.A27S9   813'.54   81-14449
ISBN 0-89407-049-5 (pbk.)   AACR2

Sincere thanks to

    The Dorothea Lange Collection, Oakland Museum, Oakland, California

    National Archives, San Bruno, California

    National Liberty Ship Memorial: SS *Jeremiah O'Brien*, Golden Gate National Recreation Area, Fort Mason, Pier 3 East, San Francisco, California

    National Maritime Museum, Foot of Polk Street, San Francisco, California

    The Richmond Museum, 4th and Nevin Streets, Richmond, California

    Karen Larsen and Richard Sloss

and everyone who was so helpful in assisting us with photographs. A very special thanks to Mr. and Mrs. Elvis Horn of San Pablo, California, and to Mr. Chris Gjerde of Richmond, California, who supplied us with the cover photograph of his welding gang.

*To the women and men who interrupted their
lives to build the ships that helped defeat
the enemies of freedom, and to my grandchildren,
Heidi and Shala, who benefit from this sacrifice.*

NOTE: Written in 1943, these stories
were retrieved from a bottom drawer
in the spring of 1980.

The Permanente Metals Corporation

Richmond · California

March 2, 1944

When the history of this war is written, the fact will be recognized that the merchant ship which did the most outstanding job in helping to win the war was the Robert E. Peary. A 10,500 ton Liberty ship, her keel was laid in Richmond's Yard Number Two, November 8, 1942, 12:01 A.M. She was launched 4 days, 15 hours and 29 minutes later, November 12, 1942, 3:30 P.M. The new assembly methods, tried out the first time with the Robert E. Peary, made it possible to cut the average building time of a Liberty ship from 241 days in January, 1942, to 41 days for the nation and 28 days for the Pacific Coast in January, 1944. It made it possible to swell the Liberty fleet from two vessels delivered in December, 1941, to approximately 1800 ships delivered by the end of December, 1943. It made it possible for the shipbuilders to meet the 18,900,000-ton quota for 1943.

Today our Liberty ships dominate the seven seas. They licked the U-boat crisis, made possible the invasion of North Africa and Italy, helped regain territory in the South Pacific while supplying American and Allied troops in every corner of the globe.

These are dry facts and figures. They are good to know before you read this book which concerns itself only with the human side of the story. It is the story of a topnotch gang, the gang that assembled the Robert E. Peary. It is the story of the man behind the man behind the gun. It tells you what kind of stuff those heroes of production are made of. Nobody would be more surprised than Jason, Alibi, Pee-Wee and all the other members of the Gang on Assembly Way Five if you called them heroes. They are just housewives, salesmen, farmers, school kids. They have come from all over the country to do some work, work which is done in the best American pioneer spirit. They work and laugh, enjoy life and love—and very seldom do they realize that they, too, are fighting the war. They assembled the Robert E. Peary and thought it fun. They are, in short, an excellent example of Free People At Work.

J. A. Loughridge, Chairman
Labor Management Committee
Richmond Shipyard No. 2

CONTENTS

I Become
One of Them

One day I found myself walking through a gate under a huge sign: REMEMBER PEARL HARBOR. I didn't need to be reminded, for on that day I had been bombed out of home and business. And not in Hawaii, but right off the main street of Omaha, Nebraska. I was a salesman of vacuum cleaners. It was a job I liked—traveling all over the States, seeing the country, talking to people, listening to their stories—that's my dish. Suddenly, all that was left of the vacuum cleaner business was the vacuum.

Then I learned they were building ships out on the Coast, in a new sort of way, preassembling them as you do cars. They needed workers, lots of them, and it wasn't necessary to know anything about a ship. All you needed were two hands, and if you had only one, they'd find a job for your one hand.

So I packed up and headed out. Sunny California, here I come.

15

At the Richmond hiring office a couple of hundred guys stood in line. Some had white collars and some had no collar at all. Some looked as if they had been waiting in hiring offices all their lives, and some looked lost like rookies.

Finally my turn came up and a guy asked me what kind of a job I wanted. I told him I wanted to build a ship.

"Take it easy now," he said. "It takes sixty trades to build a boat. How about becoming a flanger?"

"Okay with me. What does he do?"

"Beats me," he said. "Just report to work tomorrow and they'll tell you."

Next morning at 6 a.m. I rolled in merrily. It was still pitch-dark and all the highways were dotted with headlights. You could see the dandiest limousines next to the oldest jalopies and small trucks still marked with the name of a firm which had given up for the duration. It was a good feeling to belong to this stream of workers.

And so I found myself walking through the gate under that REMEMBER PEARL HARBOR sign. A procession of tin hats, overalls and lunch boxes, crowding into a new world— piles of steel plates of all shapes and sizes, shacks and booths, ladders and scaffolds, posters like the one reminding you that the guy who relaxes is helping the Axis. The yard was arranged city-like: F, G, H Streets running in one direction, 9th, 10th, 11th Streets in another. It was a city without houses, but the traffic was heavy. Cranes, trucks, trains noised by. Finally, after a rather long walk, I came to the edge of the water. There were the ships—or rather, halves, thirds, quarters and tenths of ships. There was a piece of ship here and a piece of ship there, and a hole in between. And then out of a clear sky a crane dropped the missing piece of ship, big as a house, into that hole.

I was assigned for swing shift to the gang on Assembly Way Five. I got a couple of wrist-breaking

16

handshakes but most of the guys didn't bother to look up from their hammering and welding. They all looked as though they had dug coal with their bare hands and wiped their hands on their faces.

It took me just half an hour to become as dirty as they. I gave a hand to one of them, puzzled over a blueprint with another, swapped jokes with a third, and before I knew it they ceased being a bunch of guys with dirty hands and rough language. I shared with them the great adventure of helping to build ships for victory.

I worked with them for two years and have often wondered how people with such different backgrounds could have gotten along together so well. How could the gang on Assembly Way Five click? For two reasons, I think. First, we had a common purpose. Second, we got to know each other's stories. Stories beginning somewhere on a Montana ranch, an Oklahoma laundry, a California college, a garage in Michigan, a tamale stand, a mine—all flowing together on Assembly Way Five, tying us all together.

While working in this new world where you don't say Left and Right but Port and Starboard, where your nose is on your forward end and you sit on your afterpeak, I listened to these stories and saw them develop, especially when women workers joined us. And when I look aft now, it's not so much the records we broke but the stories I heard that I want to talk about. Taken together, it's the story of a little melting pot within the big melting pot, America.

The Gang On Assembly Way Five

SHIPFITTERS
SANDY, an architect, New York, New York
CHUCK, a globetrotter, San Francisco, California
PINK and PIPSQUEAK, two college kids
                    from Berkeley, California
COOKIE, a high school graduate, Lafayette, California
CHERIE, a student from the Sorbonne, Paris, France

FLANGERS
JASON, a rancher, Montana
PEE-WEE, a housewife, New Haven, Connecticut
GOSH, an old shipfitter, Maine
BRUCE, a high school teacher, Los Angeles, California
JOE, a vacuum cleaner salesman, Omaha, Nebraska

WELDERS
ALIBI, an auto mechanic, miner and hunter,
       Minnesota
TINY, a kid from the Canton area, China
LOVELLA, a waitress, Salt Lake City, Utah
DIMPLES, a movie starlet, Seattle, Washington
SPARKIE, a high school graduate, Lafayette, California
BULGIE, a minister's wife, Oklahoma
MA HOPKINS, a grandmother, Los Angeles, California
CINDY, a manicurist, Oklahoma

BURNERS
OKIE RED, a launderer, Oklahoma
HAPPY, a railway cook, South Carolina

CHIPPER
SWEDE, a disabled war veteran, Arkansas

WELDCHECKER
MIGGS, a lawyer's daughter, England

19

The Girl with the Sledge-hammer

One day out of our clear California sky comes the sudden news that women will start working in the yard tomorrow. Sandy, the shipfitter leaderman, grins, "We'll have to watch our goddamn language, fellows," winks, and trots along. "Gosh," says Gosh, the flanger. He puts his sledgehammer down, pushes his hard hat back over his head and spits through the gap in his yellow teeth. That's what he thinks of it and he's as sparing with words as though he were cabling them overseas.

Our gang is working a second-deck unit, one of those forty-ton babies for the jigsaw puzzle called Liberty Ship. Okie Red, the burner, shakes his head as he watches his machine cutting the steel like a piece of cream cheese. "Women in the yard!" He sounds as though he wouldn't be surprised to find Lana Turner joining the commandos next. Tiny, our Chinese welder boy, shouts "Girls!" like a moviegoer on Wednesday night shouting "Bingo!" He feels everybody's eyes on him, blushes, jerks his head sharply so that his hood comes down. He begins to weld furiously, flashing like a press photographer at the White House, and all of us have to turn our heads away.

But for the most part we have little to say. Steel and skirts. The idea is too big. Steel and skirts. The thing isn't right. Powder puffs and iron. It won't work.

We look at our dirty overalls and our hard hands. Women in the yards? We try to feel the steel with our feet through our steeled safety shoes. Women? Just wait and see. We are all of us confused but we go about our work. Yet each little job we do we look at twice. Maybe we've done it a hundred times before, but now it looks strange to us. Women?

Swede the chipper makes all talking impossible. His business is steel against steel, cold steel being cut by a driven chisel. But even he isn't able to chip the girls out of our minds. When he stops his racket, Chuck the fitter's voice is heard at a shout, "Why not women? English women have been working all along. In Russia and China they fight. How about it, Jason?"

Jason is the flanger quarterman's delight. He works like a horse. He handles a sledge like a woman a comb. At chuck's question he lets out a terrific snort.

"Hell, no!" He hits a 300-pound beam and it moves three inches. "They can't work. They'll loaf and make you loaf with them. They'll make you carry their tools and do their work. All they'll do is collect their paychecks, and yours too, you suckers."

That's as final as a blockbuster for Jason. Flanging's a job women can't possibly invade, anyhow. He feels safe.

22

The next afternoon the yard hums its usual tune: the chippers, the hammers, the welding machines, the warning signal of the cranes. And yet, something new has been added. The boys, when they are sent out for a template or a truck, keep their eyes open— and not only for the steel plates swinging in the air. It's hard to spot a girl because there's only one of them in a thousand. Most of them are welders, and you wouldn't care to look at someone who's welding, even if it was Rita Hayworth, because all you'd get is a flash which feels like your eyeball is polished with sandpaper. All the boys can see is a brand new leather suit here and there and a bit of a red bandana under a hood.

But our gang doesn't have to go around looking for a red bandana. We've got a girl right in with us, and she isn't a welder, not by a jugful. She is a flanger and is assigned, of all things, to be Jason's helper. You'd call her a shrimp. She and Jason together look like an exclamation point. The biggest part of her is her eyes, deep and blue. Her hair is carefully hidden under a flowery kerchief and crowned by a silvery hard hat with the inscription: FLANGER'S HELPER. She wears a simple working suit, safety boots and heavy gloves. She seems interested in everything and asks everyone questions. To her the yard is a museum.

The afternoon sun is still hot, but that's nothing compared with the temperature Jason has reached. He's a regular keep-out sign and tells everyone who cares to listen, and some who don't, that he's through with this kind of job and is going to quit unless the girl is transferred to another platform.

Next thing you know the girl is there, asking why he refuses to work with her before he even knows how good or bad she is.

"No hard feelings," Jason tells her, "but a skirt's a skirt and can't do a guy's work."

23

She throws her head back and says, with flashing eyes, "Forget that I'm a girl. I get a guy's wages and I'm going to do a guy's job."

He looks at her as if he's going to put her in his pocket next to his small change, then his chin shoots out and he says, "All right, get that hammer."

There are four-, six-, eight-, and ten-pound hammers and Jason, on principle, always carries the tenner. But, for the girl, the tenner is about a tenth of her own weight, and she trudges kind of lopsided behind him.

Our assembly platform is a scaffold about four feet high, with beams running crosswise like the lines of a crossword puzzle. You have to walk on those beams like a tightrope walker or else you'll find yourself in the meat wagon going full blast to First Aid. But still it's a picnic to rope dance on top of the beams if you compare it to crawling underneath them, which you also have to do once in a while. The big steel plates that are laid down on the platform will curl and buckle after welding so that they look like a caterpillar unless you hogtie them from below. That's what Jason's doing now and he takes the girl along to help him. The sun has been shining on the plates all day, and being below them is like being in an incubator. The ground is a rubbish heap of scrap steel and welding glass. You can't stand and you can't sit. You have to kneel.

Happy, our black burner, who has painted his hard hat bright red and his shoes to match, shakes his head sadly, "Jason ain' quit yet but she sho will." Chuck and Okie Red, working together above the spot where the girl has gone down, look uncomfortable as they listen to the hammer blows from underneath that blend into the deafening shipyard din.

The lunch whistle blows and Jason and his helper come climbing up again. She has a black spot on her nose and cheek, and her face is flushed with heat. She

24

puts her hammer down and leaves the platform while we settle down to eat lunch. There is no special place to eat. We just sit down on a piece of steel or a six-by-eight, talking men's talk. It's not so much a rest for the legs as for the ears, unless there is a dinner concert. Some like it and some don't, but even the most unmusical guys agree that the worst boogie-woogie is better than the best chipper on the job.

Anyway, we eat, and it's everybody's guess that the girl is probably looking for a table set with napkins and flowers, when she appears with her lunch pail and sits down with us. The spot on her nose is gone, she has taken off her bandana and the hard hat and shows a barrage of curly brown hair. Her hands are soft and clean as though she had just come out of a tub. There's a lull in our conversation, but she doesn't seem to notice it and asks, "Won't somebody please tell me how these boats are built? I mean, how can you build them in a month instead of a year?"

"That's none of your business," Jason grumbles, "we just build them."

"I don't agree with you there," says the girl. "It's my business now, whether you like it or not. If I do something, I want to know what I'm doing. I don't mind hammering, but I want to know what. And if I learn that I've hammered something worthwhile, I might even enjoy hammering."

There's a short pause while her words sink in. Chuck looks at her with open approval, and Gosh releases his one rare word, "Gosh," he says. The others just eat their sandwiches and pour coffee from their thermos bottles, but every look they exchange seems to say, "She's all right." Even Jason is taken by surprise and begins to feed the sea gulls that always come around at lunch time as though they had a watch under their wings.

Then everybody is talking at the same time. What pours out are the kinds of explanations you get from people

25

who have done a job a hundred times but never thought of explaining it. It's a mixture of slang and technical terms, sprinkled with "well's" and "you see's," all hopelessly muddled like a dish of spaghetti. It's the sort of information you can safely give to an enemy spy.

At last Bruce, who used to be a teacher in his pre-flanger days, speaks up. He's the type of guy who can explain things even if he never did them himself. "It's all very simple," he says. "Instead of building the boats on the shipways, which is rather precious space, we assemble parts all over the yard on assemblies. It's done like this: the welders weld it, burners cut everything to size, chippers clean up. When the unit is assembled in all details, the crane picks it up and drops it in its proper place on the boat. That's all."

"That ain't the story," argues Chuck the shipfitter. It's really like this: the fitters, after studying the prints, are the ones who know what has to be done and where. The flangers, welders, burners and chippers just do what they are told."

"Heck," says Alibi the welder, who looks like a picture book with his arms full of tattoos, "flangers and fitters just give us a start. It's the welders who . . ."

"I get the general idea," says the girl. "Anyway, I'm going to like it."

This one shocks Jason. "It's a man's job," he insists. "Why the hell did you pick flanging, of all things?"

"They needed flangers," she explains. "Did I do so badly this afternoon, Jason?"

Jason is busy with the sea gulls.

"I'll do better tonight," the girl promises, "and still better tomorrow. Just give me a chance."

The whistle ends the half-hour for lunch. "Come on," urges Jason, getting up.

"Wait a minute," says Red the burner. Reaching for a bucket of yellow paint and a brush from a shipwright's outfit, he plants himself in front of the girl and paints with big letters on her silver helmet: PEE-WEE.

It's like pinning a medal on a hero's uniform.

After the break everyone keeps an eye on Pee-Wee. Jason makes her work, all right, and boy, does she work! New plates have been laid on the assembly. Red has burned them to size, and now it's Jason's job to move them next to each other so they can be welded. Just try and move a plate thirty feet long, seven feet wide and half an inch thick! Try it when the heaviest job you've done was wash dishes or go shopping with your ration book without home delivery. You have to stand straddle-legged like a catcher and ram a sharp pointed bar about the size of yourself into the wood beams of the assembly. You have to hit a point close to the edge of the plate you want to move. With the pointed end of the bar firm in the wood, you have to pull the other end sharply, pushing the plate an inch or two, then do it all over again until you get the plate where you want it.

If you watched Jason you'd think it was as easy as playing a pinball machine. But Pee-Wee has a heck of a time. Sometimes she misses the wood beam and the weight of the heavy bar throws her a couple of steps forward. Or she hits the beam but the bar slips and she topples. Or the bar holds but she simply can't budge the plate. Her face is flushed and wet but she hardly ever stops for so much as a breath. Bruce and the others want to help her but they know she wouldn't appreciate it. This is her fight and she's got to fight it, alone. She doesn't get much done but you can't say she didn't try.

At last the plates are lined up. Pee-Wee takes off her goggles and wipes off the sweat. You can see her lips trembling with weakness. She gets an encouraging grin from Chuck and an admiring nod from Happy, and she manages to smile back, but you can see that even the

27

smile is a strain on her. She leaves the platform and is back after a short while, looking pepped up and smelling of cologne. She walks right up to Jason who's busy with a tacker, lights a cigarette, and asks him to name some good books on shipbuilding. He, of course, guffaws at the idea that you can learn flanging from a book and rubs in what a flop she was today.

"I want to know everything about shipbuilding," she insists, "and I am going to learn it the hard way, right here in the yard. But I also want some background. I'm not going to stay a flanger's helper all my life, and the more I know the quicker I'll advance."

Jason takes the pipe out of his mouth and spits. "That's women for you. First day on the job and all set to become a big shot."

"Sure," says Pee-Wee, "why not?"

Jason looks relieved because he'd rather see her as a big shot somewhere in an office than as his helper. But when Chuck asks him how he'd like to have Pee-Wee as his leaderwoman some day, Jason looks as though he has been whacked by his own sledge.

Next afternoon the bets are five to one that Pee-Wee won't show up at all, but she gets in just one minute ahead of the whistle. She had trouble getting transportation and wants to know whether someone is living near her place with whom she could ride. It turns out that Jason is the only one on her route, but he claims he has a full load.

Swede's sharpening his chisels on a grindstone, the welders and burners are dragging their lines crisscross on the platform to the place where they're going to work, everyone is checking out the tools he needs. Pee-Wee shows up with a four-pound hammer and Jason looks at her like at someone set to carve a Thanksgiving turkey with a safety pin. He says nothing. She'll see. There are about twenty stiffeners to be set right. He begins on

28

one that is about two inches off, and goes to work with his ten-pounder. Pee-Wee, meanwhile, studies the next stiffener which is also a couple of inches off. She doesn't do anything, just looks and frowns. Then she calls Tiny and tells him to weld a little clip next to the stiffener, sticks a small wedge between clip and stiffener, taps it lightly with her four-pound hammer, and the stiffener slips like magic into the right place.

Jason walks over to see what's going on.

"The principle of Archimedes," she explains.

"What was that?"

She obviously is pleased with herself. "He said where there is one body there can't be another body. So one body just pushes the other body away. It does the work for you."

"Who said that?" asks Jason.

"Archimedes."

"Huh," he grunts. He doesn't like the idea of not knowing a guy who knows something about flanging. "You do it your way and I do it mine." He shrugs and goes back to his stiffener.

A stiffener looks like a steel rail, only it's five times as high. You have to set it along a line and flush to the plate. The trouble is the plates are always full of crinkles and the stiffs are seldom straight. When you've knocked the stiff to the line at one place, it's way off a few inches farther away. All you can do is weld-tack the spot where the stiff is on the line so it can't slip away there, and then go on a step further and make line and stiffener meet there too. You have to inch forward that way from one end of the stiff to the other.

That's what Jason and Pee-Wee are doing now. Each one has a different stiffener. Tiny is tacking for Pee-Wee, Alibi for Jason, and soon we realize there's a race on between Jason and Archimedes. Jason pounds away like a 105 mm howitzer and soon has a lead of two feet. Then he hits a snag and Pee-Wee catches up a bit. She doesn't seem to hurry, always studies the situation, frowns, and then puts her wedges in, once from this side and then from the other. Tiny feels as if he's in the running too, and when Pee-Wee points to a spot, he welds it so fast that you barely have time to hold your arm before your eyes as you automatically do to protect them. For about five feet the two race neck and neck, tack and tack, but after that Pee-Wee gets a clear edge on Jason. Sandy, the fitter leaderman, is startled, and Chuck who works with him on a layout can hardly stop himself from cheering the girl. Alibi, although tacking for Jason, watches Pee-Wee's progress keenly and flexes the muscles of his arm to make the tattooed devil's face grin. Tiny's Chinese black-button eyes already shine in anticipation of her victory.

Pee-Wee looks up and sees Jason hammering away like mad, two tacks behind her. She wrinkles her forehead. Nobody is staring straight at her, but she knows everybody's watching. Although Tiny spurs her on excitedly, she takes her time. Jason finishes first.

The tension of the past few minutes eases up. Sandy and Chuck, the two fitters, are busy punching lines. Happy dips a brush in a bucket of red paint and begins to give his shoes a new coat. Swede starts his chipping again.

Jason looks over the stiffener Pee-Wee has set. He's the boss. There is a shade of a smile in his eyes as he nods his approval, "It's O.K. Now the next."

Bruce helps me carry some brackets. "Smart girl, that Pee-Wee," he says.

Next day is Jason's day off, and when he shows up the day after, he's a sorry sight. He looks badly mauled, his upper lip smashed. Pee-Wee meets him sympathetically but turns away when she smells his breath. "Why does he do that?" she asks us.

Okie Red shrugs, "His idea of a good time. That's what he likes and he does it."

"He always picks a fight when he's drunk," Alibi reports. "I saw him a couple of times in a saloon down in East Oakland. You'd be surprised how little he can hold. It makes him sick. But he fights swell."

Pee-Wee wants to know why we're not doing anything about him, and Alibi tells her that's Jason's business and nobody has a right to poke his nose into what Jason does on his day off. As long as he shows up for work everything is hunky-dory.

Pee-Wee doesn't agree but she's not sure what she can do about it. She works silently and that's okay with Jason. When they get ready to set up stiffeners again, she challenges him: "Well, let's see how good you are today!"

This time she's made up her mind to lick him so he'll know he's licked. That's not hard today because pretty soon he loses his temper and pounds the stiffs so madly that he can't set them right to the lines. Pee-Wee is through before Jason is half done, and it turns out that he's way off line. So Swede has to come and chip out the stiff.

Swede was gassed in the last war and can't hold his hands still. They're always trembling, and for years he couldn't get a job. But they found out that for a chipper it doesn't matter whether his hands are steady because the chipping gun shakes so much that it makes the hands shake anyhow; so he got the job. And a darn good chipper he is, too, always anxious to work because, as he puts it, he has to make up for the twenty years he lived off state charity. He comes over to Jason's stiffener with his heavy air hose, his gun and chisels, and starts to chip the tacks off the stiffener. When he's got only a foot or so left, the last tack breaks and the stiffener keels over. Swede doesn't jump away soon enough and the stiff comes down on his foot with a bang. The gang rushes

31

toward him. Alibi lifts the stiffener, Chuck takes Swede's shoe off, and Bruce calls First Aid. Swede is pale, and as he watches the blood pouring from his smashed toes, his hands tremble helplessly. Then the ambulance comes and two men in white take him away on a stretcher.

This is an accident that may happen in the yard at any time and no one can really blame anyone else for it. But Pee-Wee says she can't help thinking that if Jason hadn't been drunk he wouldn't have put that stiffener on wrong, and Swede wouldn't have had to chip it off and gotten hurt. Red tells her that if she hadn't made a race of it, Jason wouldn't have hurried and made a mistake. Pee-Wee maintains that competition is something sound and drunkenness isn't. There's a hot little argument and the upshot is that Pee-Wee says she wishes someone would do something to prevent these accidents.

"Why don't you go ahead and do something about it yourself?" Alibi asks her, and starts oiling up a welding line. Pee-Wee frowns and says she'll think about it.

Next day Pee-Wee is busy with Happy burning out queer shapes from scrap metal, and during the meal break she comes out with her invention. It's a little plate with the outline of the stiff burned out so you can slide it over the stiffener like a ring on a finger. With one of these holders on each end, a stiffener can't keel over. With that thing around the stiff you feel as safe as a kangaroo baby in mama's pocket. The gang has to own up to that. Sandy the fitter is all aflutter about it and tells Happy to burn a dozen more of them. He's going to turn the gadget in to the labor-management committee which awards monthly prizes for the most useful ideas of yard workers.

Jason, meanwhile, is back to normal. That means sober, hard-working and anti-female. I begin to wonder about that guy because he shows as much interest in women as a horse betting on a horse race. And a guy built like that sure must be a bite and a snap to the girls.

32

Well, if you're interested in a fellow, you can always find someone in the yard who has known him since he was a kid and who, with the right line, will tell you all about him. So I buy Bud, a shell-riveter, a couple of drinks and get the lowdown on Jason.

Jason, he tells me, comes from a ranch in Montana. His father is the senior edition of himself, and still runs the ranch. Jason had two brothers. One is in the air corps and doing fine. The other one—well, that's a sad story. He fell in love with a girl and married her, but she turned out to be the wrong kind. She spent more money than they had and, in the end, ran off with a banker from the city. Well, Jason's brother, to keep up with his wife's demands, had mortgaged the ranch behind his father's back and then shot himself.

Jason had been going with Pudgy, who was anything but a gold digger. She just liked to dress nicely, go out and dance, and have a good time. After the tragedy, however, Jason got suspicious. With every new hat Pudgy bought, Jason would squirm. He foresaw ruin, like his brother's. He turned skinflint and the girl broke off with him. For Jason, this was final proof of her bad character. He volunteered for the air corps but was rejected. The army classified him 4-F because of stomach ulcers, and the doctor warned him to keep off alcohol. Jason had never cared for liquor, but now he began to drink. "That guy is a natural fighter," Bud concludes. "Since the army turned him down, he picks his own fights. And he relieves his anger with the sledgehammer. But he's not as strong as he used to be. Don't kid yourself—it's a slow suicide. And there's nothing anyone can do about it."

After that I see Jason in a different light. You can work with a man for years, hear what he says, see what he does, and form your own opinions, but you don't know him. Maybe we should inquire a little more about

33

those around us, but who cares for his neighbor unless you fall in love with him or you've lent him money. I wish I could find out more about Pee-Wee, but she comes all the way from New Haven, Connecticut, and nobody in the yard knows her.

There are more girls in the yard now, but it's still a mere trickle, even though I hear the welder and burner schools are full of them. After a while we get two welder girls, Lovella and Dimples. Lovella is a not-quite-natural blonde who'd like to be as beautiful as Dimples really is. Lovella shows up every afternoon in a stunning dress, her golden hair hanging down and a hat on top of it that looks like a parachute on a forced landing in a corn field. For work she changes into a welder's suit, but for lunch she wears slacks and sweater, and Alibi the welder leaderman asks her if she thinks she is in a shipyard or a fashion show. Dimples looks like a Hollywood star but she tries hard to hide her glamor. When she talks or smiles or just eats a sandwich, dimples keep coming and going on her cheeks and chin and around her lips like raindrops on a lake.

With these two girls in our crew, Pee-Wee isn't quite as much of an attraction, but she does her work so well that soon she is considered an old-timer. She belongs. Even Jason doesn't mind her and treats her the same as any of the other helpers. She even comes to work in his car now—there always had been one extra seat.

Swede's back at work again. He missed a week and still limps. He's pleased to see that Pee-Wee has invented a gadget because of his accident. Then one day, Pee-Wee's name is broadcast over the loudspeaker during break time and printed in the yard weekly, *Fore 'n' Aft*, because her idea has won her the third prize of the month, a fifty-dollar bond. Since she is the first girl given a prize by the labor-management committee, there is a lot of hullabaloo, and a photographer takes a picture of Pee-Wee, together with Jason, fixing her gadget onto the stiff.

Everything is okey-dokey now, and the daily routine on the assembly is just a merry-go-round for us. Still, something is awfully wrong. Pee-Wee is as downhearted as a crack shot classified 4-F.

When she first came to our yard and had to fight for Jason's recognition, she was as sure of winning as the ace of trump. Now, when she is the swing-shift queen, she seems to feel like a deuce. She got a prize, was pushed from helper to trainee way ahead of schedule and even had the satisfaction of seeing Jason come to work as dry as a dog biscuit for three weeks straight. Yet something's wrong. One night we send her off to order out some lifting clips far down at the burners' school. It's close to quitting time and she isn't back yet, so I go and look for her and find her off in a corner crying.

"What's the matter, Pee-Wee, are you hurt?" and I wait for her to say something.

She shakes her head. "No. At least, not the way you mean it."

I sit down and talk to her, but she insists it's no use.

"Listen," I say. "It's too easy to say 'It's no use.' You remember when Alibi told you it was no use trying to stop Jason's drinking?"

At that she begins to cry harder. She's not crying for a lost doll. These are tears of someone whose heart is too full to hold it all. "Aw, come on," I tell her, "let's have it. There's a way out of every mousetrap and two heads are better than one."

She wipes her eyes with the back of her hand but can't control her sobbing. I quit coaxing and let her make up her mind whether she wants to talk or not.

"Well, Joe," she says at last, "I'm in a spot."

Just then the noise of the yard dies down as always before a shift ends. You can set your watch by that abrupt silence. Then the whistle blows and the workers rush past us, streaming to the gates. Pee-Wee gets up. "I have to get my timecard," she says.

"Forget the whistle and the card," I tell her. "There's no law against staying in the yard after work. Let's go over there."

The night shift has taken over and again the iron coughing of work drowns out all conversation. I take Pee-Wee to the outskirts of the yard. The yard was built on swamp and pasture land. The world of steel has spread within a year, but if you pass the last assembly way, the new plate shop, and the depots, you find yourself in the middle of grassland, with flowers, crickets and a couple of sleeping cows.

Pee-Wee and I settle down on an apple tree stump. Her wide eyes are turned inward and I wait patiently until she is ready. Suddenly she lets out a nervous little laugh, shrugs, and says, "Well, I guess I'll start with the big news: Jason wants to marry me."

I had expected worse and hasten to say so. She shakes her head sharply, "You don't understand, Joe. I've been married for twelve years."

This gives me quite a turn since I didn't think she added up to more than twenty-five in all. She takes off her silver hat and bandana and tosses her hair back. "You see, I married at eighteen, to the surprise of everyone including myself. I finished high school with my head full of ideas. I wanted to go to college and study journalism and was set on becoming a newspaper-woman someday since I had done a lot of writing for our high-school paper. I wanted to see life and write about it. Then George came along and I forgot about my ambitions. George and I made a home, and we had many friends. I've been told more than once that we had one of the happiest homes in New Haven. Once in a while, though, I felt a pang. I asked myself, 'What would have become of me if I had gone to college? I would be a reporter by now, maybe editor.' When I read about some conference and saw the pictures of the newspaperwomen in the magazines, I imagined being one of them. The thought always fascinated me, but I never did more than daydream about it because my husband wouldn't have liked the idea of my taking a job.

"Then the war came and changed everything. George joined the navy. I was left to myself, wondering what the life of a working woman was like, how good I really might be. I was sure I could tackle any job. I read about the labor shortage on the West Coast and the readiness of some shipyards to try women. I heard some so-called experts express doubts if women could do the job. I made up my mind to try to take up where I had left off on my wedding day. Be a working girl. See life. The work had to be done, and my husband was somewhere in the Pacific anyhow.

"It wasn't a picnic at first, and you know it. But you know only half the story. I didn't have a single friend here, and I missed mine more than I ever would have expected. I read a lot and took courses, but I longed for someone to talk to.

"Well, Jason was the last one I thought of. He was my boss, the damper on all my ambitions. When I started to ride in his car, he began to look more human. He surprised me by showing interest in my shipbuilding books. He asked me about the course I took and eventually joined me. We often discussed flanging problems. We were a good team because I had the theoretical knowledge and he could solve the practical side of it.

"I couldn't have wished for a more ideal companion. He never so much as held my hand. I had no objections when he asked me to go to a dance with him. He behaved a bit funny that night. He watched me anxiously every time a waiter asked for my order or when a flower girl

37

offered flowers or knick-knacks. He seemed relieved when I refused them. He took me out a few times, and sometimes some friends of his and their girls came along. We danced and talked in the most impersonal manner, and he always seemed strangely stingy.

"Then, a couple of days ago when he called for me at noon, he awkwardly handed me a small package. You could have knocked me down with a whiff when I opened it: inside was the most beautiful and costly diamond ring you ever saw! For the first time, he took my hand, pressed it gently, and there was a light in his eyes I never had noticed before. 'It's a surprise to me, too,' he said. 'I haven't talked much, but I want you to know that I mean every word of it.'

"He smiled happily and took me down to his car where his friends were waiting. Nobody remarked about it, but everybody seemed to know. They were in holiday spirits, and I had a lump in my throat ready to uncork itself any minute. We went to a restaurant and Jason ordered the most expensive lunch and wine, and everybody drank but him. Bud took me aside and told me how happy they all were because I was a swell girl and a lifesaver for Jason in every sense of the word. He was surprised that I didn't know that another year of drinking would have killed Jason as sure as shooting.

"Well, Joe, that's the story. I'm glad I could talk about it, but you can't help me, nor can anybody else. What can I do but tell Jason that I've been married all along. And he's not the guy to understand. You can figure out yourself what he's going to do. Remember when Swede was hurt and I told everyone it was Jason's fault? Well, if Jason starts drinking again and is a dead man next winter, it'll be my fault as sure as if I'd put poison in his food. Blame me for everything. Jason seemed such a safe companion. He didn't even notice that I was a woman, and it made me proud that he appeared to have forgotten it. But I should have known better. I am just a

38

little goose who, after twelve years of marriage, knows nothing about men."

The moon peeks over the horizon and the skyline of San Francisco sparkles brightly. The cows are dark lumps sleeping in the sundried grass. The noise of the crickets is louder here than that of the distant chippers. Twelve half-finished ships in the cages of their staging are sharply silhouetted against the starry sky. Cranes move like huge giraffes and stoop from time to time to pick up a mouthful of steel. Welders and burners sprinkle the yard with an ever-changing pattern of sparks.

Jason doesn't show up the next day. The day after, he comes in all battered like a tomcat. So she has told him. Pee-Wee is busy as usual, but when she occasionally takes off her goggles to cool her temples, you can see shadows under her wide eyes. There isn't a day now that Jason doesn't come staggering in like a sailboat in a tornado. Even Alibi, who considers drinking a sign of manliness, disapproves. "What's the idea, him coming loop-legged to work every day?" he turns to Okie Red. "If he can't take it, he'd better knit socks for the Red Cross."

Of course, nobody is much worried about him except Pee-Wee, Bud and myself. And it comes as a complete surprise to everyone when, one evening, in the middle of his work, Jason falls in a faint. Okie Red takes him home and we don't hear from Jason for several days. Even Pee-Wee knows nothing and Bud, his pal, refuses to talk to her.

The first news about him comes from an unexpected source. A pretty brunette dressed in a welder's outfit comes up our assembly and looks around until she finds PEE-WEE written on a silver helmet. She walks up to her, gives her the once-over and says, "I only wanted to see how a woman looks who steals men from other girls." Pee-Wee doesn't say anything. She manages to look as if

39

she doesn't know what the girl is talking about, but I can see her lips pressed together.

At that moment the newcomer turns around and I see the name "Pudgy" scrawled on the back of her jacket. That doesn't mean anything to any of our gang, and I keep the story of Jason's first love as tight as the weather bureau's forecast in time of war. But I wouldn't mind knowing more myself, so I walk over to the shell assembly. Bud is hotter than any of his rivets picked right out of the hot-pot, and he starts spluttering before I have a chance to ask questions. "Some dirty rat wrote Pudgy a letter telling her that Jason spends all his time and money with Pee-Wee and that he wants to marry her. I saw that letter with my own eyes. Typed and no signature. Son of a bitch! It's a jumpy machine and the m's are all flying above the lines. If I ever get hold of the man with a machine like that, I'll break his leg and make him eat every bit of it."

That's about all Bud has to say, except that Jason is in bed and pretty sick.

Life at the shipyard rumbles along. Every week a ship slides off the skids and even as the champagne splashes against the bow, the keel for the next boat is dangling from the crane, ready to be laid in place. Then Jason is here again. He swings his sledgehammer, but the old strength is gone. He pretends to be Goliath himself, but more and more often he has to stop for a breath. He and Pee-Wee avoid each other, and I suspect that there's more cooking than meets the eye.

Bud is stewing. "That fool," he shouts. The next few paragraphs are censored. When he cools off to a degree where his language can be quoted again, he tells me that Jason got out of bed against his doctor's orders because he didn't want to be dependent on a woman. Jason hadn't saved a penny, so Pudgy had stocked his larder out of her own pocket and had also started cooking for him.

Everything seems messed up until one day Pudgy shows up in a fur coat even though it's hot enough for a swim, and on her finger glitters a diamond ring. She's going to quit working and is taking a course in dietetics. If he keeps his diet, she tells us, Jason will even be able to continue on his job.

The next morning before work, I'm at Pee-Wee's place because she promised to help me fill out a questionnaire we got from the yard. She has a cozy little one-room apartment full of books and knick-knacks and a woman's touch all around.

"What do you think made Jason change his mind?" I ask her.

Pee-Wee looks as happy as the day she won the prize for her gadget. "Oh, nothing much, I guess," she says. "Just the natural course of things. Jason never was in love with me. I was very much relieved when I found that out." She glances lovingly at a picture next to her couch showing a man in a navy uniform. "Jason isn't the compromising type," she goes on. "He's like a sledgehammer himself. If you swing him, you have to swing him all the way. It's hard to stop him in the middle. After the disaster with his brother, he lost faith in all women. When he found out there were women who work like a fellow and are fairly reasonable, that gave him back his faith in women."

"Sounds simple enough," I admit. "Too simple. A guy like Jason doesn't cross-switch women like tires."

"He didn't." Pee-Wee is sure of what she says. She must have thought it through. "He was in love with Pudgy all along. When he declared war on women in general, he found a thousand faults in her. But after he calmed down, she had just one fault: she was a few hundred miles too far away."

"You're a smart kid," I tell her, "which reminds me why I came. There are a thousand questions in that questionnaire."

41

"Sure," she says. "Give it to me." She opens her portable, puts the questionnaire in and off she goes. Suddenly I can't help drawing a sharp breath: it's a jumpy machine and the m's are flying above the lines!

She looks up, sees that I have guessed, and laughs.

"Some problems you can't solve with a sledgehammer," she says. "Even Jason's beginning to realize that."

Tiny
Giant

When Dimples starts working in our gang, we all think she must be a beauty queen or a movie actress, and a couple of months later we find out she really is both. One day, our yard weekly publishes her picture and a story on how she won a beauty contest in her home town of Seattle and was called to Hollywood, then dropped her movie career to start working in the shipyard. There's a buzz of excitement around her that afternoon, and everybody keeps asking her why she didn't tell us.

"If I had been an auto mechanic before," Dimples replies, "I would have told you. Being a movie actress is nothing to brag about when you apply for a welding job." She is actually mad at the reporter who let 15,000 men and women in on her secret but nevertheless displays a firework of dimples. "If you say you're an actress, everybody thinks you can't be good working with your hands," she explains, "and you can be as busy as a windshield wiper, and still they'll say you're no good."

Alibi, her leaderman, claims it makes no difference to him as long as she turns out a good strong weld and a decent footage. As far as he's concerned, he wouldn't even mind Hedy Lamarr around here. Lovella, our second welder girl, wants to know how on earth Dimples ever could leave a gorgeous Hollywood career for a dirty job like welding and whether she ever met Charles Boyer in the flesh. From that day on, Lovella copies Dimples' hairdo, and if there were a way of copying the dimples, she would copy them too.

Naturally, every guy on our Way makes even bigger fish eyes at her than before, but Dimples is the one with the fish blood. She just clamps down her hood and strikes her arc as bright as concentrated sunshine and there's nothing you can do but raise your arm and hold your hand between the flash and your eyes. If a Nazi spy could peek into our yard, he would report triumphantly that we *heil* each other with the fascist salute, not realizing that we are just protecting our eyes. Anyway Sandy, the fitter leaderman, claims that Dimples is the only welder in the yard who can give a man a flash even when she's not welding.

But Dimples isn't interested. She notices neither Jason's muscles nor Alibi's romantic tattoos. Pink and Pipsqueak's college lingo and Bruce's philosophical chatter are so much slag. Chuck, the globetrotter, could still be in India for all her wanting to hear about it. There's only one male in our gang she pays any attention to, and that's our little Chinese welder, Tiny. Tiny is a kid, probably not more than eighteen. His straight black hair is always carefully trimmed and he seems more fussy about keeping his clothes from getting messed than anyone else. But no leaderman has to ask him to do a job twice, and he's faster than all the other welders. He's so tiny that he disappears completely when he has to go under the assembly, and that's not more than four feet high. He always has a heck of a time trying to hoist himself up again but never wants any help. And when that foggy lunch whistle blares out its welcome note, Tiny always eats alone—that is, until lately. Now Dimples has joined him.

We wonder what the two are sticking their heads together about, especially since it's hard to understand Tiny because he talks English as though he had a layer of glue between his teeth. They are always scribbling something on the steel plates they sit on, but wipe everything off before lunch is over. Alibi, who acts as if he isn't interested in all these goings-on, has worked himself up about it, and his favorite joke is to tell Tiny that he thinks Tiny isn't Chinese at all, but a Japanese spy in disguise. Tiny never says a word to that, but one day Dimples speaks up after Tiny has gone for some new welding rods, "I wish you'd cut that out. Tiny has more reason to hate the Japs than all of us. His father was killed by them and he still has his mother and two brothers in China. Maybe they're being bombed by the Japs the very moment you're kidding him about being their spy."

That quiets everyone but Alibi, who says roughly, "If he hates the Japs that much, why doesn't he go and fight them?"

Dimples' cold stare turns to an icicle, "That's his business, not yours. But if you have to know, he tried and was rejected because of his size."

She continues like this, always sticking up for Tiny, and sometimes, when she has to wait till Chuck and the other fitters mark a unit up for weld, she murmurs to herself, or she takes out a sheet of paper and stares at it. Red the burner says maybe she's nuts—he knew a guy like that once and the last he heard of him, he was in a nuthouse.

A week later, Dimples appears with Chinese signs on her hood which Tiny painted for her. This isn't so surprising because welders paint almost anything on their hoods, from crazy names like BO-PEEP to signs that say KEEP OUT or YES, IT'S ME. Others paint their hats with ship symbols: BOW in front, STERN in back, PORT and STARBOARD on the sides. But we eventually find out that what Tiny and Dimples are scribbling and mumbling is Chinese, and that's Greek to most of us.

I did some asking around about Dimples. Some people collect stamps and some play poker, but my hobby is to find out about people and see what makes them tick. Although I'm a nosey sort of a guy, I usually keep my trap shut, and no harm's done. It's not easy to find out things about Dimples—the only man who knows anything is the reporter who wrote up that piece in the shipyard paper. Her folks, he tells me, are plain folks in Seattle, and they had a devil of a time because there were more mouths to feed than jobs to be had, but now everything is okay. Her father is working, her sisters are married, and her brothers are in the army. Dimples is the youngest and was engaged to Kenny, a Seattle boy, who is now in the merchant marine. The whole affair was upset when she won a beauty queen contest and went to Hollywood. After a while, stories appeared about her going out with a famous composer. But here my inside Sherlock fails me, although I do find out that some gossip columnists would pay cash for a clue to her whereabouts. The reporter said he was sorry he wrote that story but it was only in a local sheet that nobody reads except the guys in the yard.

Well, there it is. I know more than the Hollywood scribes but I'm still on machinery casing number 76 without a blueprint. Why, for instance, does Dimples learn Chinese and why is she so concerned about Tiny's self-confidence? We hear her giving him pep talks, mentioning Napoleon and Mickey Rooney. And she tells him that he is a valuable welder because he can crawl into the tight corners where no other welder can work at all. Tiny always listens politely and keeps smiling, but he's not kidding anyone. He's only hiding the hurt of always being considered an egg of "B" quality.

The sun's working overtime, fourteen hours a day and seven days a week, a shining example of being on the job. When we start our swing shift, the steel plates are so hot you don't dare touch them with your bare fingers. The welders in their heavy leathers, their faces covered with stuffy hoods and holding hot rods in gloved hands, feel like they're fried alive, especially when we're working on inner bottoms.

An inner bottom is the belly of the whales we call Liberty ships. Imagine that belly divided into steel compartments like egg-box partitions, thirty inches square in midship and smaller at the ends and a lid clamped tight on it. A mouse might be comfortable in that whale's belly. For a man to work inside of it is a struggle for a Jonah.

The place swarms with fitters, flangers, chippers, burners, pipefitters, and lots of welders. Nobody likes inner bottoms when you have to climb from one little compartment into the other. The temperature is hot enough to fry a hamburger on the steel plates, and the chippers thunder right into your ears. Still, we on the assembly have something to be thankful for. We work in the open, so the welding fumes don't bother us much. As soon as the inner bottoms are lifted to the boat, the rest of the work has to be done in closed compartments full of fumes and noise, and you can't climb over the egg-box partitions anymore because the cover has been placed over them, so you have to crawl through the connecting holes, fifteen by twenty-one inches big.

This, of course, is the spot for Tiny, and Alibi is always using him wherever a job needs to be done in one of those corners too small for a full-sized man. But does it

47

make Tiny feel important as Dimples would like him to feel? Not by a long shot. He always goes around looking like a little dog who has stolen a frankfurter.

One day I visit a friend in San Francisco, and use the afternoon ferry to go to work. There are no more busses running from San Francisco to the yards, and if you don't drive or ride with someone, you have to take the good old ferry which came to life again for shipyard workers only. Naturally, the ferries are packed, everyone with his helmet and lunch box. Some use the hour's ride to nap on a bench, some read the paper or have a quick snack at a counter, others just talk. Couples are holding hands or hugging each other, and a few play cards or shoot craps. A course in First Aid is offered, and once in a while, the First Aid people hunt for a victim among the crapshooters to practice on.

About a quarter of all passengers are Chinese because a big crowd in the yard comes from Chinatown. You can see them all over the boat, and some youngsters are bunched around an old man with twinkling eyes who's playing the accordion. The kids dance as though they're getting paid time and a half for it. One girl, small and cute, looks like the queen of the gang. Everybody wants to dance with her, and they fight for her like football players for the ball. She laughs and darts from arm to arm, light as a feather. Tiny, as usual, sits apart and watches, but there's something in his eyes that's new to me. It's like worship of a goddess or, if you like, the admiration of a hungry man for fried chicken.

I ask Lim, a burner on the forepeak assembly, who that girl is.

"Oh, that's Sylvia," he tells me, amazed at my ignorance.

"Quite a dish," I say. "Everybody seems to like her."

Lim's ready nod doesn't exclude himself.

"How about Tiny?" I venture.

48

Lim curls up his lip. "That fool," he says contemptuously. "He's always trailing her, and he knows he hasn't got a chance."

"Why not?" I pretend not to understand a situation which is only too clear. "She is a shrimp herself, no taller than he."

It's an effort for Lim, but he manages a smile. "It's different with a girl. A girl can be as small as a doll and still make a giant crazy. Besides, Sylvia was born in this country."

I nod knowingly, but now I can't see the point.

"She's a citizen," Lim explains. "Tiny came over a couple of years ago and can never become a citizen. He's just a refugee."

By now Lim feels he has definitely wasted too much time on me and joins the dancers. For a moment he gets a chance with Sylvia, then she's snatched away by some other boy.

I still can't quite make out what the festivity around the girl is all about until another Chinese fellow enlightens me.

"Don't you know? Sylvia's been picked by the management to launch a boat which is named after a great Chinese poet."

His eyes shine, and I wonder if he is more proud of the poet or the girl. I go over to Tiny. "Well, what good news," I begin, "a Chinese launching!"

"Good news," he repeats. He doesn't take his eyes off the girl. There is something desperate in his voice. Suddenly I understand. The honor of launching the boat has carried Sylvia still higher up, beyond his reach and, indeed, beyond his hopes. If he ever had a spark of optimism in his heart, the news of that honor had killed it so completely that it even tore away the mask of a smile from his face.

Well, it turns out that the boat to be christened by Sylvia is the one we assembled. It's true that there are

49

thousands working on parts that go on that particular boat, and we are a gang of only twenty, but we feel as though we had hatched "our" boat from an egg. There are many parts in a ship we have nothing to do with, for instance, the shell, the fore- and after-peaks, the deckhouses and masts, which are assembled by special crews all over the yard, many hundreds of feet from the place where the boat is actually built. In fact, some people work on parts and never even see the boat. But we on the assembly are right in front of the ship. We watch it grow from nothing to an enormous hunk of steel that eventually changes its number to a name and then goes down the skids leaving a hole in the staging that is filled with a new boat—it makes you feel like patting the boat on its afterpeak just before shoving it off. Pink and Pipsqueak, our two college kids who are full of practical jokes, never miss a chance to hide a four-leaf clover in some hole before it's welded solid, just to make sure a boat they built will never get torpedoed.

There's always excitement before a launching, and I hear that Sylvia's going around San Francisco smashing empty beer bottles against walls just to make sure she's got the right swing. Everyone knows that a ship will have bad luck if the champagne bottle fails to break, and Sylvia is not taking any chances. That launching is going to be the highlight of her career, something to remember for a lifetime, as sweet and passing as an icecream cone, and she has made up her mind to enjoy every lick of it.

The big day arrives and with it the usual hustle. The ship is ready, with her final coat of gray paint and her name printed in large letters on her bow. A string of flags is flung from end to end, and down the bow, on a red, white and blue streamer, hangs the bottle of champagne, all wrapped up in thirty-six yards of grosgrain ribbon of a patriotic hue. The launching platform with the desk for the speaker is brought by a Whirley crane, the loudspeaker set up, the balustrade draped with American flags. But all that is only what meets the eye. Down below, the work that really counts goes on. It takes one second to pull the trigger that releases the boat, but it takes three hours of the most exacting teamwork for the launching crew, the midwives at the birth of the boat, to get ready for that second.

A hull rests on two sets of blocks. The lower set is built firm and is used for every boat launched from that shipway; the one on top is loose and slides down with the boat; and between the two is plenty of grease. The boat is held in place by hundreds of shores which have to be knocked away gradually, block by block. If they all came out at once, the hull would crash to the skids upon which it finally rides out to sea.

While all that knocking and preparing is going on, the maritime commission gives the ship a last checkup— without the okay of the maritime commission no boat can be launched. Every rivet is looked over, every tank is tested, every foot of weld examined.

Meanwhile, we are assembling parts for the next boat when one of the welder bosses comes running down to Alibi and talks to him in great excitement. His arms wave as though he is sending out flag signals. Alibi gets as red in his face as the heart tattooed on his arm, and tells Swede the chipper to cut the racket. Then he calls his gang around him and tells them they can start looking for another job because one piece of weld in an inner bottom they had welded was found hollow inside and is as good as not welded at all.

"The launching is off," Alibi announces.

At that, the welding boss looks as if a Japanese submarine had just sneaked into our yard and the torpedo had hit him personally.

"Whataya mean, off!" he shouts. "Do you know what kind of a launching this is?"

51

"No," says Alibi. "What's up?"

The boss cools off a couple of degrees and admits he doesn't know himself, but something is going on because the place is swarming with cops, and the yard manager and all the other big shots are here, but he'll be damned if anybody tells him anything except if something goes wrong.

At that Dimples, who stands right next to Alibi, speaks up. "Why don't you just send someone down there and weld it good and solid?"

The welding boss looks at her like a man who has been bothered by a mosquito and is getting ready for the kill. "Send someone down!" he snarls. "There's room enough for a rat down there but only if you cut off the tail." He cools off a little because no man can look at Dimples' smile and stay mad long.

"We've got a man who can do it," Dimples insists. She reaches somewhere behind her and pulls out Tiny like a rabbit from a hat. The boss stares at him and something like a smile crimps his lips. "Naw, not even this guy. It's just a little corner on the side of the boat and all blocked with pipes."

"He can squeeze in anyplace," Dimples assures him. "I'd try if I were you."

"Even if he could get in, he would choke to death by his own welding smoke and burn to death by his own welding heat."

Tiny stands very straight, "I'd like to try, sir," he says.

The boss looks him over, surprised. "It's dangerous, really dangerous," he shakes his head. "The safety department wouldn't allow it."

Tiny shouts something in a high-pitched voice. I don't know if it's English or Chinese, but Dimples understands it. "He says," she interprets Tiny's outburst, "there's no safety department in China when soldiers fight a war."

52

The boss scrutinizes Tiny with growing interest. Then he goes off with him and we find out later that he took him to the big shots, then the bigger shots and finally to the biggest shot, and everywhere he goes, Dimples goes along like Mary's lamb. Everywhere she interprets what Tiny says, and explains to him what the others say. They must be pretty desperate because in the end they agree to let him try. Tiny is bursting with happiness and is impatient to get going. They give him the best set of welding stuff there is: a long line, a gadget that will pump fresh air down to him, and a hose through which he can try to breathe. They explain to him where he is to go and what he has to do and how to handle the emergency signals. Then Tiny disappears into the belly of the boat.

Meanwhile, the guests for the launching arrive and fill the platform at the beflagged bow of the ship. A number of cars have arrived, many more than for a customary launching. All kinds of rumors go around the yard and most of the guys believe that the ship has broken in two. The visitors are warned that they may have to go home again, and little Sylvia, in her best dress and her black hair full of white flowers, looks like a kid who's been told Christmas is off this year. Only a small group of people knows what's going on and that the whole launching now depends on Tiny.

The reports from the battlefront are not so good. The airhose gets pinched and the little corner where Tiny is welding is so full of fumes that they have to haul him out. He's unconscious, breathing heavily, and when he comes to, he coughs so much we think he's coughing his lungs up. He tells us he's only half through with his welding and wants to go back down right away. The doctor looks doubtful and talks to the yard superintendent. There's lots of whispering and glancing toward the main gates of the yard where more cops are trooping in. Tiny insists he's going down again, and it seems he won't take no for

53

an answer. His lips are pressed together, and his black-bead eyes burn in anger. After new instructions, the doctor gives his okay, and the minister, who's here to bless the outgoing boat, takes off his hat and moves his lips.

Our gang, meanwhile, works in a half-hearted manner; everybody is discussing whether Tiny will make it, and the bets are three to one he won't. But he has certainly improved the relations between China and the United States as far as our gang is concerned, and we agree that the Chinese are a brave people who fight with their bare hands and shoot at planes with homemade slings. Suddenly Pink slaps his hand against his forehead and says to Pipsqueak, "Guess who I just saw in that car? The President!"

Pipsqueak shoots a glance toward the car that moves slowly toward our boat, and shouts, "It's him, all right. Hi, Franklin!" Perhaps the President heard him because he flashes his teeth in a big smile—or it might have been just the automatic reaction to a photographer who clicks a snap.

Lovella takes off her hood and fixes her curls excitedly. "I wonder if I could get an autograph." She flicks an eyelash tentatively, like a singer trying her voice before appearing on the stage. Gosh just says "Gosh," and that exhausts his daily word ration.

The limousine stops and the President laughs and chats with the men who are with him, then he looks over the yard, the assemblies, the ships on the Ways, the traveling cranes, the stacks of plates, and the working men and women. Just then Alibi comes running along, his cheekbones and ears all flushed. "He did it," he hurrahs. "He's more dead than alive, but he did it!"

Jason the flanger points with the stem of his pipe in the direction of the President's car. Alibi's eyes follow, and when his mind grasps what he sees, his cheekbones and ears turn white, and the unexpected happens: Alibi, the he-man, passes out.

54

The whistle announces break time and the launching ceremony begins on schedule. Since this is our boat, we can climb up on the piled units we have assembled for the next hull, and we have a better view from our ringside seats than even the President from his limo below. The yard superintendent is the master of ceremonies and the speeches are broadcast throughout the yard. He points out that we, today, enjoy the highest honor and the most distinguished guest any shipyard in this country has yet enjoyed. And he doesn't forget to mention that today's launching was made possible only through the heroic deed of a little Chinese welder who may claim the title of not only the world's "smallest" but also the world's "bravest" welder.

Sylvia is introduced as "one of our workers who was picked to christen the boat and who can be proud of her countryman whose name the ship honors as well as of the one who made it possible to launch it on time." The maid of honor, another Chinese girl, is also introduced, and both girls are presented with huge bouquets of flowers. Sylvia looks as nervous and happy as though it were her wedding day. Only thirty seconds to the launching, it is announced. Only twenty seconds to the launching . . . ten more seconds. Sylvia's silvery voice sounds through the loudspeaker as she christens the boat. A flash bulb flares. The champagne bottle splashes. And then, after a second's hesitation, the big hull begins to move. Slowly, then gathering speed, it slips down the greased skid. The customary shouting, "There she goes!" sounds through the yard, hands are waved, hard hats are thrown into the air. At the ends of the Way, the boat gracefully dips into the water with a great plunge that is like a sigh of relief, and some of the spectators who had the best seats close to the water get soaked from head to toe. Pink and Pipsqueak, who anxiously followed the ship down the Way with their eyes, report triumphantly, "She's floating!"

Most of the workers in the yard turn back to their sandwiches and to the next boat, whose keel is already dangling from the Whirleys over the rather naked-looking shipway.

The visitors come down the flag-draped stairs, pass by the President's car, and the President is busy smiling and shaking hands. Sylvia and her maid of honor are introduced to him. Sylvia, holding the mahogany box containing the broken bottle, looks as thrilled as though she were shaking hands with Santa Claus himself. At that moment Tiny appears, walking under his own steam but supported by the doctor and the yard superintendent. He's held up to the President like a child, and I can see the President saying something to him that makes Tiny's pale face beam with pride. A flash bulb flares, Tiny is lowered again and disappears in the crowd.

When we leave the yard at the end of the shift, early morning editions already carry the story and the picture, and—at least in Richmond—Tiny gets more publicity than the President. If the papers can make a mountain out of a molehill, they certainly can make a giant out of Tiny. He's labeled "The smallest welder in the world," and that's going to stick to him till the end of his days.

During the following days, Tiny changes as fast and thoroughly as the sky during a sunrise. As a matter of course, he joins us at lunch time and we're proud to have him with us. Everybody treats him like an envoy on a goodwill trip, and he seems to expect it. He has only one sandwich and a quart of milk in his pail, but Pee-Wee is offering him dried apricots, Bruce some candies, Chuck a deviled egg. Jason says he's sorry he's on a goddamn diet and hasn't got anything but a jar with farina. Lovella, who changed for the half-hour rest period to tight-fitting slacks and a flaming blouse, is nibbling a package of dates. "How about a date?" she offers Tiny. "When?" he asks in a matter-of-fact tone.

56

Not only our gang pays him respect. Lim tells me that Tiny had a dance with Sylvia on the ferry that afternoon and nobody dared to cut in. She appreciates the way he saved her launching, and is convinced he did it for her. Besides, she considers the President's praise better than citizenship papers. After all, that's just a law and nobody can do anything about it. Even Madame Chiang Kai-shek couldn't become a citizen.

But in all his glory Tiny doesn't forget Dimples and that she's responsible for his luck. Things didn't turn out so well for Dimples—in fact, she's in a hell of a mess. The whole story has given her some publicity too, and publicity is the last thing she wants.

The same day, after work, some of our gang go to the cafeteria for a midnight snack. The cafeteria is part of the yard, but you can enter it only from the outside. You can eat there only before or after work. Before every shift the place is crowded, but after work everybody rushes home, so it is a quiet hangout now. Dimples is here and Tiny and Lovella and Chuck and Pee-Wee, and we all have ice cream and some gossip to go with it. Tiny, of course, is the center of our circle, and he is no longer afraid to say anything that we might not understand. He just talks away like everybody else and has an opinion on everything, and amazingly enough, the more he talks the more we understand him; his words don't seem to be glued-up anymore. Pee-Wee has given him a leather-bound scrapbook and, in her friendly way, is showing him how to paste the clippings in. Tiny has been busy cutting them out from all the papers he could get hold of. Jason has brought him a clipping from his Montana home paper, Bruce has one from Los Angeles, and I have a little item for him from my Omaha Gazette. Red promises one from Oklahoma City and Pee-Wee has friends in Boston and New York and she'll get him a few clippings from there, too. Tiny feels big. He enjoys being the smallest welder in the world as much as he had resented it in the past, which goes to show you that it's not so important what you are, but how you feel about it.

But there is also a story in the paper that a certain distinguished composer has arrived in San Francisco, and that makes Dimples' conscience boil over and she spills her story drop by drop.

Well, to our disappointment, and especially to Lovella's, it turns out that Dimples was not a success in Hollywood after all. Beauty queens from all over the country find their way to Hollywood but, according to Dimples, 999 out of every thousand either go home again or become waitresses in a bar hoping one day Alfred Hitchcock will buy a drink and give them a break. If we can believe Dimples, the whole Hollywood business is something like a hit-and-run raid, one making a hit and the others running for a job.

It seems that Dimples had about decided on the bar bit when she met the big composer whom she calls Magi. When Dimples speaks of Magi her eyes go dreamy. He's a guy of nearly sixty and one of the few real geniuses of Hollywood's Who's Who. Dimples says he can make an immortal tune out of a baby's sneeze, and everybody is so worried about not disturbing his peace of mind that even his cook doesn't have the heart to leave him and get married though her fiancé keeps sending her ultimata. Well, it seems Magi has only to say "hoodoo-voodoo" and the doors of Hollywood society fly open, and he said it more than once for Dimples. She had the time of her life, met people up and down the society page, and even got some nibbles from the studios.

Then, to top it all off, to her utter consternation Magi asked her to marry him. One doesn't say no to Magi and, besides, she was dazzled. More doors flew open, including those of Metro-Goldwyn-Mayer. Did she have it? The answer, she found out, was negative. Not that her face wasn't photogenic, or her voice too nasal, or that she couldn't act. These minor details can be fixed up by the Hollywood magic mill which puts in an ugly duckling on one side and, presto! out of the other side comes a swan that can tap dance. What Dimples didn't have was the ability to fit into a life that sounds glamorous only in the gossip columns. She was raised to pinch every penny, and here people were making more money in one week than her whole family in a year, and spending twice as much. She couldn't get used to people who say the opposite of what they think, who look at marriage as a stepping stone to a career—in fact, they marry so often, and mostly to someone who just got divorced from a friend, that Dimples claims Hollywood is just one big family related by marriage.

One day Dimples woke up and realized she didn't belong to that family. She hated herself for believing that being a star was more important than being herself. And she admitted to herself that whatever "successes" she had came not because of her talent but because of Magi. A great longing for Kenny gripped her—Kenny whom she had hurt by being her honest self and writing him about Magi and life in Hollywood. He had been shipped overseas, and she had been too busy to see him off. Now he was somewhere in the South Pacific. Even if she had known his whereabouts she couldn't write him.

Suddenly she wanted to get away from it all, and get away fast. She tried to talk to Magi about it but couldn't do it. She found it just as hard to level with him as to stay another day in Hollywood. So she did the cowardly thing and disappeared. She knew Magi would find her if she went back home to Seattle. So she used the Richmond shipyard as a hideout. That was one place Magi would never suspect.

What follows makes us all blush. It's Dimples' declaration of love for us, no less. She says living with us is like going to a fresh, clean mountain place after living in the dumps. Not that we're angels, not by a long shot. But if we have a beef we say so, and if we don't like someone we fight him with our fists. And if a guy loves a girl, he tries to marry her, and if he feels like kissing a girl, he takes her out for a dance and tries to make her like him. Dimples admits she may be prejudiced because she comes from folks who work for a living and never have a cent unless they sweat for it.

She doesn't want to talk about Hollywood even though Lovella tries hard. She wants to forget that chapter of her life and prepare for the future chapters with Kenny. She remembers his plans. He had wanted to help win the war, and afterwards work in the American service to rebuild the world. Right after Pearl Harbor he had gone to officer's school and learned Japanese so that he could work in the postwar administration, somewhere in Manchukuo or Formosa, with her as his wife. He had talked to her of his dreams which, for a while, had been *their* dreams—and now he's somewhere in the Pacific, alone. All she can do is to learn Japanese so next time he comes home on furlough she can tell him in Japanese that she is ready to go with him to Manchukuo. So, she's taking classes in Japanese, and since Japanese has many signs taken from Chinese, Tiny is a great help to her.

But now the tough part is to face Magi and tell him, sorry, it was all a mistake. That's beyond Dimples. Who is she, anyway? If she were Greta Garbo or Eleanor Roosevelt she could go to him and talk to him on the same level. But being who she is, Dimples, she feels like a snowflake that wants to go up to the sun and give it the cold shoulder. That's the problem in a nutshell, but it's an awfully tough nut to crack.

"Speaking of nuts," says Chuck, after a short pause, "the joke's on you. If a man wants to marry a girl, and

60

the girl doesn't want to, I don't care who he is and who she is, the only thing to do is to go to him and say so. It'll hurt him, and here I speak from experience, but he'll get over it."

Dimples' voice is so small you could put it in a thimble. "But I can't do it," she says. "That's one thing I can't do."

Here, Tiny, who's been quiet till now, speaks up, "Don't worry," he announces slowly, "I'll take care." Then, with finality, he declares, "I go speak to Mr. Magi."

There are all kinds of noises from all sides that, translated into English, mean: "But Tiny, you can't do that!"

Tiny speaks carefully, and you can see he's thought it all out. "Mr. Magi," he explains, "is famous man. Newspaper write about him. I am famous man, too. Newspaper write about me. President shaked hands with me. Maybe he not shaked hands with Mr. Magi. I can speak with Mr. Magi."

There is so much confidence in Tiny's words that it knocks us over. A whiff of a giggle is on Lovella's lips. Dimples looks shell-shocked, and Chuck is speechless. It's Pee-Wee who finds words first.

"That is sweet of you, Tiny," she says tactfully. "But remember, it's a very personal affair between Dimples and Magi."

"I know," replies Tiny. "But I am very personal friend of Miss Dimples, no I not?"

Dimples, with effort, turns on some of her dimples. "Sure you are," she says, "but still, you can't possibly . . ."

Her voice fades away and we all take over the arguments why Tiny can't possibly. The arguments are so obvious it seems silly to voice them, but they're lost on Tiny. His mind is made up and he can't grasp the idea he may be wrong. He appears to get harder and harder like an egg after the third minute. From time to time he assures us we needn't worry anymore because he'll take care of the whole matter, and his word sounds as final as a Supreme Court decision.

Eventually he resolves there has been enough talk and now it's time for action. He leaves, and there's nothing for us to do but leave too. Dimples seems relieved about the turn of events, coward and fool that she is!

I admit I worried all the next morning, and the others tell me they felt the same way. In the afternoon, worse comes to worst—Dimples doesn't show up for work.

Tiny is all smiles, but we know that's a mask. We wait to see whether he'll tell us anything, but he keeps quiet. Finally Lovella can't stand it any longer.

"Everything is all right," he reassures her.

"What do you mean, 'all right?'" Lovella pounces on him. "What happened?"

"I spoke to Mr. Magi," says Tiny in a matter-of-fact tone. "Very nice man. He read about me in the paper. He knew all about me."

"Never mind yourself," Lovella snaps, "what about Dimples?"

"I not see Miss Dimples," Tiny reports. "I told Mr. Magi. He say it's all right. He go back to Hollywood. Very nice man."

That's all we can get out of Tiny. He's busy welding in all kinds of corners and between pipes. Dimples' absence makes us wonder what kind of a mess Tiny has made of her affairs. When she shows up the next day, however, we feel relieved because she seems to have dug a few more dimples in her cheeks, and she shows them all in a big, wide smile.

She stands at her toolbox, putting on the leathers over her jeans and taking out her stinger, brush, pick hammer, hood and heavy gloves. We drown her with questions. She turns on her welding machine and adds a driblet of noise to the prevailing din.

"I am so grateful to Tiny," she says.

"He really did it?" asks Lovella, removing the wrapper from a piece of gum with her teeth.

Alibi passes by. He seems mad. "Get ready, you two," he shouts. "They took Tiny away from us, those hen-snatchers! They claim they need him on the deep tanks. As if we don't need him here too! Now we've got to get along without him. We've got to finish welding bulkhead 68 before lunch!"

"He did as much for me as I did for him," Dimples reports. "I made him go down and weld that hollow seam. And he made me go and talk to Magi. When he said he'd go and talk to Magi himself, I simply saw no other way but to get there first. It wasn't half as bad as I thought it would be. Suddenly I knew exactly what to say and said it."

"Hey you!" Alibi bellows through the increasing noise. "Are you on vacation?"

"Coming!" Dimples shoulders her coiled hose and drags it up the platform. She dumps it and sets the stinger. "I guess there's a spot in everyone where he feels tiny until someone comes along and shows him that he is just as big there as he wants to be." She bobs up her head, drops her hood, and her welding flash blends into the dazzling pattern of our shipyard.

United Nations

The first woman shipfitter who joins our gang is a goodlooker. Our flanger girl, Pee-Wee, and Dimples and Lovella, our welders, are all excited about the way the newcomer's overalls fit. The men just whistle. Gosh says "Gosh" and Sandy, her leaderman, gives her a handshake like a candidate before election and tells her how glad he is to have her with us. Pink and Pipsqueak, the two college kids who spend their weekends working in the yard, buzz around her like hummingbirds around a snapdragon. Pink jumps at a chance to punch some chalklines with her and returns to Pipsqueak going pit-a-pat.

"Is she really French?" Pipsqueak wants to know.

"As French as a fried potato," Pink assures him. "Latest model from Paris."

Only Chuck, second in command, looks like a turtle that has retired into its shell for the duration. And Chuck

65

isn't one who is prejudiced against women. Not him—he's prejudiced for them. But he steers clear of this one as though this potato was not only fried but sizzling.

After he works with Bruce a couple of hours, silent as a movie in the twenties, Bruce can't stand it any longer and wants to know what in the world is the matter with him. Chuck puts down his two-foot square, looks straight into Bruce's eyes and asks, "How many women are there in this darned world?"

"A billion, I'd say," guesses Bruce, a bit surprised.

"A billion!" Chuck kicks the two-foot square against the girder he is working on. "And of all the lousy places, this one must be just here!"

A welder flashing next to them snaps open her hood and turns out to be Lovella, our private gossip columnist. She can hear a scandal ten feet away, even through the worst chipper's noise when nobody else can understand what's being yelled right into his ear. Lovella seems to hear right with the tip of her tongue. If you tell a story near her, you might as well broadcast it to the whole yard. But Chuck doesn't seem to mind, and while putting a cargo hatch together, he unloads a cargo from his heart.

We all know that Chuck has been around because he never forgets to tell us how they do this in China and that in Brazil. He's the only one in our gang who has seen a Nazi in the flesh, and he keeps telling us how it feels to live under a dictator and claims that nobody around here has any idea what it's like. He says it's like a toothache, and you can't describe it to someone who's never had one. That toothache theory seems to be an obsession of Chuck's. He had to find out everything himself. That's why he never settled down to a job but whirled around the world to see what it was like. Born in San Francisco, he worked a sailor's way to China as soon as he was old enough to pass for sixteen. He was a newsboy in London, a waiter in Rio de Janeiro, a dishwasher in Bombay; he returned to the States and then shipped out again.

In 1938 in Paris, it happened. She was a student at the Sorbonne and they called her "Cherie." To be truthful, it didn't happen then. They just had a swell time, the sort of time you could have only in good ol' Paris. He went on to London and met Margaret, the daughter of a big-shot lawyer, whose ancestors had been lawyers and probably had some part in the murder case of Abel vs. Cain. For Margaret, Chuck was quite an experience. He couldn't sit still even while smoking his pipe. He called her father "old man" and cheered in the opera so enthusiastically that the audience watched him more than they watched the singers. Margaret showed him off to her friends as proudly as though he were a pet panda. But Chuck never liked being a pet in a cage and escaped.

Back in the States, he began to get letters from Cherie and he answered them. After a while, they both knew that they had fallen in love with each other and they decided to make San Francisco their nest. He sent her a ring, a steamship ticket, and an affidavit to enter this country. He counted the days to her arrival and anxiously watched the Germans closing in on Paris. He didn't hear anything for weeks. Then he got the letter he least expected. It was mailed in Marseilles. Cherie wrote that in these past few weeks, fleeing from Paris, she had met someone else who had come to mean an awful lot to her. She would give the world for the past three weeks to be wiped out of existence but those things just didn't happen. She felt utterly unworthy of all the fine feelings he had for her but hoped with all her heart he would eventually find happiness. Enclosed was his ring—but not the steamship ticket and affidavit.

That letter hit Chuck right between the eyes. He had been the "one and only beloved one"; now "someone else" had appeared and everything which was "meant forever" was wiped off like the dust on a piano. That again was a new kind of toothache to him, something he had

67

heard about a thousand times but had never gone through. The more he grieved about it, the more he thought of Margaret. Whatever you may say against the British, they're firm of character. Look how they take the aerial blitz of their homes! He wrote to Margaret and Margaret answered. He found a great deal of comfort in her letters.

And he found more. It seemed the German bombs had not only destroyed the walls of English houses, but also the walls Englishmen often build around themselves. She no longer saw him as the funny little American, but a friend across the ocean who was in the same boat. He and she were different but if they didn't row together, their boat would sink. Margaret had never worked in her life, but now she was busier than a school-corner cop, evacuating children from London. She went into the slums of London and met We the People. That made her see a new side of life, and it made her think. And the more she thought, the more she wondered what America was really like, that country where they had written a whole constitution for We the People.

So she jumped at the chance to accompany children to the U.S. Chuck met her in Chicago. She was surprised that the people in Chicago were not so different from the people in Liverpool or Birmingham. After a diet of American movies, she had expected to find every man in Chicago talking out of the side of his mouth and with a bulge at the left hip where he carried his gun. Still more of a surprise was Chuck, who told her that he had given up bumming around and was working at a shipyard near his California home town. Being British, Margaret was attracted more by shipbuilding than by anything else. They spent an unforgettable evening together talking about all kinds of unimportant things but telegraphing their mutual admiration by way of the international code of the eyes.

Margaret left for England the next day, but when she brought another bunch of kids to a Midwestern town, their letters had softened up their defense lines sufficiently and

68

Margaret went on to San Francisco. There she was, all ready to say the fateful "I do" when, out of the billion women on earth, Cherie turned up in our yard.

"She wants to explain things," Chuck concludes his story and shrugs. He laughs unexpectedly, and it sounds like a hiccup. "You see, she used the steamship ticket and affidavit I sent her. She claims it was the only chance she had—a lifesaver—otherwise she would be stuck in Marseilles, and I don't doubt that part of her story. But what gets me is she didn't just use the papers I sent her as my fiancée for herself. No. She had the crust to bring that guy along, that 'someone else,' that son of a gun. He's a Russian by the name of Dubrovnowski. He's a swing-shift welder up on the boat!"

Lovella obviously enjoys that twist and studies Cherie with interest. The French girl is on her knees punching lines which Pink and Pipsqueak are snapping across the plates. You have to punch every line on the assembly because the chalklines are gone in no time, but you can find the punch marks any time you scratch the rust off the plates. Every time Cherie hits her punch with her little hammer, a blonde lock pushes its way through her brown hair and falls over her forehead, and once in a while she pauses to toss it back. There is a second blonde strand near her left temple and Pink claims that her eyes have the same color as those two locks.

The boys are tickled to have someone like Cherie to order around. "Will you hold that chalkline for me, cherry," and "Get me some spinach, cherry," and so it goes. When she's confused about the spinach business, they take great pains to explain to her the difference between a spinach and a dog which are two types of steel clips. Bruce, who can't stand the wrong pronunciation of the girl's name, tells the boys that her name is French and not pronounced "cherry" but "shairee," which means "darling." Pipsqueak says that she may not be a cherry but she certainly is a peach. He goes up to her and asks her,

69

"Will you please get some bolts and nuts for me, darling?" whereupon the girl lifts her hand and slaps his face. Pink gets a kick out of that slap, but from then on Pipsqueak treats her as cautiously as a faulty welding line.

During the meal break Cherie sits down on a six-by-eight and soon a guy in welding leathers joins her. There's nothing much you can see in two people munching their sandwiches, but since Lovella has lost no time spreading the story, everybody is discreetly staring at them, like at the Maharajah of India traveling incognito. The Russian is a tough-looking fellow, but who isn't in welding leathers? For a while we try to pronounce his name but soon we call him Ski which is the only part of his name we can agree on. Chuck calls him various unquotable names and wants to know what this guy's got that he hasn't. To which Pipsqueak says, "The girl."

Two days later the story takes a turn from muddle to huddle. We get a new weldchecker, a girl who goes around the assemblies and the boats and writes down how many feet of weld are done by each crew, so that the man-hour office can juggle the figures around and find out the best crew to prod the others on; they also figure under what circumstances a welder is at his best. Then they put out charts of their findings. Welding becomes more and more the bottleneck of production because, with all the prefabrication, you can build a ship in exactly the time you need to weld the pieces together. With our manpower limited, we have to get out of each welder as much footage as possible and maybe ten percent more. That's where the weldchecker and the man-hour office come in, but there are those who think that if all the people in those departments would do some welding themselves, we might get more footage yet. However that may be, a weld hasn't got a chance to cool off before it's measured, classified, catalogued, indexed, alphabetized and whatnot—and the place swarms with weldcheckers.

A new weldchecker, therefore, is no greater surprise than a new egg on a chicken farm. This one is a properly dressed girl, looking like an illustration from a handbook for safety inspectors: no rings, no laces or bows, no cuffs on jeans. Only when she takes off the hard hat and kerchief can you see her dark, shiny hair, with a triple garland of curls all around her head. The guys call her Miggs and she is friendly yet distant like a full moon, except to Chuck. To him she's like a new moon—nonexistent.

You don't have to be a quiz kid to guess that Miggs is slang for Margaret, and the words she pronounces smack of the Thames. Lovella doesn't have too hard a time drawing the latest dope out of Chuck, because Chuck's about as full of steam as a pot of boiling water.

Well, it seems Cherie has had the desire for a straight talk with Chuck and insisted on explaining things to him and on paying back his expenses for steamship ticket and affidavit, including the postage. Whenever Cherie makes up her mind, you can't stop her any more than you can stop Gandhi from fasting. She went to Chuck's apartment, accompanied by Ski, and unfolded her story in front of Miggs who had no inkling of the existence of a Cherie in Chuck's life. Miggs was all sugar and honey in Cherie's presence but turned to vinegar as soon as little Frenchie left.

So, Chuck was engaged all along, and only when he had been turned down was he good enough to remember her. Ha! Miggs' eyes spluttered bullets of hurt pride into Chuck who listened with a rapidly rising temperature. When she stopped for breath, he threw in his two cents worth of libels. After some chain-talking, Miggs came to the conclusion that Cherie's explanation of coming to California just to pay for the steamship tickets was as fishy as a parachutist in the neighbor's garden. Cherie probably wasn't sure, after all, whether she liked the Russ better than Chuck and just wanted to have a good look at

71

both before she decided. You never can tell about a girl who once found "someone else." She might find someone else any time, or go back to her first choice.

This one hit Chuck squarely on the jaw because he, too, had asked himself what he'd do in case Cherie wanted to get rid of Ski and come back to him. He didn't know the answer but suspected that the desire to get even with Ski might have something to do with his decision. Miggs sensed his doubts and wanted to see clearly for herself. So she went to the shipyard and got herself a job as a weldchecker—and not just to check welds.

There they are, four jumping beans in a box of TNT. It goes without saying that Miggs has no use for Cherie, and Chuck none for Ski, and that works the other way round, too. But there's also no love lost between Miggs and Ski, and neither Cherie nor Miggs are on speaking terms with Chuck. And to top it all, one day Lovella reports that Cherie has broken with Ski because he is jealous of Chuck and wants her to leave the yard. But Cherie insists on staying until she has earned enough to pay Chuck back what she owes him. So Chuck has lunch with us, Miggs with her weldchecker crew, Cherie all by herself on her six-by-eight, and Ski somewhere on the boat. Nobody knows much about Ski anyway.

One evening the sun sets behind the Golden Gate bridge in a glory of violet and lemon, and everybody feels full of pep. The steel plates on the assembly are strewn with debris from the day shift, and Cherie and Pee-Wee are busy sweeping them off with brooms. Pee-Wee seems to enjoy that job, and when she's sweeping a 40-ton upper-deck unit you half expect her to put a doilie on the stiffeners and a vase with flowers on the hatch-end beam.

We usually have one-hour crane service when swing shift starts so the completed units can be taken to the

72

hull and new plates brought to be assembled into new units. It's a busy time for Sandy the fitter leaderman. He has to figure out the best way to make use of the space on our assembly without wasting too much of the crane's time, which is as carefully measured as your ration of sugar. Each Way, besides having little cranes like choo-choos and doodlebugs, has one Whirley on each side. A Whirley runs on rails along the whole assembly and the whole boat, which is about 600 feet long. It can pick up anything from the assembly and drop it in place any-where on the hull. One Whirley can carry forty tons, but our inner-bottom unit weighs more than fifty, and so the cranes to our left and to our right have to join forces. The rigger stands on top of the unit and talks to the operators, each in his cabin higher than the hulls. He talks the language of the riggers, sometimes raising his finger and boring a hole straight up into the air, sometimes circling his hands around each other, sometimes joining them as if in prayer, and sometimes thumbs up or thumbs down. There's even a signal when the rigger puts his hand on his rear end, which means "go aft."

This evening our two Whirleys hold our inner bottom left and right like daddy and mommy taking junior out for a walk. They lift it a bit, always on a level, higher and higher, until the whole unit is above the staging built around the hull. Then, ringing the warning signal, both Whirleys travel along, taking the unit right over our assembly.

Alibi's powerful voice shouts a warning, "Heads up!" over Swede the chipper's noise. Chuck and Sandy signal to Pee-Wee to get out of the way, and Okie Red taps on Lovella's hood, because a welder under her hood can't see or hear much. Jason drops his sledgehammer. "Let's get the hell out of here," he says to Okie Red. Red looks up at the 50-ton unit sailing towards them and pats his hard hat. "Nothing can happen to me," he grins with a wink,

73

"I've got my hat!" Everybody leaves the platform which darkens in the shadow of the passing Whirleys. We follow the traveling unit with our eyes and Pink admires the huge number he has painted on it.

Up there, the crane operators calmly steer their load which could destroy the assembly and everything on it if it crashed. We have a good man piloting our Whirley, Clif, who used to be an ace in World War I when he flew a plane and won a bunch of decorations. He's a silent sort of guy, but who wouldn't be high up there? It's a ninety-foot climb straight up in the air, where no one drops in for a chat. Most of the kids envy him that job, especially those who are taking up flying.

"One nice thing about being up there," Pipsqueak muses, "he's not likely to get hit by a falling bolt." Cherie points to her hard hat. "He can wear a soft hat," she sighs dreamily, for God knows, she has worn a different style back there in Paris.

Meanwhile, the danger has passed and everyone goes back to work. That inner bottom no longer is one of our worries; the shipwrights on the hull will set her in place, join her to her neighbors, and have her welded in.

Suddenly thunder fills the air, so loud it drowns out the din of the yard. Immediately after, the hum of work dies down and it gets as quiet as it usually does only before the whistle. Everybody stops working and listens.

"Something must have crashed on the boat," Dimples says, but Bruce shakes his head. "That was an explosion," he decides, his face clouded with worry.

At that moment the sirens begin to shriek. It sounds like a jive session in hell. There's a long wail and a short interval—and every time you think it's over, on it goes again. Fire trucks whizz by, one after the other, whining like screaming bombs, and then we see a flame leaping from our boat up against the sky.

Workers from all the Ways come to find out what's going on. Pee-Wee suggests we seek shelter under the hull as we are supposed to do in case of an air raid. Bruce, our trained warden, assures us that this is no air raid warning because the sound of the siren didn't go wailing up and down. Miggs says that in London during the blitz she learned to tell the difference between all kinds of alarms, and this one is, without a doubt, a fire alarm. Lovella suddenly shouts that she can see Jap planes high up in the air. Jason looks up calmly and says, "Japs, hell. That's a couple of sea gulls."

There's confusion, and still more curiosity, until they broadcast over the loudspeakers that there has been an accident on Hull Number Five, but the fire is being brought under control and everyone is to go back to work.

So everybody gets going except that our minds are still on that fire. It's our boat that is burning, and everybody is speculating how on earth it could have happened. Cars are streaming in, filled with police and soldiers and big shots and plain-clothes cops. Cherie, who at the first sound of the burst had been running toward the boat now returns through the cordon of police. We crowd around her. Her face shows deep concern.

"There was—" she pauses to look from one face to another. "There was a bomb in the unit they just took up the boat."

"A bomb!" It comes from all sides, a mixture of disbelief and indignation. But Cherie doesn't seem to notice the crowd around her waiting for more details. She turns to Chuck with a gesture of desperation.

"Oh, Chuck, you've got to help us!" She puts her hand on his arm. "They think Ski did it."

That gives Chuck quite a turn, and I don't know which startles him more, the accusation or Cherie's appeal. Gosh manages a breathless "Gosh"; we others are speechless. It's little, quick-thinking Pee-Wee who asks the question that is on all our minds. "Why do they think he did it?"

"Oh, I don't know," Cherie waves her hands impatiently. "Just *stupidité*. Ski was around when the thing exploded. But anyone could have put it there. Anyone here on the assembly." Her forefinger sweeps through the air and seems to point at each one of us. "And anyone on the boat. But they all know each other, and Ski's a stranger." She shrugs. "Someone shouted that he's a communist and communists are terrorists. *Voilà*."

"Is he a communist?" Lovella wants to know.

"That's not the point," Cherie snaps angrily. "They're wild. They'll kill him."

Chuck, who hasn't said a word, looks as if he wouldn't mind that. A wave of anger sweeps over Cherie's face, and she stamps her foot.

"This is no time for jealousy!" she shouts. "Come on and tell them."

Chuck looks restive. "I don't know that guy myself."

"But this is abominable!" Cherie spreads out her ten fingers in desperation. "You know me and I know him. Isn't that enough?"

Chuck gives a short laugh. "I'm no good character reference for him."

Cherie seems to be at the end of her self-control. As if driven by an inner explosion, she flies at Chuck, grabs both his shoulders and shakes him like a man you want to wake up.

"Chuck," she cries, "be yourself! There's a saboteur among us, a man who throws bombs into our ships. Do you want to let him run amuck only because I've hurt your pride?"

There's a short pause while Chuck's jaw twitches. "The cops will take care of that," he says eventually.

Cherie doesn't waste another word on him. She pivots around and pushes her way through the crowd. Chuck stands there looking forlorn. Suddenly Miggs is next to him.

76

"That wasn't fair," she declares calmly.

Chuck comes to life again. "What do you want me to do?" he asks scornfully. "Stick my neck out for a guy I've only seen twice and didn't want to see even once?"

Miggs' expression is so quiet in all that excitement that it's a relief to be near her. "You could find out who threw the bomb," she prompts him. "That's what the Chuck I met in London would do."

"You are all just plain crazy." Chuck jerks his head toward the platform, "Let's drop the monkey business and get to work."

But this is no day for work. Our Way is full of people asking questions, taking down names, looking the place over. Every one of us is a suspect and inevitably you find yourself looking around, wondering which of all these guys could have been the traitor who planted a bomb in the boat we are building together. And it dawns on us that we know nothing about the people with whom we have been working all these months. Any one of them might be an escaped convict, a fascist, a spy, a saboteur. But it's hard to believe. Bruce's train of thought must have been on the same track. I overhear him say to Pee-Wee and Dimples, "You see, that's the difference between a dictatorship and a democracy. In a dictatorship everybody suspects everybody. In a democracy nobody suspects anybody."

Even the big Whirley stops working, and if a Whirley quits, all work within its reach stops, because a modern shipyard without a crane is helpless. The proud giraffe neck of our Whirley is stooped as though it had a guilty conscience. Clif, who never leaves his high spot, not even during lunch hour, is down on the ground. An FBI guy takes him into the hull foreman's office which is used as headquarters for the investigation where we all are taken to see whether we can provide a clue. Clif usually wears a disgusted expression on his face—or maybe it's just heart-

77

burn. If he talks, nine times out of ten it's a story about the last war, of how he blasted a German out of the sky or dropped a stick of TNT on a munitions depot, and now he has that dull job up in the Whirley.

His eyes burn angrily. "Have I seen something!" he shouts. "I'll say I have. Before the shift started, a bunch of loafers were busy electing their committee, the one that's going to decide whether a guy can take a day off. Try and make them come to work an hour earlier, and you'll hear some howl from the unions. But when it comes to making speeches, balloting, voting, wasting time and all that crap, then they are right there. If a guy has no more sense than to lay off because he's drunk or has wasted his money on a girl, then by golly, kick him in the pants and he'll remember. And if he doesn't remember and lays off again, beat the stuffing out of him."

The officer taps the pencil against his knuckles. "It has been decided by the labor-management committee to fight absenteeism through elected representatives of the workers themselves. There was nothing wrong with that election."

"Election! Committees!" Clif snorts. "Can't that damn yard be run without them?"

The tapping of the pencil grows more impatient. "Maybe it can. But what we want to know from you is whether you saw anyone monkeying with that unit you took up the boat this afternoon."

"No," Clif grumbles. "I didn't."

The officer turns to us. "Has anyone seen anything suspicious?" A chorus of no's is the answer. Then, to the hull foreman, "What about that welder you told me about?"

"He was the first one to go down with his welding machine and a box in which he claims he had his welding rods."

78

"Did anyone see him go down to that compartment where the bomb was planted?"

"No. That compartment was all finished on the assembly. That's why nobody was seriously hurt."

"And the guy who was down there, was he hurt?"

"No, sir."

"What kind of a guy is he?"

"We don't know much about him. He's been working in the yard only a few days. He's not a citizen but was checked by the FBI before he got the job. He's a Russian."

The officer looks up. "Russian?"

"Yes, sir. We have taken him into custody."

"All right. Bring him in."

The little room is crowded with our gang. Lovella, of course, stands in front, her eyes taking snapshots and her mind recording every word for later rebroadcasting to her friends. Pee-Wee, on tiptoe and leaning on Jason's arm, jumps up from time to time to see better. Happy, our burner, is squatting in a corner, giving his red helmet a shine.

When Ski is shoved through, Cherie is with him, every inch the Fighting French. The officer behind the desk looks straight into his eyes and Ski returns the glance. Ski's wide cheekbones are pale. The two men stare at each other silently for what seems to be ages. Then the officer takes down his name and address. Putting down his pencil and settling back, he asks, "Why did you leave Russia?"

Ski answers without hesitation. His father couldn't get used to the new regime and left for Poland. Ski stayed behind and worked on a collective farm until his father fell ill and wanted to see him. Ski couldn't get a permit to leave Russia but decided to see his father anyway. Once in Poland, he couldn't go back to Russia. So, after his father's death, he went on to Paris where he worked in a factory until the Nazis came.

"Do you regret having left Russia?"

"Yes, sir." Ski's voice sounds grave. "I now regret it very much." The hull foreman looks grim as though he were saying, "Ah! Just as I thought!"

The officer seems puzzled. "Why?" he asks.

"Because I want to fight for Russia on Russia's soil." It sounds simple. A proud smile slips across Cherie's lips. The officer relaxes.

"Do you believe in the institutions of the Soviet Union?"

"In most of them."

"Are you a communist, then?"

"I'm against force," Ski says, "but for state ownership of vital industries."

The hull foreman looks bewildered. "Well now, are you or are you not a communist?"

At that moment Cherie, who's had a hard time keeping quiet, speaks up, "And if you decide, *messieurs*, he is a communist, would that prove it was his bomb?"

The officer smiles at her with his eyes. "You're the French girl, his fiancée?"

Cherie gives him a double nod. "*Oui, monsieur.* And I was with him when he fled from Paris to Marseilles. You come to know a man pretty well when dive bombers are after you and the road looks like a graveyard. After that, you know that he wouldn't try to blow up a ship which is built to fight the fascists."

The officer, the foreman, and some of the big shots who haven't opened their mouths so far, stick their heads together and announce that we can go back to work. Ski is to be taken along for some more questioning. Cherie turns on the danger signal in her eyes. If she were a rattlesnake, she'd raise her head and hiss. Being Cherie, she says, "*Mais, messieurs*, this is preposterous."

There is some shuffling in the back of the room and Chuck appears before the desk. He fingers the leather tool

80

pouch on his hips, then looks straight into the officer's face. "If you need some character references, sir," he says, standing at attention, "I have known Dubrovnowski and have heard about him quite a bit through Mademoiselle. I know Mademoiselle very well. You can trust her."

The officer gets up quickly. "Thanks, I may need you later on. I may need you all later on." He picks up his papers and the whole party, including Ski, walks out of the room. Chuck is still standing on the same spot, looking peeved. Cherie slaps her hard hat down on her chestnut and gold-sprinkled hair.

"*Imbéciles*," she says with contempt; then she turns to Chuck. "That was *magnifique*, Chuck. *Merci*."

Chuck slowly comes to life. "They can't do that to us. Who the hell do they think they are?"

Cherie puckers her nose. "Now," she smiles. "That's more like yourself. What are we going to do?"

"Find that fascist skunk who did it, break every bone in his body and send him to the police as a jigsaw puzzle."

"*C'est bien*, but how?"

"Oh, I don't know. I'll go around and ask the fellows. Perhaps someone has seen or heard something."

We know that's brave talk but useless. The break whistle goes off, but it's a silent meal. Everybody is munching sandwiches filled with gloom. Only Happy has something to cheer himself up, a small red ribbon, half burned, which he tries to use as a bow around his neck to match his red hat and shoes. Sandy, just to break the depressing atmosphere, asks him where he got it, and Happy says he found it up on the boat.

"Where?" asks Chuck. "Anywhere near the blast?"

"Just about," nods Happy, beaming at the attention he is getting. Everybody is examining the little ribbon. Bruce shrugs. "A piece of red tape may be responsible for a lot of trouble but not for an explosion."

"It has a funny little pattern in the middle," Chuck says.

"Let me see," Pee-Wee reaches for the red tatter and studies it carefully, a deep crease appearing on her forehead. "I don't know where, but I've seen that design somewhere here in the yard. Maybe on a bandana or a scarf the girls wear."

"*Cherchez la femme*," Cherie remarks.

"We can't go on sleuthing during the whole shift," Sandy grumbles. "We have to finish that deep-tank unit, bomb or no bomb."

"It's our only chance, though," Chuck insists. "If we don't catch him now, we'll never catch him."

"Oh, you just want to go around looking at girls' bandanas," Bruce says.

"I can take care of that," Miggs offers. "I've got to walk around anyway checking the welding. Besides," with a side glance at Chuck, "a woman has a better eye for a girl's—bandana."

We finish our deep-tank unit. When Miggs returns, her communique reads, "No bandana, no design, no soap." Pee-Wee still has that faraway look in her eyes.

"I've been thinking all evening," she says. "I'm sure I saw that pattern somewhere in the yard. And it seems to me it's the design of a hand."

"Wait a minute!" Bruce closes his eyes and, with both hands, waves away all disturbances. "A hand! I've seen it too. A fist, as a matter of fact. Oh, I know. I know! It's a funny little flag in the rigger's office. Red, white and blue, with a fist in the middle."

"Right! That's where it is." Pee-Wee is all set and raring to go, and so are most of us. But Cherie puts on the brakes.

"Let's not make this a march on the Bastille," she says. "Let me handle this."

Off she goes and is back ten minutes later. This is the story she has to tell. There's only one woman in that

82

office. We all know her and call her Sharky because she always looks as though she would like to bite off your leg as soon as you come near her. When Cherie comes in and begins to beat around the bush, Sharky points to a poster that reads: STATE YOUR BUSINESS AND SCRAM. LOAFING IS TREASON. Cherie carefully reads that poster, which is just beneath the flag with the fist, and so it seems quite natural to ask about the flag.

"It's an American flag," Sharky snaps. "I don't expect you to know that. You're French, aren't you?"

Cherie admits that she is, and tells Sharky that the French colors are red, white and blue too. She adds that she's never seen one with a fist in the middle and what's the fist for?

"That's none of your business. If you have to know, it's for strength. America Invincible. And that means work, not talk. What is it you're after?"

Cherie makes some excuse of wanting some crane service, and Sharky points out that this is not the proper way to get it, but then you can't expect foreigners to know.

"That's all," Cherie finishes. "Not much of a success, *n'est-ce-pas?*"

Chuck whistles a scale of surprise through his teeth. "I have a notion we're smack on the right track. I'm going to see Pigeontoe, and I want a few of you to come along as witnesses. Only don't make too much of a hullabaloo."

So Cherie, Miggs and I go along. Pigeontoe is an old rigger and as good a man as any when it comes to a difficult lift. His hands and neck are brown and creased like bark and his face would look natural carved out of redwood. The Whirley happens to be busy setting a bulkhead in place. That's the job of the shipwrights and gives the rigger a chance for a breather. Pigeontoe, as usual, is chewing tobacco when we involve him in a friendly chat.

"By the way, Pidgy," Chuck drops casually, "didn't you tell me you joined some patriotic club the other day?"

83

Pidgy spits expertly and nods. "A mighty fine club, too. America Invincible."

"Yes, I thought that was the name," Chuck throws a meaningful look at us. "What kind of an outfit is that?"

"Oh, I dunno. Just American, I guess."

"I know that. We might join, you know, but naturally we want to know what it's all about."

"It's only six bits a month," Pigeontoe says. "You can afford that. You better talk with Clif about it. He's the president."

"Clif, eh?" says Chuck. "Many members there?"

Another spurt of brown tobacco juice lands on a two-by-four. "No, just a handful. Clif doesn't take everyone. Has to be careful. Only really good Americans."

"Hm, I see. You don't remember anything they talked about?"

"Well—they said there's too much talking and meddling instead of action. And that America is the greatest country on earth. It was a fine meeting."

Pigeontoe gets ready for his next lift and we're left alone. Chuck looks serious. "A fascist outfit! You bet Clif has to be careful how he picks his members. What can he get but skunks or dopes. I wonder what Pidgy will say when he finds out that his six bits have bought a share in that bomb!"

We're a silent bunch as we enter the hull foreman's office. He raises his eyebrows when we ask him to send his secretary out. Then Chuck tells him what we know.

The foreman laughs angrily. "Ridiculous," he says. "Clif risked his life for Uncle Sam when all of you sat in your highchairs. He volunteered in 1917. Clif and a bomb! That's a good one!"

"But I tell you he is the president of a fascist organization!"

"Fascist, my foot!" The foreman kicks back a pile of papers, annoyed. "Clif loves America, and he's proved it."

84

The mercury in Chuck begins to rise. "Listen, buddy," he goes off, "I've been around a bit and seen all kinds of birds who loved their country all over Europe. Many of them were dirty liars, but quite a few believed the bunk they preached. Some of them were such crackpots that everybody laughed at them. There were some who disliked Hitler, but they disliked someone else even more—the workers, or the rich, or the Jews, or some goddamn bunch they had a beef against. To put one over on them, they'd have made a pact with the devil. So, Hitler grabbed the country. By the time those dopes realized what they'd done, they were already up to their necks inside the Nazi crocodile."

"All right," snaps the foreman. "All right. I've heard these stories a hundred times. That can happen over there but not in this country. Clif is a topnotch American and all out for the U.S."

"But for the wrong kind of U.S.," Cherie remarks.

"Let the FBI decide that, will you?" The foreman's head gets redder by the minute. "Now, get!" he shouts. "And if I find you snooping around anymore, I'll have you fired, all of you."

"I am curious if he is in it too," Cherie wonders as soon as we're out again, but Chuck shakes his head. "Just mental gout. His mind has everybody tagged like the animals at the zoo. A communist is a communist and an American hero an American hero. To him a word means more than a man."

"Let's go and tell the FBI," Miggs suggests. Chuck shrugs. "What can we tell them? A hunch, no more. Besides, I think we should tackle this thing ourselves."

"Now you're talking," Cherie cheers. "But how? What can we do?"

"I'd like to go up there in that cabin in the sky and use the fist of his own flag right on his nose," Chuck scowls, but he knows that's no good.

We stand around the problem in helpless frustration. Once in a while, one of us bursts out with a brainstorm, but it's scrapped before it's well aired.

Suddenly Miggs snaps her fingers. "I saw a movie once where the inspector trapped a man he suspected. He mentioned in the man's presence that fingerprints had been found near the scene of the crime. He set an appointment with the fingerprint experts for two hours later. The stupid fellow rushed in to wipe off the 'evidence' before the expert arrived—and the fingerprints that weren't there got him into jail."

"That's marvelous," Cherie pokes Miggs' arm. "A cute *ruse de guerre!*"

"Might work," Chuck decides. "What do we have to lose?"

We plant the rumor of the fingerprints by mentioning it in the presence of Sharky and hope for a speedy crop in our victory garden. Sure enough, no sooner are we out of sight than Sharky sneaks to the Whirley and uses the telephone up to Clif's cabin. She seems to be getting instructions because she listens intently and nods a couple of times.

Chuck rubs his palms and we retire to a hideout near the place where the fingerprints are supposed to be. It's deep in the belly of the boat. Everything is twisted by the explosion. Workers are clearing the damaged units so that they can be taken out and replaced by new ones. Naturally, the explosion is still the headline of all conversations, as far as you can converse with hundreds of people chipping and grinding the words from your lips. The longer we wait, the less we feel like Sherlock Holmes. When we're about as low as fifty despair below zero, a figure appears whom we least expect. It's Angel, the Mexican painter, who never rushes—not even out of the gate after shift—because his philosophy is: "If I'm not in the yard, I'm somewhere else. If I'm somewhere else, I spend money. If I'm in the yard, I make money." He's saving money for his old age—he's 75 now.

He dips his broad brush in the rust-preventing red paint and begins to cover our precious spot with slow, broad strokes. Chuck jumps at him and breaks out in red spots all over.

"What's the matter with you?" Angel asks when he has regained his balance. "Have you been stung by a wild bee?"

"What are you painting here for?" Chuck demands threateningly.

"I got an order," Angel explains, and produces a little slip. That's how we work it at the yard. We write our orders on a pad outside the painter's office, so that a painter, when he's through with one job, can find out where he is wanted next. The order Angel presents is written in straight block letters.

"Did you ever paint an inner-bottom unit inside a boat?" Chuck shouts over the din.

Angel shakes his head.

"Then you don't have to paint this one either."

Angel again shakes his head, this time grudgingly. These youngsters nowadays! They don't know what they want themselves.

"A new way to get rid of fingerprints," Chuck mutters. "Sherlock Holmes had an easy time with his criminals. We're in business with chiselers who send out painters!"

"What about fingerprints?" Scotty bellows. He's the shipwright in charge of setting the units right when they are lowered on the boat.

Chuck tells him. He has to let out steam somewhere. He tells his story at the top of his lungs. In the end he's hoarse but feels better. Scotty's eyes get big and round like saucers.

"A flag? There was a flag on the unit when it was

brought out. I saw it and my whole crew saw it. There was something like a fist on it."

Chuck grabs his shoulder and shakes it like a cigarette machine that has cheated you out of a quarter. "Jesus Christmas! Why didn't you say so? That's what we've been looking for!"

A riveter goes off right next to us; he drills through our nerves and words. Nobody tries to say anything while the riveting is at its height. A horrible light is breaking in on Scotty. "How could I know . . ." is the next thing we hear from his pale lips. "How could anything so ghastly come out of an American flag?"

It's not easy to get through to the FBI man. Night shift is streaming in and swing shift is slowing down. Chuck gives a dramatic description while the FBI man takes notes.

"We'll check on that," he promises.

"Check on it!" Cherie shouts. "You've arrested my fiancé on much less evidence, haven't you?"

The FBI man does a lot of telephoning. Finally he winks at Cherie. "We'll get him, all right. Don't worry." He hesitates a second before he continues, "Swell team, you four. Would you care to come along?"

Bet your life we would. We troop along with the FBI man and the cops—Miggs and Chuck, arm in arm, Cherie next to them and obviously wishing she had Ski with her. I really don't belong here. Ski should be here with them. The FBI man is right. Swell team, those four.

Just as we reach the Whirley the whistle blows and Clif climbs down the ladder. It's a long ladder, straight up high. We're standing quietly, watching Clif come down. About twenty feet from the ground he sees us, and for a moment he stops. But there's no escape. He comes down, step by step. When he touches the ground, the FBI man goes forward and says something to him. Clif looks sullen.

88

"Okay," he shrugs. "So you know. A man who doesn't stick to his conviction isn't worth the air he's breathing. I don't want to hush it up. I want to shout it into everybody's ears. That bomb will do its part to wake up America and rally the country around strong men. When that time comes, I'll get my reward. Then American boys won't have to fight for foreigners. Then Uncle Sam won't go on being the Big Sucker, feeding and coddling the whole world."

"The hell with those catchwords," thunders Chuck, and his veins swell on his temples. "If you'd ever use whatever you have in your head, you'd see we're fighting for our very lives."

"This is a clever man," Cherie adds, "who refuses to help repair the first floor because *he* lives on the second."

"Come on," the FBI man pushes Clif on. Two cops have a good grip on him.

"Don't you know what's going on?" Clif shouts. "We are being sold out to the English peers, the Russian generals, the Chinks, the South Americans, the African nigger chiefs, the kicked-out kings! They sell you out, and you vote for them. Vote—that's all you can do. And now here, too! A committee to cure absenteeism! What we need is a strong leader to get us out of this mess!"

"You can write another *Mein Kampf* in prison," Miggs tells him. "But the world will be on guard against people who write autobiographies in advance."

Sharky passes by, in the grip of two cops. She is holding up her fist in a demonstrative salute to Clif, her eyes burning. The crowd begins to guess what's up.

"Come on," urges the FBI man, alarmed, "get going."

Word is spreading that we've caught the man who planted the bomb. There is a sudden rush and the next minute we are the center of a whirl. Threats are hurled at Clif. Shrill whistles and more policemen. I can see Chuck

89

struggling for Miggs and Cherie pushed around, a huge cop trying to protect her. I feel elbows and fists all around me and have a sensation like drowning in a wild ocean. Next thing I remember is the First Aid station with a room full of casualties. Chuck, his overalls torn, is holding Miggs' bandaged hand, and Ski is leaning over Cherie whose cheek is red and swollen.

"We managed to get Clif out of the yard in one piece," Chuck reports. "But the people did their darnedest to thank him for his services. It was a shock to them."

"To him, too, I bet." Ski is holding hands with Cherie. "He thought he was a hero."

"He certainly did," Miggs agrees, smoothing down what used to be a carefully groomed triple garland of curls. "Otherwise he wouldn't have been stupid enough to plant his flag on the bomb." Then, with a faraway look in her eyes, she concludes, "I only wish people would remember that bombs may come in patriotic wrappings."

The Story
of
Seven
Tattoos

Among the unwritten laws of the yard is one which says
you can't sit down or put your hands in your pockets even
if there's nothing to do. Another forbids you to leave the
assembly before the whistle blows. But work drops off
before the shift changes. Burners coil their hoses, welders
turn off their juice, flangers check in their sledges. So
there you stand around your leaderman, and as soon as
the whistle goes off, you grab your timecard and run. I
don't know why you rush, but you do as sure as in a
New York subway.

One day the welders are flocked around Alibi when
he lets out a noise that sounds like a man gargling TNT.

He throws the timecards about like confetti and, leaving a blue swathe of language behind, jumps off the assembly and on a guy in welding leathers who's walking by with a girl. The two men exchange ten words, nine of which don't look good in print. Then they're at it, swapping punches, and man I mean punches. Did you see the movie sequence of the bout in *The Spoilers*? Well, this is it. Meanwhile the girl stands by fixing her hair with the unconcern of a cat licking her paw.

Red tries to break it up but finds himself kissing a pile of brackets. No one else dares to interfere until suddenly a cop appears. A uniform does wonders, and in a moment the puff-faced Alibi and his equally battered sparring partner are held arm's length apart like two roosters with their feathers still bristling. Only then do I see that the cop is a woman.

Alibi pulls back and tries to get away, but the policewoman seems to have a grip like a Whirley.

"Stop it, buddy," she advises him. "Take it easy now."

She's a tall girl with smooth fair hair under her police cap, and eyes as green and refreshing as lime sherbet. Alibi still tries to shake her off. "Let me go," he yells. "You have no business protecting that two-timer. This is a free country. We have a right to slug it out. Toots is *my* girl and that fork-tongued low-lifer took her out for a dance for the third time this week. Of all the double-crossing rats!"

"Loose talk costs lives," the cop snaps. "A girl can go dancing with anybody she pleases. This is, as you said, a free country. There goes the whistle. Scram."

To the other guy who sneers at Alibi, she adds, "And that goes for you too, Mister."

She gets two glances of pure vitriol and Alibi declares, "God only knows why but I never hit a woman. Lucky for you, too, or you would be carrying your front teeth home in your handbag."

This is the first, but by far not the last time the lady-cop takes a hand in our affairs. She is stationed next to our assembly and is as good a watchdog as a jealous husband. She seems to sense approaching trouble as sure as radar picks up approaching planes. She usually shows up just when the tempers are about to boil and, with a grin or a wink, turns the gas lower. Moreover, she has other means. In her pocket is a batch of quit slips and she uses them as effectively as her brothers of the highway, the only difference being that you don't write off a quit slip with two or ten bucks. You're fired.

Not that we are at each other's throats all the time, but if you work a year or more without a holiday or vacation, you collect a lot of gripes, and they are liable to pop out at any moment. And there's that thing called love. Alibi is suffering from it right now, and Alibi in love is no Ferdinand the Bull smelling a flower. He's Ferdinand stung by a bumblebee. So the cop-girl has lots of trouble with him, and he has lots of trouble with her. Her name, by the way, is Juanita, and if you wonder how a Spanish girl can have fair hair and eyes like a pail full of fresh water, I'll let you in on something: she is not Spanish at all, but Irish— Irish descent and temperament, with a Spanish name.

But I'm not thinking so much of Juanita as of Alibi and his Toots. Something is haywire between them and Alibi shows it. He's as easy to upset as a paint bucket on a ladder. As a welder leaderman, he has to keep his mind on the job, especially with more and more welder girls floating in. Cindy used to work in a beauty parlor and isn't used to a job where you have to bend or kneel all the time. Ma Hopkins, close to sixty and looking even older, came to work in the yard after she was notified that her only grandson had been killed in action. Bulgy is about as wide as she is tall and deathly afraid of walking on the assembly with all its booby traps of loose scrap and tangled

93

hoses. All these new welders are a problem to their leaderman. Before the war it used to take a couple of years to become a welder, but now it takes a couple of days. The girls are rushed to the job as soon as they have learned not to be scared by their own arcs. Alibi has to show them the tricks and help them drag their heavy lines across the assembly. These lines are a hundred feet long, filled with electricity and likely to burst into a flash when you least expect it.

A welder leaderman is supposed to be a patient guy, and that's one thing Alibi is not, at least not right now. About half the time he's frothing at the mouth over a trifle. His old hands, Dimples and Lovella, are used to it and even seem to get a kick out of it, but his manner frightens the newcomers. When it gets too hot he tears off his shirt. Then we see that there are six tattoos on his arms and shoulders with the chances that there are more under his undershirt. He has a handcuff painted around his right wrist, a picture of a woman on the inside of his right forearm and a devil's mask on his right shoulder which he can twist to a grimace when he bulges his muscles. On his left arm you find a heart with an arrow pinned through, a ship, and a landscape complete with palm trees and moon. Each of the six tattoos bears the name of Toots.

Well, I figure, if a man goes through all that trouble for a woman he must mean business, and no girl has a right to blow hot and cold at a fellow who has half-skinned himself for her and made a picture album out of his two arms. So I decide to have a little see-here with Toots.

Toots is a welder in the plate shop. That's a huge hall running across nearly the entire width of the yard. There the plates are cut and marked and simple assembling jobs done. It is filled with the deafening screech of machines and clouds of welding smoke. If you work in the plate shop for some time you get used to the noise, but your ears keep ringing for hours after.

94

I pick lunch time for my chat with Toots. She's surprised because she hasn't seen more of me than an eyeful here and there. By now I've gained some experience in sticking my nose into other people's affairs, and so far my nose has always come out unscratched. When I start talking to Toots she takes pieces of cotton out of her ears explaining that this is the only way she can stand the din. She's swathed from head to toe in a welder's suit, her head is turbaned, and from her ear lobes silver earrings jingle.

"Well, Toots," I set out, "I've come to you because I'm worried about Alibi."

Judging from the girl's expression, I see I haven't touched the friendliest chord. "First of all," she snaps, "I'm no Toots. My name is Mary. That's a pretty good name too."

"Sure, sure," I agree readily. "I didn't know. Alibi always calls you . . ."

"Alibi does a lot of things I don't like," she says. "I don't want to have anything to do with him. That," she adds, "you may quote."

I scratch myself around the ears. "Maybe it's just a quarrel, a whim of love, you know."

My suggestion is lost on Toots-Mary. "Nope," she sets me right. "It's sure and final." She bites resolutely into a tomato.

"Well," I say, "your name is written all over him in several colored inks."

This one thaws her somehow. "Yes, I know," she sighs. "That's how it all started. It was a thrill. But now . . ."

I'm busy with my sandwiches.

"Maybe you think I'm a playgirl," she goes on, "but I just want to have a good time while I'm about it and wait for the right guy to settle down and marry."

Her voice trails off and her eyes turn inward—looking at her off-shift self, getting ready for a date, holding a new

95

dress temptingly in front of herself, her feet tapping in anticipation of a dance. I'm still eating sandwiches when the whistle ends the break.

The next day when Alibi shows up for work Juanita grabs his arm. "Let me see your lunch box," she demands. Before Alibi knows what's up, she gets hold of his lunch box, opens it, takes out his thermos, pulls out the cork, and sniffs. Then she nods, puts the cork in place and hands the thermos back to Alibi.

Alibi has followed all this with amazement. "Well, slap me down!" he bursts out. "Are we in the United States or in a German concentration camp?"

Juanita shrugs. "There've been plenty of accidents because guys are coming to work loop-legged. We have orders to watch it."

"Oh yeah?" Alibi sneers. "You think if I wanted to take whiskey along, I'd hide it in a thermos? If I feel like getting drunk, I get drunk. I am no frigidaire that gets lit behind closed doors. Look here, Miss Smarty." He reaches for his back pocket and produces a bottle which he dangles in front of her nose.

Juanita's eyes get cloudy. "Cut it out," she orders. "No drinking on the job."

"Oh, no?" He takes a deep breath, and down it goes. But before you can say "Cheers," Juanita has snatched the bottle from his lips. Alibi stares at her, his veins swelling. We expect he'll at least slap her, but he just stands still, panting. Juanita walks slowly toward him like a lion-tamer about to perform the head-into-the-lion's-mouth stunt, takes the cork from his fingers, closes the bottle, and puts it into her pocket.

"You'll get it after shift," she tells him. "If you want to eat arsenic and old lace in your time off, nobody'll stop you."

Alibi doesn't even open his mouth, but for the rest of the day we steer clear of him.

96

At break time a guy from the plate shop comes up to me with a message from Mary. She'd like to see me after shift.

At eleven then, I pick her up at the gate and we have some ice cream in the cafeteria. She looks cute in her slacks and white blouse. Her slightly tanned throat is circled with a necklace to match her earrings and her white hands are fragrant with some lotion.

Ice cream affects some girls about the same way a drink affects some men, and she begins to talk. I'd shown some understanding the other day, she tells me, and maybe I can help her—get rid of Alibi. She's made up her mind, once and for all. "I'll tell you why," she says, "and you'll see."

Mary is one of the few native Richmond folks. When her father first arrived in 1905, the whole village had no more than seventeen houses. In the spring of 1941, when war was but a cloud on the horizon, the town numbered 20,000. Still, it was a sleepy place and its chief attraction to outsiders was the auto-ferry to Sausalito across the Bay. Suddenly came war and with it four shipyards and an influx of 200,000 people. Just as suddenly came the saloons, movies, clubs and dance halls. The old life of Richmond was disrupted and carried away in the deluge.

The first batch of newcomers were tough cookies, adventurers of the gold-rush type, exciting—but none you would care to meet in a dark alley.

Mary lived with her parents and used to go out with Kelly who helped his father run a hotel in town. Business was good, every room taken and guys begging for a bench in the lobby. Kelly had the idea of hiring a band and throwing a dance every Saturday night in the hotel lounge. He had every reason to regret his brainstorm because it was at the first of those dances that Alibi met Mary.

Alibi just sat at a table and looked at Mary all evening. He didn't dance with any other girl. He sat and drank and watched Mary dancing with Kelly. Wherever Mary went his eyes went along. It made Mary a bit wobbly in the knees. At one a.m. he suddenly sidled up to her and her partner and before they knew what was up, he was waltzing her about the floor.

Kelly protested, but Alibi just said, "This is my favorite tune, and this is my favorite gal," and went on dancing. Kelly cried, "You're drunk," and tried to push him away. The fight was short. Alibi finished the dance with Mary.

That was the beginning of a beautiful romance. Alibi swept Mary off her feet and whirled her right over his head. He danced, talked, sang, played the accordion, he splashed his money about and gave her the time of her life. One thing he didn't do was sleep. They used to dance all night, and toward morning, while Mary, on buttery knees just managed to reach her bed, he was into over-alls and leaving for work. When she woke up he stood under her window playing the accordion and singing while she dressed. Then they drove around, saw a show, went to a dance and talked. Alibi had seen the whole country and parts of South America and Alaska, and so it was a thrill to listen to his stories.

He called her Toots, and she didn't mind. She didn't mind anything at that time. Alibi was a possessive sort of a guy. She had to give up her curls and part her hair in the middle for him; he brought her a special brand of perfume and didn't allow her to use anything else. He bought her a beautiful red evening gown and wanted her to wear red all the time, with a certain kind of nail polish to match. He insisted that she call him Alibi. It was a strange but exciting time. He topped it all when one day he tucked up his shirt sleeves and unveiled six tattoos, her name written on every one of them. Alibi let the devil's face grin and put his wrist with the handcuff against hers and let her feel the crusts that were still on the new tattoo of a ship. "They'll fall off in a day or two," he promised. "I got the most expensive tattoos I could find." He won her mother over in a jiffy, and he and her pop were great pals.

Alibi had their whole life mapped out. He took her to the church in which they would be married. He described the wedding dress and the jewelry she would wear as clearly as if he had already bought them. He drew a sketch of the house he'd build. In fact, he was very fussy about that house. He spent hours explaining to her where the kitchen would be, and what furniture the dining room would have. He seemed to have figured out every stair, every door, every window.

"Just wait till I get rid of that mud job," he promised. "As soon as the yard gets under way I'll get myself a job as a welder. I'll make big money in no time. Then we'll build our house and get married."

The yard at that time was merely a plan in some-body's office. There was just an orchard and a stretch of the Bay which they were filling up with dirt. A nearby hill was being carried off, truckload by truckload, and poured into the Bay. As the hill disappeared the site of the future yard grew. Alibi worked as a pile driver at the wet end. He claimed piles weren't driven at Richmond, they just sank out of sight. One day, he told her with a twinkle in his eye, a new helper had given a pile a light tap with the driver; it went down so fast that the suction pulled the whole crew in after it. They hadn't had such wet bottoms since they were six months old!

But after a while the yard was ready and the first keel was laid. As Alibi had promised, he switched to welding and bigger money. He continued talking about the house and pushing his accordian, and when he wasn't making music, he was jitterbugging to someone else's. In fact, the

99

change from pile-driving to welding hadn't changed Alibi one bit. Mary was beginning to see that living by his side would mean dwarfing her own personality. When Alibi felt like singing ear-splitting songs in the middle of the night, he sang them. When he felt like dancing with Mary on MacDonald Avenue, he danced. When he felt like punching someone in the nose, he punched. "It's a free country," he said.

But it wasn't a free country for Mary. She had to do whatever he wanted. For a time she got a kick out of being looked after like a seven-year-old kid. After a while, however, it got on her nerves. She got tired of always wearing red, of parting her hair in the middle, using the same perfume and of being called "Toots"; but Alibi made her life miserable if she didn't. She got no support from her parents whom Alibi had won over completely. She got no support from her friends because Alibi wanted her for himself all the time. And she couldn't so much as glance at a man without having Alibi in a fighting mood. All these things, to be sure, had pleased her in the beginning, but now she knew she couldn't stand them for the duration of a lifetime, perhaps not even for the duration. To talk things over with him was impossible. To talk things over with someone else was impossible too, because Mary found herself isolated. Her girl friends snubbed her, her boy friends were frightened away, and Kelly was overseas in the army.

One day Mary threw away all the red dresses Alibi had given her. She ditched the perfumes and the nail polish and did her hair up in curls. Then she hopped a train and left town. She got herself a job as a waitress in Sacramento and spent three happy days there. Then, one night, Alibi walked in.

"Where's that skunk?" he asked.

"There is no skunk, except yourself," she said bravely.

She was sure he would hit her, but he didn't. He looked humble. She never dreamed he could look like that. "I've

100

traveled all over the continent to find the girl I wanted," he muttered, "only to find that she doesn't want me."

He promised to be reasonable, and she went back with him to Richmond. They prepared for the wedding. Soon, it started all over again. He was tyrannical about every detail. She was to wear a veil twenty feet long. He went around to pick twelve little girls who were to carry the veil behind her. He was going to throw candy among the wedding guests. He was going to parade to church with the whole crowd, playing the wedding march on his accordion. Mary resented the idea of making a Fourth of July out of her wedding, but Alibi was as persistent as a cold in the head.

So, before there ever could be a wedding, something in her snapped. She found a place where the newly thrown-up houses, the highways and the parking lots, the piles of wood and half-finished scaffolds, had left a little patch of grass with a bench. She threw herself down on the bench and let her tears flow.

"What's up?" a deep voice sounded.

She had to tell someone.

"I wouldn't worry," the stranger advised. "Let that crackpot go."

"Nobody can help me," she sobbed, "he knocks down any guy who just looks at me."

"I used to be a prize fighter," the man grinned. "My friends call me Tiger."

Mary called him Tiger too, and he persuaded her to join his crew as a welder. "We need welders," he told her. "Besides, I can keep an eye on you."

He kept an eye on her, all right, on and off the job, and there were a series of fights between him and Alibi; but Tiger could not be frightened away. He stuck by his promises to Mary.

"There is only one way to get rid of that poison ivy," Tiger prompted her. "Let's get married."

101

That was yesterday, and Mary tells me she's made up her mind to marry Tiger because he's kind and gentle, except when he has to fight Alibi, and she can have her curls anywhere she wants them and pick her own wedding dress. But Alibi's sure going to make trouble.

Well, it seems just my luck to have to go around and tell toughies they can't marry the gals they want. I'm puzzled that I still have all my teeth and no bent-in ribs. But somehow this job is the worst one I've tackled. You see, I was never a prize fighter or even a fighter, prize or no prize, and I begin to play with the idea of taking Juanita along as a bodyguard. Then my manhood gets the best of me and I begin to figure in which bar Alibi would be least likely to break a mirror if we sat in a back booth—because I plan to let Alibi in on the sad news over a friendly drink.

Two nights later, after work, we go out on what starts as a little toot, but I soon begin to suspect that Alibi must have had at least ten years with the Czar's army. He drinks but doesn't get drunk; he's unsinkable. One broadside of scotch is followed by another, and finally I hear him order a triple-shot with a highball chaser. The bartender eyes us suspiciously but Alibi is too busy talking to take notice.

"Women!" he exclaims in disgust. "Don't tell me about them. They're all bitches. Trouble is we can't live without them. That makes our life a devil of a jackpot. Look at that glass," he goes on, holding his glass up. "As long as you have a grip on it everything is okay. But if you let go—" he drops it to the floor and shrugs, "it's gone. A woman and a glass are forever in danger. Someone always tips them over."

After a few more drinks he can't talk about girls without getting sentimental. He takes off his shirt and looks his tattoos over. He points to the landscape with the name of Toots across the palm tree and the moon.

102

"I used to love her very much," he mutters.

"What d'you mean, used to?" I try to talk in a joshing sort of way.

"It's all over," he says merrily, "and it was all my fault."

I manage an uninterested stare.

"I'll tell you what a fool a man can be," he takes off. "It was down in British Guiana . . ."

"Eh?" It sort of pulls the ground from under me.

"In Guiana," he repeats. "A couple of years ago. I worked as a cement finisher at the airfields they built in the jungle. We were the big bosses, the colored guys did all the work. Still, it was a hell of a job, and white women were as scarce as a holiday. But Jim and I, we had a couple of swell dames. Spanish, you know, with pearls all over and earrings so big a tiger could jump through. But I don't go for that, so I made mine arrange her hair in a decent way. After that, she was just something you wanted to pick up and run for the hills with. To save my life, I can't remember her name. I just called her Toots, and we were all set to get married. I'd be taking her to the States and we'd build our own little house in Minnesota. Our life was all mapped out like a commando raid—and then I pulled a boner.

"Trouble was, y'know, Jim didn't make any headway with his woman. He carried the torch so high over his head that he stumbled over his own toes. She had a weakness for a Brazilian composer who went around playing the mandolin under her window. He'd written a love song for her, and that song simply made her swoon. You know how women are. Every time she heard that sob ballad, her eyes went dreamy and you could just see her heart melting away. And that damned song was getting around like fleas. There was hardly an evening when some fool didn't exercise his tonsils with it.

"Now, everybody knew that the Brazilian was a jerk, but a skirt in love has to find out the hard way. Jim was

103

sighing and doing nothing about it. So I decided to step in.

"One night the four of us were sitting on the porch sipping a drink when sure as payday that song pops up from nowhere. Well, I'd cooked up a little story which would cure a skirt from getting a molten heart every time she heard that melody.

"'You hear that tune?' I set out casually, pointing with the stem of my pipe somewhere into the night. 'There's a funny story behind it. I happen to know the guy who wrote it.'

"I let that sink in and can almost hear her heart pound against her ribs. 'He isn't much of a composer but he's written one good song—this one. Maybe he was in love when he wrote it.'

"'He sure was,' she sighs.

"'Yeah, he probably was,' I admit. 'But he works it nicely. Know what he does? He goes around and plays that song for rich widows and gets himself invitations to dinner; and he plays it for little dames and makes them fall in love with him. But the topper is that he manages to make every one of them believe he's written that song specially for her.'

"There's a long silence—just the music. Suddenly she jumps to her feet.

"'Jim,' she blurts out, 'you asked me this afternoon if I want to marry you. The answer is Yes.'

"Jim dives into a tornado of happiness, and I think I have all the reasons to rub my hands. How about a celebration? Not tonight. The lady is tired. Off she goes, followed by Jim.

"Remains Toots and myself. No sooner are we alone than tame little Toots goes wild. If ever a girl scratched a man's eyes out with words, Toots did it that time. 'You can't dish that malarkey to me and get away with it,' she shouts. 'Slinging dirt on a genius like Lorenzo! For *me* he wrote that song! I was his girl till you came along. I've had enough of you and your house and your big plans. I want to live my own life and I'm going back to my Lorenzo.'

"She pulls no punches. She blames me for all and everything, a thousand little things I hadn't even noticed. You wouldn't believe what an amount of gripes a sweet little girl you thought all yours can store up in herself.

"I sure fought for her, but one day it dawned on me that it wasn't worth it. The hell with it. That wasn't the girl I had been looking for all my life. But then, sometimes, I don't know. Maybe she was. You never can tell."

Alibi downs the rest of his drink. "Well, Joe, that's the story of a lie which split two people apart and glued two together. Yes, I saw Jim and his woman. They live down in Texas, beak on beak."

Alibi shakes the dice absentmindedly, shoots five and orders a couple of drinks.

I chew on a question which has been stuck in my throat for quite a while, "So all those pictures on your arms go for the Guiana girl?"

He laughs. "Heck, no. This devil was for a doll in Alaska, this heart for one in New York, this woman for an Arizona skirt. And this handcuff—" his voice goes soft "for one in Minnesota."

Now it's time for me to down a drink. "And the name of each of them was Toots?"

He shakes his head. "I just called them that. Makes everything easy." He jerks his chin toward his right forearm, to a picture of a woman with a head like a mushroom, all in red and blue. "Take this one, for instance. I sure thought she was the real McCoy. I was working in a copper mine in Arizona, as a rock crusher. Y'see, you've got a rock as big as a cottage; you find your self a concave to put your blasting stick; then you go to an electric exploder, far enough away to be safe; you touch two wires, and the whole works goes off. Well, when I first saw Toots behind that tamale stand, in her red dress, her

105

hair parted in the middle, dishing out the food with that million-dollar smile of hers, two wires inside me banged together and I felt like the rock going to pieces. There were about a dozen men after her but I really went to town. I'd saved six hundred bucks and I blew every bit on her. That's a lot of dough-re-mi, but I didn't care. Gee, what a doll she was! She didn't want to come with me to Minnesota, and I didn't mind building our little house right there in Arizona. I bought the lumber and was about to start on the house when, one day, Toots disappeared."

Alibi downs another one and stares at his tattoo gloomily. "I'm a goddamn sucker for women," he says. "I even had given her my machine and had to hitchhike when I went after her.

"One day I pick up a ride with a skirt from New York," Alibi goes on to tell me. "A Woolworth salesgirl on her first vacation in five years. Her boy friend's just given her the brush-off and now she's driving around in a daze. I tell her my story and it gets her all worked up. By that time I've tracked down my Arizona Toots pretty well, and the New York girl takes me to a village where she's supposed to be hiding. But when we get there, Toots has made off again, to another town fifty miles ahead. The girl drives me down there too, and we hunt around the whole day and eventually dig up a clue that leads in the opposite direction.

"To cut the story short, that girl spends her whole vacation with me, tracing Toots cross country, and she turns out to be a good sport. She isn't exactly a beauty, but she's as cute as a squirrel and eats peanuts right out of my hand. Just when her vacation is about over, we happen to hit a carnival. Toots's track has fizzled out and well, maybe I don't care. Anyway, I decide I owe a little thank-you to the New York skirt before we say good-bye. So I give her the time of her life, with merry-go-

106

rounds and ferris wheels, drinks and dances, fire- and other works. I win her three big dolls, a bear, an alarm clock, a cane and a Mickey Mouse. In the end there's just time enough left for her to drive all night to be back on her job next morning. Everything's fine, but there's just one catch to it, and I have to break the news to her: I had no money for all our fun, so I sold her machine. When she hears that, she goes flooey. She leans against my shoulder, sobbing, soft and small as a kitten. I ask her if it wasn't worth it, and she says it was worth everything, but if she isn't back on her job by tomorrow morning, she'll get fired. I tell her she needs no more jobs. I'm going to take care of her, because from now on she's my Toots.

"I really wish, Joe, you could have seen her that night, loaded with dolls and the alarm clock, balloons floating above her head, her face softened up with tears, with the merry-go-round music blaring all around us. She doesn't know herself whether she's crying because she's happy or because she's miserable. Y'know that type: a timetable creature, choo-chooing through life and stopping only to take in some rest and fuel. She keeps gabbing about Woolworth's and her landlady and some bills she can't pay. I put my arms around her shoulders and tell her, 'Watch me, Toots, I'll fix that up for you.'

"I grab her dolls, the cane, the alarm and the Mickey Mouse, and talk some pie-eyed guys into buying them for their dames. I collect ten bucks and walk over to a joint where a crap game is going on. To Toots gambling is as wicked as murder. However, she keeps her eyes peeled on the bills that come trickling in. I'm sitting and she's planted right behind me, her hands on my shoulders, and whenever the dice hop along the floor her fingers dig into my shoulders till it hurts, and I can feel her breath coming in hot waves over my cheeks when she bends down to watch. When we have fifty bucks she wants me to quit. But not me. On we go. I feel like a thousand dollars, and a

107

couple of hours later I'm worth it, too. Yessir, if you try and tell me you started with ten bucks and ended with a grand, I'd send you out to find yourself a sucker for your fish stories. But that was one of those nights. I buy Toots a honey of a machine from a guy who's losing his last shirt and wants to get another chance. I load Toots and all our stuff into it and drive ahead. Toots just curls up and falls asleep, peaceful as a baby.

"We arrive in New York next morning just about in time for her to show up at Woolworth's. I get myself a job as a winch operator in Brooklyn, and I find out that New York isn't a bad place to have some fun. I fix Toots up with dresses, rings and bracelets, and everything a girl needs to be happy and make her guy happy, too. We're both saving for the furniture of the house we're going to build in Yonkers, and I have my lumber sent from Arizona.

"Everything's looking up when one day a guy blows in who tries to sell me the story that he's been Toots's boy friend for six years and that they're going to be married any day, only she's afraid to tell me. Naturally I knock the guy down the stairs. Then I go and see Toots and ask her what the hell's the matter with that guy—he must be cuckoo or something. Toots is all tears and sobs and spills the story; the guy told the truth, and now I've gone and broken two of his ribs. Before I can argue with her, two cops turn up and when I wake up in the can with a head like a sandbag, my cellmate tells me they have funny laws in New York. You're thrown in the clink when you knock someone down. And if you hit a cop, you don't have to worry about your room and board for the next few weeks.

"When I get out, Toots is a married woman, and I'm so fed up with skirts that I don't want to see nothing of them. That's kind of hard in a city like New York and since I don't like their laws anyway, I make up my mind to beat it. A guy tells me he knows a place in Alaska where women just ain't, and if you want to see some long hair you have to look at the grizzlies.

"That's where we go, shooting fox, martens and ermines through the eyes so we don't spoil the furs. It's a grand place for a man with a broken heart because the only females you see you shoot and skin. But after a while—I don't know. You've dreamed of a house of your own, you have the lumber all ready in New York, the blueprints in your head, and now you find yourself living in a sod igloo. You have whale ribs as walls, and a sealskin for a roof, seal gut for windows and a reindeer skin as a door. You lie in a ditch in the frozen ground staring at a stone seal-oil lamp, which is also your stove, with a piece of moss as wick and some blubber as fuel, and you listen to the blizzards outside. Then you look at all those furs you've collected without a chance of putting them around a girl's shoulder—and you feel silly. Women, they say, are like drinks: you know they're poison, but you can't keep away from them.

"One day I go to the nearest town, a hundred miles away." Alibi muses over the devil's face on his forearm and makes it twist. "That's where he comes in. I don't exactly remember what happened that first night in town but there must've been some awfully big guys around because the next thing I knew was a clean bed in a hospital, a bandaged arm, and a chin that felt the size of a spittoon. When I'm able to peek through my lids, what do I see? The prettiest little nurse bent over me, giving me a sweet look like I was a baby in a crib. Gone are the pains in my arm, and my chin shrinks to its normal size. I open my eyes as wide as I can and grin.

"'So you're a man who fights for his woman?' she whispers dreamily.

"'You bet,' I say, and we have a long talk and I give her all the works I've had stored up in me in that lonely

109

igloo. She insists that I stay in the hospital for a week, but nothing doing! We have a date the same evening and I'd like to see the guy who tries to stop me. We sneak out of the hospital and really go to town that evening and she admits she had more fun that one night than in all the other nights of her life put together. It turns out that she used to be engaged to some guy in Canada, but she walked out on him just when the wedding bells were being tuned. Well, this is a new one on me, being on the receiving end of a runaway bride. She calls me 'devil' but from her lips it sounds like angel. The higher we step the more she likes it. It's sort of funny that I found her in Alaska where I went to forget all about women.

"We grab our fun like candy from a sack, and pretty soon she looks and behaves like the Toots I've always dreamed of. We're talking more and more about what our life is going to be like; we're going back to Minnesota, and I'll have the lumber sent there from New York. I do most of the talking and she does most of the listening, and I feel like shouting from the rooftops.

"Maybe it won't surprise you, Joe, but it sure sent me to the bottom when one day she, too, walks out on me. I don't know what's wrong with me. I give those skirts the time of their lives, but when it comes to settling down and getting married, they disappear like an Italian battleship.

"This time, however, I get a note. It's from a guy in Ottawa, a college prof. It's a darn nice note, the kind that butters you up so you can't even get good and mad and toss it into the ashcan. The upshot of it is, in plain American, that he's the guy Toots was engaged to. It seems she couldn't get used to the idea of rotting in some hick town with no fun in store for her. She dreamed of a romance like you see in the movies starring Charles Boyer, with maybe a shot of Humphrey Bogart. She got it from me all right, but she couldn't take it. It frightened her back to 'security' and her old yawndaddy. He actually

110

thanked me for 'giving her a lesson,' and everybody was happy."

Alibi tosses the dice into the air and catches them. "Then I came down here, to Richmond. You know what's happening. S.O.S. Same old story. I find myself a Toots and then she walks off with that ornery-looking hombre. I might as well give up. What's the matter with me? I'm a dud. I look like a blockbuster and am nothing but a heap of scrap. Something's wrong with me. Someone sabotaged me when they put me together. Someone's tossed a monkey wrench into my motor. But where? I wish someone would tell me."

He looks his tattoos over gloomily. "That ship's the latest. It's for Mary, my Richmond Toots." But then I notice that his glance turns gradually on his wrist and he begins to finger the tattoo of the handcuff. Maybe the drinks I've had made me bolder. Anyway, I push out with, "How about the handcuff?" And then I wish I hadn't pushed out.

"Shut up," Alibi barks. "That's my business." And he orders another triple with a highball chaser. But you can't drown troubles that have learned to swim. For what seems like an hour he guzzles silently. He gets moodier and seems to have forgotten me. Suddenly he flings a bill on the counter.

"Come on," he orders harshly.

He crawls into his car and I hardly have time to sit down by his side when he starts off as if he's going to escape from past and present, and in a hurry. He whizzes out to the Bayshore, leaves the road and jeeps across a bumpy field until he comes to a stop. It's a clear night. The lights of the yard speckle the sky with a pattern bright enough to make the stars feel jealous.

Alibi picks up the accordion from the back seat, climbs on his fender and, his knees drawn up, plays a sentimental tune. He plays softly as if trying to lull himself to sleep. Then he starts talking again.

111

"When I first saw her she made me feel like tossing my hat in the air and yodeling. She wore a red dress and red earrings. Her blonde hair was parted in the middle, and when you came near her you got a whiff of a perfume you'd never forget. She stood behind the counter where I'd been eating my sandwiches for months. But instead of fat old-lady MacIntrye, the girl was there, with a giggle like a kiss and a wink like a hug.

"I was twenty then, and there had been no girl in my life I wouldn't gladly have swapped for a Model T. But this one was different. Her name was Toots. I was running a filling station and doing some repair work on the side. My station and the MacIntyre joint was all there was within eight miles. People kept coming and going, but I was the only steady customer at the counter. It was a cinch that Toots should be my girl.

"But I'll be jumped if I could have so much as a date with her. If I wanted to see her I had to eat a sandwich or drink a beer. Mr. and Mrs. MacIntyre were around all the time. Only on Wednesday afternoons they took off and went to town and then I could have a word with Toots. She liked me, all right, but whenever I asked her to go out with me, she shook her head. Did she have a boy friend? No. Didn't she like to dance? She loved it. So why not spend Sunday afternoon with me in town? Mr. MacIntyre didn't like it. Who the hell was MacIntyre? Her father? No, not even a relative. I couldn't figure it out. I had to go on eating sandwiches and drinking beer.

"One day I hear loud voices from inside the joint. When I come over I see Mr. MacIntyre bawling Toots out. The girl looks frightened and her eyes are red. What did she do? Threw a cigarette butt on the floor and a piece of paper caught fire. Not worth talking about, but the MacIntyres make a big fuss.

"'She's so goddamn careless,' Mr. MacIntyre says. 'We've got to watch her.'

112

"Next Wednesday when I come over for our little eye-to-eye talk, the joint's closed. I've been looking forward all week to Wednesday afternoon, and now Toots is gone. Maybe gone for good and I'll never be able to find her. I don't feel like working that afternoon and I take a stroll.

"When I get back I hear a whimper in the back of my tool shed. First I figure it must be a stray cat, but when Toots stumbles out you could knock me cold with a flip of your little finger. She has a scared look in her eyes and is shaking all over. She flings herself against me and I feel her wet face on my shoulder. Her arms hug me as a drowning man would hug a plank. It takes a while till she's able to talk.

"'Someone broke into the place,' she sobs, 'and stole money from the cash register. Twenty-six dollars.'

"I feel relieved and pat her head. I would gladly pay a lousy twenty-six dollars for every pat she'd allow. 'That's nothing to get all worked up about,' I say, 'You just tell them what happened.'

"She looks up, with eyes wrapped in gushes. 'I can't. They wouldn't believe me. Oh, you don't know. I stole something once. I was stupid. They put me in jail and then let me go, on probation. I have to report to the police every week. It's hard for me to get a job. MacIntyre gave me a chance. If they find out that the money is gone, I'll have to go to the jug for years.' A new burst of tears, some more pounding at my chest with her two fists. 'I don't want to go in again. I don't want to!'

"'Nobody can throw you in the clink if you haven't done anything.' I back her up. 'It's in the Constitution.' I take her fists and hold them firmly.

"She relaxes and her hands in my palms get soft and helpless like a baby bird. 'They won't believe me,' she says. 'How can I prove that I didn't take the money?'

"'Just tell them where you were!'

"'Oh, I don't know myself,' she shrugs. 'I just run about in the woods when I get fed up with my job.

MacIntyre keeps telling me how kind he is to let me stay. I can't do a thing without getting a sermon. I have to be on the job all the time, and on my day off I've got to stay home. It's just like prison. I want to get out of that rut and have some fun. I'm young, ain't I?'

"She looks straight into my eyes, her fingers still locked in mine. Is she young, oh boy! Her lips tremble. Before I know it, I'm knee-deep in a kiss.

"Then I sit down next to her on the bench in my garage. The world's as bright as a headlight. 'Don't you worry,' I tell her. 'I'll weasel you out of this. Just listen: you weren't taking a stroll this afternoon where nobody saw you. Five minutes after the MacIntyres left, you came over to me. We had a date. I made love to you. I kissed you. Like this.'

"I show her. 'Let's go over it again,' she says, 'so I won't forget when the cops question me.'

"We make sure neither of us will forget as long as we live.

"'Well,' I go on, holding her tight, 'after that I asked you to marry me. Do you remember, what you said?'

"'Do I remember!' she cries. 'I remember every word of it. I said *YES*.'

"I jump up, grab her hand and run with her to my machine. I lift her up and put her on the front seat. The next moment we're off. 'Now get that straight: we decided to get married right away. I knew a place where we could get a license.'

"She cuddles up close against my shoulder. 'And that, Your Honor, is the truth and nothing but the truth, so help me God!' she sighs.

"Well, Joe, it worked. We came back next morning because we didn't want them to think that Toots had gone over the hill. They questioned her but couldn't do anything. She had a bombproof alibi." He stops playing the accordion and stares toward the Bay.

114

"From that day on she called me Alibi."

He puts the accordion beside him and leans on it. It gives a squeak and goes off the air.

"Toots wanted to forget the MacIntyres and all, so I gave up my filling station and bought another one on the highway," Alibi continues. "When I left my old place, Mr. MacIntyre got hold of my buttonhole. 'You watch her,' he said. 'She's a good kid but goddamn careless.' I was too happy then to even kick him in the pants. I had my station and Toots helped me by running a sandwich counter. I built a little house for us. It was a honey of a house and Toots was a honey of a wife. When we felt like running wild, we closed our station and had a good time. When we felt like working, we worked. There were no restrictions and no rules. That's the way we wanted it to be. We were bound to each other but to nothing else in the world. That's what the handcuff on my wrist means.

"It lasted a little more than a year, then everything went up in smoke. Our house burned down, and we couldn't save Toots. They say the fire was started by a cigarette butt."

There was nothing to say. Alibi squats on the fender holding his knees close and staring toward Richmond. His thoughts must have flown from his first and original Toots in Minnesota to his last Toots in Richmond, for when he speaks up again, it's about Mary.

"You know, she's getting married tonight?" he blurts out. "That bitch!"

I swallow a couple of times, then I take off. "You can't blame Mary," I tell him. "You can't blame any of those girls for walking out on you. You never gave them a break. You just tried to revamp them so they'd look and behave like the one girl you really cared for, your first Toots in Minnesota. You can't do that to a girl. A skirt wants to be loved as she is. It's a take it or leave it proposition."

115

The next minute I'd have given my little finger not to have opened my mouth. Alibi gets hold of the front part of my shirt and shakes me like a cocktail.

"You goddamn shyster," he shouts. "I'll show you, scooping me out and then calling me names!" I take a flight through the air and make a forced landing on a rock. Two red spots bob up in front of my eyes, get smaller and disappear—the stoplights of Alibi's machine. It's tough to hobble three miles with a smashed bottom.

For a couple of weeks Alibi doesn't talk to me. When he thinks I'm not looking I can see him watching me, but he keeps clear. He works hard and his crew has it easier now. He brings a knee pad along for Cindy, and he helps Bulgy balance her weight safely over the beams of the assembly. He keeps telling Ma Hopkins that she's becoming a top-notch tacker and the young girls can take her as an example.

"Something's wrong with him," Dimples says, "he's getting human."

One day I hang around a while after shift to help Red collect worn out files and discarded bits of wood and pipe. He spends his time-off grinding and putting together knives for the soldiers in the South Pacific. I'm just ready to quit when all of a sudden Alibi is next to me.

"Busy?" he asks.

"No," I say. "I haven't got a thing to do."

He doesn't seem to know how to begin. When he talks his words gush out like he wants to get it over with. "I got a new place to live," he splutters. "How about coming over to see me?"

"Okey-doke," I agree. "Have you had your lumber sent from New York and built your house?"

He seems a bit uneasy. "No. It's something else. Let's get going."

I look around for his car, but he says we don't need a car. "It's right over there." He points to a trailer camp in

116

front of the yard. There are a couple of hundred trailers lined up village-like around the office buildings with a recreation room and showers. Some owners have built themselves a little porch by putting up some mosquito screens, others have made a pathetic attempt at a garden by fencing off a piece of the dried-up soil next to their trailers. Most of these people come from the Middle West and are unable to find a place to live. So they decide to make the trailer their home for the duration.

As Alibi and I walk through that camp, the swing-shift workers have just come home. We hear them taking their showers.

Alibi stops at one of the trailers with a bright light shining over the door. Its coat of green paint can't hide the fact that it's a patched-up secondhand job. Alibi's car is next to the pole with the plug for electricity. We've got to stoop when we enter the trailer under a big sign: WELDER'S IDYLL. Inside, the first thing that stares me in the face is a grizzly gnashing its teeth. Its fur covers a cot and its head is a pillow. A little shelf holds green and black rocks and transparent crystals. The accordion is resting on a gas stove. And that's about all there is room for.

Alibi tosses his lunch pail into a corner and his shirt on top of it.

"Come on," he says, "make yourself at home."

I sit down on the cot and pat the grizzly's head, wondering what Alibi's up to. Suddenly a cop appears in the door. It's Juanita.

"How often have I told you," she hollers, "not to park on Lot 17. Yours is 16 and you have to park there!"

I hardly trust my ears. "For heaven's sake, Alibi, is she bossing you off the job too?"

"You bet," he says. "She sure makes a nuisance of herself."

"Oh hello, Joe," Juanita waves in my direction. "I didn't know Alibi brought you home."

117

"I wanted to show him something," Alibi nods. "You know, Juanita, he's a hell of a nosey guy. He never said so, but I bet he'd give next week's paycheck to find out if I have a tattoo on my chest. So I decided to show him."

With one move he takes off his undershirt. He has a chest like a rock but on that rock blossom roses—a whole bunch of them. And clear across them a name is written. Not "Toots" this time, but "Juanita."

I'll be jumped if I can breathe a word out loud. Alibi laughs and lifts Juanita high up till her head bumps against the ceiling and her police cap drops off. When she comes down again he kisses her good and long.

"We were married last Saturday," he explains.

"It takes commando training to stand his high-powered romance," Juanita pokes him in the ribs. "But I can take it."

Alibi sits down next to me. "Come on, Joe, come to. Pinch yourself, it's all true. D'you remember that night by the Bay when you told me I didn't give those skirts a break? Well, you were only partly right. I wasn't giving myself a break either. I thought I could go ahead and make myself a Toots out of any woman. I was wrong. There was only one Toots and she's dead. But there are thousands of other gals, some of them pretty hot stuff." He gives Juanita a big hug. "You just have to see them as they are. Thanks, Joe. You took the hood off my eyes." He laughs happily. "So I decided to get rewelded. And it'll last."

A thousand thoughts whirl through my head. I can't tell why I pick just this one. "What about your lumber in New York? Haven't you had it sent out here to build your house?"

"Forget the lumber," he says. "I gave it away."

A sweep of his arm encloses the cot with the grizzly, the rocks, the accordion, the gas stove, Juanita. "Does a guy need more than this?"

118

Don't
Play
Hookey,
Cookie

One foggy afternoon our flangerette Pee-Wee comes to work a bit late, and giggling. She missed her ride with Jason and, living in a neighborhood where a bus is but an unconfirmed rumor, she hitchhiked. Not that she wanted to hitchhike. In fact, she was a little afraid when the first car she thumbed stopped for her. But she'd bravely clambered in, hoping the guy at the wheel wasn't one of those Richmond Romeos. He wasn't. He must've been over seventy. He wore a pince-nez, a well-tailored overcoat and all the doodads the well-dressed gentleman of the good old pre-yard days used to wear. He looked like a college prof.

"Thanks for giving me a lift," Pee-Wee said. "Just drop me off on San Pablo. I'm going to Yard Number Two."

"Why, I also work in Yard Two," the old man replied cheerfully. "I shall deposit you at the gate."

On the next corner they picked up another passenger. He could have been the old man's twin brother except that he looked a bit younger. Instead of a lunch box he carried a leather folio.

"We have a new rider with us today," the first man said. "I picked her up at the corner."

The second man turned his head slowly and stared at Pee-Wee through his gold rims. "I don't approve of hitchhiking, but—" his face hinted a smile, "unusual times produce unusual circumstances, eh Malcolm?"

Before they got to the yard Pee-Wee learned that Malcolm and his friend were exactly what they looked like, college professors.

"Imagine!" Pee-Wee says, giggling. "They're spending their vacation helping Uncle Sam!"

The two Malcolms aren't the only ones. Vacation time washes quite a wave of school kids and teachers into the yards. Our assembly is ably represented by Pink and Pipsqueak who are now working full time. And yesterday we got the Spears girls fresh from Berkeley High. They're redheaded twins, and when I say red I don't mean auburn or copper, I mean red, and lily-skinned and daintily freckled. Cookie's joined the fitters and Sparkie the welders and it's a good thing for us, otherwise we couldn't tell them apart. As it is, if Miss Spears wears a blouse and overalls it's Cookie. If she is in hood and leathers it's Sparkie.

On their first day on the job, Sandy gives Cookie the "we-sure-need-you" line. But Cookie hardly needs a pep talk. She's a package of five hundred volts raring to go ahead and build a whole Liberty hull by herself. She's a bit disappointed that we don't push out battle wagons, but Sandy tells her that without those Liberty ships our best soldier boys would be stuck somewhere on a flea-

120

bitten island. That makes her feel good again and she's ready to go down on her knees and get busy with her hammer and punch. And down on her knees she goes.

She takes her first breather at the meal break when she and Sparkie join the rest of the gang.

"Gee," says Sparkie, "this yard is terrific. Absolutely tops. It makes you dizzy to open your eyes."

"Look at those boats," Cookie points to the hulls behind the scaffolds. "They don't look like boats. They look like giant Model T's."

"But they're definitely streamlined over there in the outfitting dock," Sparkie splutters. "Be fun to take a trip on one of them!"

"That's what I'm going to do," Pink says.

Sparkie is thrilled. "How d'you know you'll get on a Liberty?"

Pink peels an orange with his teeth. "I'm a lucky dog. I always get what I want."

"I wonder if I could go to the outfitting dock and see a boat just before it's delivered?" Cookie is quick to ask.

"Sure," says Pipsqueak. "I'll take you. I have a friend there in an important position."

"What does he do?"

"When the boats are brought in after the launching he licks the champagne off the forepeak."

Sparkie throws a piece of flux at him.

"You can go to the outfitting dock any time after shift," Sandy tells her. "I always get a kick out of seeing how those rusty steel plates and beams become dandy cabins. Besides, it's a most pleasant way to learn something about shipfitting."

"We'll take you," offers Pipsqueak, speaking for Pink and himself.

Cherie raises a hand while she finishes swallowing a bite of her sandwich. "Don't trust those nincompoops," she warns. "They took me up the boat once, and I was

121

wondering why everybody giggled. The two *imbéciles* had hung a sign on my back: THIS END UP."

"If you really want to learn something," Chuck advises, "ask Bruce to show you around. He loves to explain things. He'll tell you the history of ships back to Noah."

"Genesis, chapter six," says Bruce, smiling whimsically, "tells you about the world's first shipwright who launched his ark made of gopher wood and caulked with pitch."

"The professor knows everything but how to hold a hammer," says Jason.

Bruce keeps looking at Cookie and Sparkie through his rimless glasses. The twins are bubbling with excitement, trying to talk to everybody at once. Bruce sits still. He always picks a place for lunch where he can rest his back and stretch his legs. He usually has a little book in his pocket which he reads during lunch hour. Today the book lies open on his knees.

"So you're a teacher," Cookie says to him. "What d'you teach?"

"Oh, all sorts of things. My main subject was music."

"Music!" Cookie edges over to him and sits down at his side. "Then you must know Doctor Lodge! He was my music teacher in high school!"

"I don't know the fellows up here," says Bruce. "I come from Los Angeles."

"Say, I didn't know you taught music," Pee-Wee cuts in. "What instrument do you play?"

"The piano and the violin," says Bruce. "Mainly the violin." He's busy with his thermos.

"Dr. Lodge also played the violin!" Cookie announces noisily. "We did quartets, Doctor Lodge, Sparkie, another girl and I. We played some Mozart quartets at commencement."

"For heaven's sake, Bruce," Pee-Wee pipes in, "you'll spoil your fingers with yard work."

122

"Gee, that's a shame," says Cookie. "They won't be as nimble when you go back to school in the fall."

Bruce looks down at his long narrow fingers covered with scratches and blisters and lines of dirt. He moves them swiftly, testing his knuckles.

"I'm not going back to school," he says slowly. "I'll stay right here until the war's over."

The whistle blares. Pee-Wee frowns at Bruce, then snaps her lunch pail shut and hops onto the assembly. Bruce and Cookie face each other for a moment. A faint smile can be seen in Bruce's eyes. Cookie responds with a timid but heartfelt grin.

"Well," he says, getting up a bit clumsily, "we have work to do."

The shipfitters are making a layout. Plates have been welded together to form a big portion of the second deck, seventy feet long. Hundreds of items go on that piece of deck: girders, beams, brackets, steel clips, each of them in its proper place, not an eighth of an inch off, else it won't fit when the unit goes up on the hull. The shipfitters snap chalk lines crisscrossing the plates, then punch those lines so you can find the punch marks after the chalk wears off. They paint numbers and names on the lines so the flangers will know which beam goes on which line and the welders will know where to weld what.

Chuck directs the layout. He looks at the blueprint, measures, squares up, figures out distances and angles. Pink and Pipsqueak, the trainees, can follow him, but they couldn't do the job themselves. Cherie and Cookie, the helpers, have only a faint idea of what it's all about. For them a blueprint is as clear as a Japanese war bulletin. They snap, punch and paint wherever they're told to. They move around like a troop of somersault artists in a three-ring circus, and that's just what Cookie likes because it gives her the feeling that she's really doing something to speed those ships off to the battle fronts. Her eyes shine, her hair sparkles, and her lips are so red and full you expect them to pop.

The layout is finished. Chuck takes Pink and Pip-squeak to another unit leaving Cherie and Cookie behind to do the rest of the punching. That's not so much fun because they have to be on their knees on steel plates still hot with the sun, and once in a while they hit their fingers instead of the punch. But it keeps them busy and that's all they care about.

"Gee," says Cookie when they're through. "That absolutely knocks you out." She takes off her hard hat, wiping her forehead.

Cherie giggles. "It makes you dirty, too. Never wipe your hands on your face." She picks up Lovella's welding hood and hands it to Cookie. "Look at you."

A welding hood has a piece of dark glass through which welders look at their arcs. That's what makes the hood popular with the girls. They can use that glass as a mirror.

"Holy cats!" Cookie says, looking into the hood at herself. "Well, it's all in a day's work, I guess. Let's find out what comes next."

The gang is waiting for the crane to bring up more plates, so Cookie goes to wash her face. When she comes back she walks past Bruce who's busy with some beams. He nods a smile in her direction, which is unusual for Bruce when he's working. He isn't as strong as Jason and hasn't got Pee-Wee's knack of doing tough things the easy way. For him the steel won't behave. It gets cockeyed, mulish, and in the end it kicks. Nobody on the Way has as many blackened fingernails and painful bruises as Bruce.

Cookie watches him for a while and her youthful face goes maternal, like a mother watching her son earning a living digging ditches. It's a mixture of pride and pain.

"It's a dirty shame for him to be doing this kind of work," she tells me. Then, with a dreamy look in her eyes she adds, "He isn't meant to be a flanger. He's an artist. I wonder why he's doing it."

Something in her voice makes me sit up and take notice. If I know anything about girls, Cookie will do her darnedest to find the answer.

Take it from me, some people are just plain lucky. If I want to find out something about someone, I have to spend half my time off snooping around, buying people ice cream or beer. But Cookie—well, the dope on Bruce just falls into her lap during lunch hour just as she gets her pretty mouth around a ham sandwich.

I've already mentioned that an old lady has joined Alibi's tacker crew. She's somewhat shrimpy and quite gray-haired. We call her Ma Hopkins because that's what's written on her hood. Shipyard guys go by the moniker they paint on their hoods, hard hats or leathers. There's a guy on Seven called Lefty. He's not left-handed; he just bought a jacket with the name on it and so he's Lefty. But back to Ma Hopkins. She's a whistle-to-whistle worker and eager in her tacking. And she's shy. It takes her a couple of weeks to join us at the break. Our gang doesn't always eat together but most of the time you'll find us sitting on the same beam or, in rainy weather, in the same shack. These days even Bruce, the hermit, sits down alongside the Spears redheads and Pink and Pipsqueak.

One Tuesday at break, Ma loses her shyness. She comes over.

"May I?" she asks. "Sure," chirps Pipsqueak, and he makes room for her on the six-by-eight.

Ma sits down, watching Bruce who's with the twins. She busies herself with her sandwich, then suddenly turns to Bruce.

"I didn't think you'd recognize me," she says.

Bruce looks up puzzled. Ma Hopkins takes the faded kerchief from her gray hair. Bruce turns red.

125

"Of course," he stammers. "You're Chris's mother. How could I forget?"

"A small world," Ma Hopkins says. "Quite a coincidence to find you here."

"Yes, quite a coincidence." Then, with an obvious effort, Bruce asks, "What do you hear from Chris? How is he?"

"He was killed at Guadalcanal." Ma Hopkins pats the welding gloves in her lap. Nobody says anything. Jason tosses bits of his sandwich to the sea gulls and everyone watches the birds as they snatch the pieces in midair.

"You can imagine how I felt when I got the news," Ma Hopkins continues. "I couldn't sit still. I wanted to fight, myself. And I was mad because I was old and a woman. Then I got an idea—be a worker, free a worker. This war has a place for an old woman. That's why I came to the yards."

Bruce pushes back the bridge of his glasses. "Isn't the work here too hard for you? I mean . . ." he breaks off.

Ma Hopkins nods. "I know what you mean," she says. "You remember how I looked a year ago. Now you can't even recognize me. I've grown twenty years older in twelve months. But Chris's death isn't the only thing that aged me."

By this time Lovella has moved nearer, and so have Pee-Wee and the other girls. They sit around Ma Hopkins like kids around grandma telling fairy tales. Only this isn't a fairy tale. It's a story of real life told against a background of steel and dirt.

"You see," Ma Hopkins now includes all of her listeners, "I was a saleslady in a store for men's wear. In Hollywood you can have pretty girls a dime a dozen and no one likes to look at a gray-haired lady behind a counter. They claim young girls sell better. But I had the job, and it was a good one. By spending much time and

126

money I still could pass for forty when I really was sixty. I had to lie about Christopher, too. I was his grandmother, not his mother."

There are sympathetic glances from the girls and I'll-be-darned headshakes from the men. Ma Hopkins folds the sandwich wax papers and puts them neatly back into her pail. "Yes," she says, "when I had a chance to get away I grabbed it. There's no need to use makeup and hair dye in a yard, and no danger of meeting friends and scaring the daylights out of them by having become an old scarecrow all of a sudden. It's quite a break, sometimes, to begin a new life and not to have to meet one's old friends—isn't it, Bruce?"

"Yes," says Bruce, abashed, "it's a break."

Ma Hopkins watches him silently. Then, taking her eyes off Bruce, she addresses all of us again. "I don't regret that I've come up here. Only now do I realize how sick and tired I was of playing the part of a middle-aged woman. I never felt as young as now when I can show my gray hair and my wrinkles."

Pee-Wee declares that working in the open air has done miracles to her health too, and Lovella wants to know what cosmetics Ma Hopkins used to erase twenty years off her face. Bruce comes to only when the whistle gives the kickoff to the second half of our working day. Cookie nibbles on her fingernails excitedly, and no sooner is Ma Hopkins back at her stinger than Cookie is with her, talking busily. Sandy has to get her back to her job, but you can see she's all hopped up and she keeps hitting her finger instead of her punch. She hardly notices it and from time to time forgets all about the yard and the punching and goes off into the land of dreams. Jason meanwhile watches her impatiently. A lot of flanging is waiting for her punchmarks and he is itching to go to work. Finally he can't stand it any longer. He grabs her punch and hammer and finishes her job.

Cookie stays in a daze the rest of the night. Once, a crane carries a twenty-ton unit right over her head. Everybody yells, but she doesn't hear. Chuck grabs her and pushes her off the assembly. "For heaven's sake, kid," he shouts. "Wake up! I'd hate to see you cause a sudden slump in the hamburger market."

One day before work, I take Cherie to a jeweler friend of mine in San Francisco to pick out the rings for her and Ski. They're ready for the plunge. Cherie is spicily dressed in a hug-me-tight sweater and a simple skirt. She's all in a flutter and keeps telling me stories about herself, Ski, Chuck and the rest of the gang. It doesn't take too long for her to give me the latest on Cookie.

It seems that Cookie's in for that certain feeling, and you don't need a tipster to see that Bruce is the one. For Cookie his mere presence in the yard is a mystery with a capital M. Why isn't he going back to teaching after vacation? It's a *secret*, so Cookie jumps at a chance to get the lowdown from Ma Hopkins.

After seeing the old lady, Cherie assures me, Cookie is even more steamed up. Why? Because her little pink ear got a loadful. The secret is out, and it's sensational. Sen-sa-tional! Cookie glances over nine shoulders before she comes out with it. Bruce was *dismissed* from school! Ma Hopkins didn't say much more, but she hinted enough for Cookie to see that there was a *scandal*.

"I tell you, the kid was crazy," Cherie chatters on, tapping her forehead to make sure I understood. "Cookie once read a story of a teacher who was dismissed because he fell in love with one of his students. So it's a *fait accompli* for Cookie that the same thing happened to Bruce. She talks about it all day. She wonders what the girl looks like, and whether she's still in love with Bruce, and whether Bruce is still in love with the girl and whether they write each other secretly. Oh, *mon Dieu*,

128

Joe, it makes me sick to my stomach, and yet I envy her. Three years ago I'd have run a temperature like that, too. Just ask Chuck about it. But after all that happened to Paris and me and my folks, life has become a serious business. When I see Cookie taking on like that I feel old and wise like grandma in her rocking chair, and I don't like it a bit. You know, Cookie's definitely decided that Bruce is still in love with the *mademoiselle* of L.A. and that he's working in the yard just to tire himself out and to try and forget her. I tell her things will take care of themselves; from what I know about men, the only way to get a girl out of a man's system is to put another girl in."

"Well, she seems to have made up her mind to put herself in," I say. "Cookie never misses a chance to be near Bruce, and for him that's just what the doctor ordered. He thinks too much, and that's his trouble. He looks ten years younger since she's around."

"Cookie sticks around him more than you know," Cherie tells me. "She and Bruce, and Sparkie and Pink are playing quartets together. Pink has joined them, not exactly for the love of music. He goes for Sparkie, as you must have noticed. *Oui, monsieur,* there's no shortage of love in the fitter's gang. Chuck and Miggs are testing wedding rings too. They're just waiting till he gets his leaderman's rating. That leaves Pipsqueak the only sane person, if you can call Pipsqueak sane. To him a girl is something to tie a "This end up" label on. He'll learn differently some day."

One late morning I find myself meandering down Broadway in Oakland. That's a favorite pastime of mine when I have nothing better to do. There's a lot of khaki and army twill and navy blue on the street, and with each uniform a girl. All those soldiers and sailors are on furlough just for a little while, and you'll be glad for their laughter. Mixed with them are a lot of Midwest farm folk who came out here to help in the yards. They feel lonely and rushed and

129

wish everything were over so they could go home again. And there are the high-school and college youngsters who see that the world is topsy-turvy and figure they might just as well find fun while it lasts. Broadway in Oakland is full of lights and gaiety but it's a gaiety you can't be too happy about.

Then I see two red-red mops. Sure enough it's Cook and Spark. But I have a hard time identifying the two guys with them as Bruce and Pink. You can work with a man in the yard for a year but when you see him in his off-shift outfit, I'll bet my prewar thermos you won't recognize him. It's like meeting the scarecrow from your victory garden in an eighty-dollar suit.

They make a big hullabaloo and insist that I come along to have a bite with them. So we breeze along Broadway hopping and singing and even Bruce hops along, although he isn't the hopping type. A sailor gets caught in our way, and Cookie slaps his back and shouts, "Go ahead pal, you sail 'em, we build 'em!" And on we go till we find a café that isn't too crowded.

The twins are rigged up in their latest and look as much alike as two Liberty ships before their names are painted on their bows. Still, you can tell them apart—Sparkie has a three-degree list toward Pink, and Cookie slants even more heavily toward Bruce. Bruce is a nice, quiet guy, sure of himself, serious, but no killjoy. He handles a fork and knife as expertly as Jason the sledge.

"You should hear Bruce play the violin, Joe," says Cookie. "We have the most wonderful quartet!"

"With and without music," Pink nods. "And sometimes duets, too, on the side." He winks at Sparkie. Sparkie flushes, fumbles with her handkerchief and drops it on the floor. Pink is quick in picking it up.

Bruce winks at me. "Isn't that funny? He wouldn't do it in the yard. Girls pick up their own handkerchiefs

130

while they're getting one dollar five an hour. If you take them out and spend ten bucks on them an evening, you pick up their handkerchiefs, too."

"That's an idea," Cookie chirps happily, "let's spend ten bucks tonight and go places."

"Cookie, Cookie!" Bruce shakes his head. "After all I've been telling you . . ."

"Oh well, those ten bucks won't start the inflation," Cookie says lightheartedly. "Besides, if I buy bonds instead, and there is an inflation, I'd have no fun and no money. So what's the use?"

Bruce silently starts modeling a figure out of a piece of bread.

But Pink takes up the idea. "Why not? Let's paint the town red tonight. How about it, Sparkie?"

"I don't know." Sparkie wrinkles her nose at him. "Last time we hit the highspots together I was so worn out I nearly fell off the assembly the next day."

"Let's have a good time tonight and not think of tomorrow," Cookie goes on. "If we're too tired, we can always stay home and get some sleep."

"Uh, uh," cautions Bruce.

"Just once, Bruce, please." Cookie puts her hand on his arm. "We never can hit it up together, having different days off. One of us always has to go to work when the other one has a chance to play."

Bruce lets out a sigh and takes her hand in his. "It's war, Cookie," he says softly, "and there are a lot of youngsters all over the world who can't do what they want to do."

"It's war, all right," Cookie nods sharply, her mop dancing, "and I think I'm doing my share. My work in the yard is hard enough, dirty enough and, coming down to it, pretty dull. And I do it of my own free will. I'm entitled to some fun. Look at them," she points with her head to the couples around us. "For them the war brings fun.

131

Even the soldiers in the camps get furlough. We in the yard don't."

While they go on talking, their hands are locked together and their fingers speak a language that has nothing to do with war and shipyards. Pink and Sparkie are busy kidding and giggling together. Bruce and Cookie are getting more and more serious.

"Yes, I see your point, Bruce," Cookie says with a do-we-have-to-go-through-that-again look. "But I wish you'd see mine. In school we never had more fun than when we played hookey. You've got to play hookey once in a while if you want to stay afloat."

Bruce takes up her fingers one by one with his thumb and forefinger, and lets them snap back while he talks to her.

"Yes, I know it's fun," he says. "But playing hookey in school doesn't hurt anyone except maybe yourself. Later in life, it's different. Everybody has a job to do and if he doesn't do it, someone else will suffer. That's true always, but you can see it clearly in wartime. If you and I play hookey for one day maybe *one* man will die. Do you think it's worth taking that chance?"

There's something in Bruce's voice that gets me. It's not so much what he's said, but how he's said it.

Cookie sits quietly, her fingers held in his, and stares in the direction of a girl in the arms of a sailor.

Pink bangs the table with his palm. "Whoopee!" he shouts. "I've talked Sparkie into a fling."

"A rationed one, till midnight," Sparkie adds, snickering.

"Then we'll skip work today. How about it, Bruce?"

"How about it, Cookie?" Bruce asks her.

Cookie squirms. She looks at Pink and Sparkie and she looks at Bruce. Then she shakes her head. The red curls dance about her shoulders.

"I'm a bit tired," she says. "Another time."

132

"Let's meet at the Hungry Tiger at six," says Pink. He pulls Sparkie out of her chair, chattering and hoping she won't change her mind. Bruce, with a warm look for Cookie, happily jingles the coins in his pocket.

"What's wrong, sis?" Sparkie says, turning from Pink's arm.

Cookie casts a quick glance towards Bruce who is paying the bill, still with a grand slam look on his face. "He wouldn't go," Cookie whispers, wrinkling her nose. Sparkie gives her a you'll-fix-him wink and breezes out with Pink.

Cookie's eyes follow them enviously. "You mustn't hold it against him," she tells me in a confidential sort of way. "You know, he had a big disappointment down in L.A."

Bruce joins us again and I beat a hasty retreat, leaving them behind holding hands.

Next thing I hear about Cookie is a squawk from Cherie. Shipbuilding seems to have disappointed Miss Shipfitter Spears. It isn't all flags, music and champagne bottles. It's staying up till midnight, never having an evening off, handling steel, dirty and hot with the sun, crawling through flux which is really broken glass, and being on one's knees going punch, punch, punch. The whole gang lays out a unit and leaves the two helpers, Cherie and Cookie, to punch it. This is what gets Cookie.

Cherie tries to tell her that someone has to do the dirty work, and it can't be Sandy or Chuck because they have more important jobs to do. "You know, Cookie," Cherie explains to her, "we're like the WACs. Girls can't go and throw hand grenades but they can free a man to throw them. Just consider yourself a shipyard WAC and you'll feel better."

But Cookie won't be sold on that. "The WACs have flashy uniforms," she argues, "and look at us. I'm not going to crawl around on my prayer-bones till my tongue lolls out."

The next time a big layout has to be punched, Cookie goes on strike. She tries to chat with Bruce, but Bruce has hardly more than a smile for anyone while he works. So Cookie takes a stroll through the yard to see the sights. She watches the spray-painters who look like men from Mars dipped in orange paint, face and all. She sees girls delivering work orders on motorcycles no bigger than scooters, weaving their way through the traffic of enormous trucks and cranes. She even watches an accident, a man lowered by the big crane on a stretcher from the upper deck of a boat to the ambulance waiting down below.

When she comes back to the assembly, Sandy her leaderman takes her aside. Sandy handles the problems on Five.

"Cookie," he begins, "you have been a darn good worker, and I sure hate to see you lose interest. What's wrong?"

Cookie tells him and Sandy listens carefully, nodding from time to time.

"I know how you feel, Cookie," he says finally. "I felt the same way when I was a helper. You want to build a ship and you stand around and don't know what to do. Then someone comes along and gives you a silly job. Something any moron could do. I know how you feel, punching all day. You get sore—and I don't mean only your knees. But just wait till you pick things up, till you can read a print. Then you'll enjoy shipfitting."

Cookie nibbles her fingernails. "I'd like to learn more about it," she says. "I know you haven't got the time to teach us. But why don't the others explain all those symbols on the prints to Cherie and me?"

"Well, you know how it is. Pink's all set to join the merchant marine and his mind's more in the South

134

Pacific than in Richmond. And Pipsqueak is taken up with his flying and his air corps exams."

"What about Chuck?" Cookie insists. "He could teach us."

Sandy sighs. "Chuck's in a rut right now," he says. "I wish he'd snap out of it. Oh, I know how you feel, all of you. But I wish you'd know what I'm up against."

"All right," promises Cookie. "Don't worry about me."

Sandy flashes a smile. "Thanks, Cookie," he gives her a two-palm handshake. "I knew I could count on you. And now I'd better run along. The shipwrights are waiting."

For two days Cookie works again in her old win-the-war spirit. You can hear her and Cherie punching away like a fifty caliber. At the end of the second day they're punching a deck unit around a big hatch. It's seventy feet long and nearly sixty wide. Chuck stands by smoking a cigarette and talking to Jason and Gosh.

"Come on, Chuck," says Cookie. "Give us a hand and we can finish it."

"I don't care," Chuck replies, waving her off. "Let night shift finish it. They'll get the credit for it, anyway."

He turns to Jason again. "Here you have another example: the shift that finishes a unit gets credit for its entire tonnage. A good leaderman works the most urgent unit first, but those smarties throw all guys on a unit that can be finished on *their* shift, and let another unit go when they see they can't get the credit for it. So what happens? The finished unit has to be stored for maybe a week, is in everybody's way, and wastes precious crane hours. And the guys on the hull wait for the unit which is stalled off, and *that* holds up production, not absenteeism. Politics! Every place you look, politics. It stinks!" He turns and walks away.

"What's the matter with him?" asks Cookie.

"He's just disgusted, I guess," Jason grumbles. "Who wouldn't be, in his shoes? He figures he should

135

have been leaderman long ago, and he'd make a darn good one, too. They always pick guys who know much less but have some pull with the big shots. I don't blame Chuck for getting hot under the collar."

Cookie is mixed up. There's something on her mind she wants to find out about. She goes up to Chuck who's gabbing with Pee-Wee.

"Say, Chuck," she calls up to him. "What's the idea, slowing down production? Someone has to do the job. Come on."

Pee-Wee puts down her sledge and leans against it. "I'm kind of lost, too," she says. "You used to walk around and preach how we have to work to fight Hitler and Hirohito & Company. And now you, Chuck, of all people, are playing their game!"

Chuck breaks into a short laugh. "Don't kid yourself, girls. It's not how fast you work that counts, but how efficient your system is. As a fitter I can save minutes, but what good does that do if the system wastes days? I'm not going to back up a wrong system. As a leaderman I could save days, and I want the big shots to realize it."

Back at her punching Cookie gets still more mixed up. Sandy makes her work seem important. Chuck makes it seem useless. She tries to think about it, but everything is all balled up. The only sure thing is her burning knees.

At meal break she takes it up with Bruce. Bruce'll know the answer as sure as John Kieran. "Chuck says there's too much politics in the yard," she tells him. Bruce sets out to answer when something strange happens—without any reason Ma Hopkins starts laughing. It's a shrill laugh and its effect on Bruce is amazing. His face goes dead and doesn't come to life for the rest of the lunch period. When we speak to him he doesn't answer. He just stares holes into the air.

136

Cookie is worried. She tells Cherie. The two girls start snapping some thirty lines across a deck unit. Each holds one end of the string and after it's snapped they meet in the middle to rechalk it and have a chance to exchange a few words.

"I wish I knew what's the matter with Bruce," says Cookie. "He's like two different men, and I sure like one of them." They chalk the line, each going to her end. They square down the line, snap it and go toward each other again.

"Why don't you ask Ma Hopkins?" Cherie says. "Maybe there's more behind his getting fired than meets the eye." They chalk, square down, snap, and meet once more.

"She won't tell," says Cookie. Then, after that line is snapped and they are chalking it up again she adds, softly, "Besides, I'm afraid to hear about that girl down there."

One more line is chalked and snapped. "Don't be silly," says Cherie. "I'll find out for you."

The rest of the unit is done in silence. Cherie has made up her mind, and as soon as she gets a chance she takes off on her reconnaissance raid. She and Ma Hopkins put in hatch brackets, Cherie holds them in place and Ma Hopkins does the tacking. When the brackets are in, the secret's out. Cookie stands on the tips of her toes waiting for the news.

"What's the score?" she asks.

Cherie takes off her safety glasses and rubs her eyes with the back of her hands. She looks tired. "Cookie," she says, "Bruce was fired because he took politics into the music room."

Cookie cheers up. "Is that all?" she cries, relieved. "Looking at your face, I thought he was at least secretly married."

Cherie stays dead serious. "It's much worse than that, *ma petite*. Here are a few things that Bruce preached: that

137

the Declaration of Independence is bunk, that we Americans are too selfish, that Christianity is responsible for the war . . .''

Cookie's hand goes up to her lips. "But that's impossible. He must have lost his mind."

Cherie shrugs. "Christopher, Ma Hopkins' grandson, was one of his students, and he fell for it. Many kids fell for it. The principal of the school told Ma Hopkins that Bruce had a whole screwy scheme worked out and felt it was his duty to teach it. *Je ne comprends pas.*"

"Come to think of it," says Cookie, "he does talk cockeyed stuff once in a while, but I never pay much attention. Still, it doesn't make sense. Why should he be working in the shipyard now?"

"To find dopes for his propaganda, of course," Cherie tells her. "That makes much more sense than your romantic explanation. I know that intellectual type disguised as a worker. We had plenty of them in France."

Next day, every one of our gang seems to know. Lovella claims she always guessed there must be something wrong with Bruce because he never kidded around with the girls like the other men. Jason says he doesn't know what the score with Bruce is politically, but as a flanger he stinks. Cookie says she thought things over and she definitely believes Bruce must have lost his mind temporarily because of that girl in L.A. And it isn't hard to guess what Gosh says.

Bruce works as hard as usual, without paying much attention to what's going on around him, and he doesn't seem to notice the glances turned at him on the sly. Besides, the gang doesn't have a chance to take a breather today. Sandy is off and George, the relief leader-man, has taken over. He's a young fellow and wants things done in a hurry. He orders the gang around and calls workers away from one job to do another, and the guys don't like it.

138

"He just wants to make a big splash," says Chuck, lighting a cigarette.

Pee-Wee speaks up for George. "It's his first week on the job and he wants to show what he can do as a leaderman. We ought to give him a break."

"He doesn't need our help." Chuck flips away the match. "He's in with the big shots."

"All right, he has some friends in the office," Pee-Wee admits. "But that doesn't make him a stooge. You shouldn't sabotage him."

"I'm not sabotaging him," Chuck replies. "I do what he tells me, but no more."

The air on the assembly is getting loaded. George feels it. His orders get rougher and that doesn't make things easier for him or for the rest of the gang.

After dark, Okie Red, the machine burner, calls Chuck. "Say, have a look at that bulkhead before I go and burn it. There's something haywire."

Chuck glances at the bulkhead. "George laid it out for burn, didn't he? He's leaderman. I'm not. I'd burn anything on a leaderman's say-so."

So Okie Red goes ahead and burns it. Sometimes he's sure of his burns and sometimes he demands a written release. But he's always been sure of Chuck. Chuck has never given him a bum steer.

The next day everybody is in a swear and a sweat. That bulkhead was burned wrong. The engineering department and the maritime commission check the unit. Every fitter boss and flanger boss of every assembly comes to see it, like attending a hanging. It's a mess.

When Sandy comes back, it takes him three minutes to figure things out. Twenty beams have to be chipped out and a filler put in, and it'll take a whole shift to fix it. Okie Red can't be blamed because a burner just burns off what the fitters tell him to. So the blame falls on George. But when Sandy learns that Red had asked Chuck about that burn, I see him blow up for the first and only time.

139

"Anybody can pull a boner," he shouts, "but Chuck knew it was laid out wrong and let Okie Red go ahead and burn it! That's dirty pool! I won't stand for that sort of thing on my crew!"

It's Chuck's day off, but when he comes back next afternoon Sandy has the quit slip ready for him. The shift has not started yet, and Jason, Alibi, Pee-Wee and I stand there with Chuck and Sandy. It's a foggy day and only when a nearby welder strikes an arc and his flash throws us into a glaring green light do I see Chuck's face. It's motionless, except for occasional twitchings of his jaw muscles. He fingers the quit slip awkwardly.

Then Bruce joins us. "Wait a minute!" he says.

"You would stick up for Chuck," says Sandy.

"I'm not sticking up for anyone but myself," Bruce counters. "I know you think I'm a saboteur, or worse. We've been a swell gang and I don't want it to crack up."

"Okay prof," says Jason. "Dish it out. Prove to us that trees are fishes."

A welding arc splutters and our shadows dance grotesquely in the glaring eerie light on a deep-tank unit behind us, changing size and shape with irregular flashes. Cookie stands close to Bruce, her eyes focused on his lips.

"I'm not defending Chuck," Bruce starts out. "He should have known better. He has seen Nazis and Japs in their backyards and he knows what our lives would be like if they won the war. But something happened to his thinking and I want you all to see clearly what it was, whether you like it or not. He wanted to become leader-man and another guy walked off with the job. That got Chuck. His thinking went haywire. What he did will delay our ship for a day. Its cargo will reach the front a day later. In simple words, because Chuck didn't get a raise of fifteen cents an hour, a few soldiers will be killed. Others will live without a leg or arm."

140

"If you put it that way," says Chuck, "I could kick myself in the pants. But there's more behind it."

"I know there's more behind it," Bruce cuts him short, "but whatever it is, it isn't worth a life or a limb. You see that now. You've just flown off the handle. And we have no right to condemn you because we've done the same thing, one way or another."

"The hell we have," says Jason.

"What about that fur coat you bought for Pudgy, Jason—instead of buying war bonds? What about those two days, Joe, you laid off and went fishing? What about the working hours we lost because you had a good time a few nights ago, Alibi?"

"That's a lot of baloney no matter how thin you slice it," Alibi growls. "This is a free country and every guy has a right to spend the money he earns and to work when he wants, and I'd like to see the goddamn dictator who tries to take that away from us."

"Nobody is going to take anything away from you, Alibi," Bruce says, raising his arm against a welding flash. "No one likes to be told what to do and not to do. But unlimited freedom is no ticket to paradise. The way I see it, something is demanded of us to which we have to respond."

"Demanded?" Pee-Wee frowns. "You mean, by God?"

"You can call it God if you are religious," Bruce replies. "Or by Life. Or Nature. I think that every situation places a demand on us to which we have to respond. True freedom, meaningful freedom, does not mean that I can do whatever I damn well please. It means I am free to respond to the demands of the moment. Animals do it by instinct. We do it by choice. We are able to respond by choices—we are response-able. That distinguishes us from the other animals. We are not only free but reponsible.

"What are you trying to say?" asks Jason. "That Chuck was irresponsible?"

141

"We all are selfish," Bruce goes on. "That's human too. The war puts special demands on us. It makes us see things more clearly—about freedom, responsibility, selfishness. War can make brutes out of people. But it can also get us closer to our true human nature at its best."

"Sounds okay on paper, professor," says Alibi. "But you'll never be able to make an inner bottom look like a deckhouse."

"Maybe not," Bruce admits. "But a human being is not an inner bottom, a thing. We can change. If people fifty years ago had started to change, we might not have had to fight this war. Maybe we can save our kids from another war."

"Let's stick to Chuck," says Cherie who has joined our group. "I know him well enough to know he's sorry even if he doesn't say so. As for the human race, I've seen enough of it in Paris, French and German variety, to tell you it's hopeless."

"That's where you're wrong," Bruce replies firmly. "It all depends on what you teach in school. You can make devils or angels out of kids. Hitler proved you can make devils out of them. We *can* make reasonable human beings out of them. I know it because I tried."

"And they kicked you out," Alibi reminds him.

"Yes, they kicked me out. But do you know why? Because the boys were so thrilled about the idea that they went home and tried to convince their old men. But it's not an idea for old men. You have to teach the young."

The whistle cuts through his words. It sounds like the alarm clock that calls us from our dreams into a dark, foggy day. The chippers are tuning their guns, the burners and welders connect their lines and drag them across the assembly. Butch, the rigger, comes up to Sandy, "What do you need?"

142

Sandy tells Butch that he wants the crane to take the unit that was completed during the day shift up the hull. He looks at Chuck for a moment.

"Chuck," Sandy says, "will you see that the unit is cleared for the take-up?"

Chuck gives Sandy a happy grin, tears up his quit slip, and goes to work. The take-up of the unit gives the rest of us a few more moments. There still is unfinished business.

"Now tell us," asks Cookie with eager eyes. "Why did they dismiss you from school?"

"What about those things you said about Christianity and the Declaration of Independence?" Cherie asks in the tone of a public prosecutor.

"Oh, you know about that, too?" Bruce smoothes his hair with both hands. "Okay, I'll tell you. I was talking about responsibility. The Church reaches people all over the world. It has the responsibility, not only to get us into heaven, but to help us establish a heaven on earth. I told them Christ's words, 'Love thy neighbor,' will have to be a political program. The Church will have to *do* something about peace, not just preach it. 'If the Church does not go in for political action,' I said, 'it will have to accept its share of responsibility for World War III.'"

"The preachers?" Jason asks. "Going into politics?"

"I got into a lot of trouble about that," Bruce admits. "People hear the word 'politics' and they think of lies, dirty deals and pork barrels. What I meant was people should get actively involved. If Americans would keep score of their politicians like they do of their baseball batters, the world would become fit to live in."

"What about the Declaration of Independence?" Pee-Wee insists.

"The Declaration is a great document," Bruce says. "But it isn't enough. It talks about independence, freedom. We have a Statue of Liberty. We need a Statue of Responsibility to match it."

143

"We have our Constitution to dish out responsibility," Pee-Wee replies. "It tells people what they can do and what they can't."

"That's exactly what I told my students. The Constitution, by dishing out responsibility, limits freedom. Not even the President can do as he pleases. It was the Constitution, with its clout, that made us a nation."

"Is that why they fired you?" Cookie's voice is thin and disappointed.

"Some teachers agreed with me. But the parents were upset. It was they who had the clout. I never could make them understand."

"You got a raw deal," Pee-Wee says. "But don't give up. You've got something."

"It won't work," I tell Bruce. "Take our gang, for instance. Alibi and Jason would just sneeze at sacrifices. Red and Lovella would think it's crazy because it's never been done. Pink and Pipsqueak wouldn't take it seriously. Happy and Gosh wouldn't know what it's all about, and the rest wouldn't bother."

"Who are you telling I wouldn't make sacrifices?" Alibi shouts. "I'm making a great sacrifice right now by not punching you in the nose!"

"Give us a chance, Joe," Pee-Wee tells me. "We're not doing so badly here." Then, seeing that the crane has cleared the assembly, she adds, "How about responding to the demands of the moment and laying out the next unit?"

"Okay," says Alibi, "let's get off the filthy dime and finish this unit before the shift is over!"

Chuck is directing Pink and Pipsqueak who are laying out the unit, snapping their chalk lines. Cookie and Cherie follow them with their punches, Pee-Wee and I are right behind them knocking the beams into place for Sparkie and Ma Hopkins to tack them on.

"Remember the two Malcolms?" Pee-Wee asks between hammer blows. "I sometimes ride with them now.

144

They've decided to stay in the shipyard even after summer vacation. One is interrupting writing a book to work on these war ships, and the other will be spending his sabbatical being a steel checker."

She gives a twenty-foot beam one of her Archimedian taps. I see Bruce struggling with a stiffener, and Cookie, with a dreamy look in her eyes, hitting her fingers more than her punch. Then my glance goes to the boat they're building from the parts we assemble. It's a beautiful boat, as good as complete. A couple of painters are finishing the coat on her bow. I know them both. One used to raise chickens in Petaluma and the other one used to sell peanuts.

Then I get a hopeful feeling about the future. If a bunch of raw hands like us can build topnotch ships like these, then maybe some day, in spite of all of our shortcomings, we'll get along together and build a nice world to live in, and maybe we won't even worry who gets credit for the tonnage.

Romance
on a
Liberty

One summer night, after a day of working on sizzling steel plates, we're standing around under the assembly shelter waiting for the whistle. I notice Pipsqueak dishing out what looks like a handbill and I wonder what trick he's up to. Then he's there, right at my elbow.

"Here!" he says.

I open the slip of paper. In letters not too fine yet suggesting a wedding I read:

PINK AND PIPSQUEAK
give you the honor to be present at the launching
and maiden trip of the U.S.S. Jellybean.

All shore loafers of the gang on Five will meet
at the ferry at 10 a.m. and will be convoyed to
the ship by Captain Pipsqueak. There will be chow
in the galley and drinks in the tanks.

If you have a date bring your jewel along!
Come as you please but please come! Make knots!
Don't miss the boat!

When I drive up the Bayshore the next morning, nearly all of our gang is flocked around Pink and Pipsqueak, and there are also guys from other Ways and people I don't know who look like college kids. Pipsqueak is rigged up in a uniform Hollywood might dig up for an admiral in a musical comedy. Pink wears a fancy cap, a khaki shirt and pants. Everybody is chatting and it's nearly as noisy as in the yard, when Pipsqueak climbs on the top of his car.

"Ladies and gentlemen," he mimics the official yard announcer, "will you please form a group and follow Ensign Pink. Don't step on boards with rusty nails. Don't fall in the water. This is for your own safety. Your cooperation will be appreciated. Thank you."

We follow Ensign Pink, wondering what it's all about. Soon we know. Ahead of us, made fast to a dock is a small, gray fifty-foot boat which is an exact copy of a Liberty ship. The shape, the masts, the deckhouses—everything is there, even a little rowboat on davits made up as a lifeboat. The bow announces her name: *U.S.S. Jellybean.*

Everything is draped in patriotic bunting and a string of flags flies across the forepart of the *Jellybean* just like on her big sisters over in the yard. A bottle dangles from the bow and a small soapbox platform is ready for the launching ceremony. While a phonograph blares a march, we crowd around the soapbox. Pipsqueak climbs up again for a speech while Pink presses a big bunch of roses into the hands of a startled Sparkie.

"One more minute to the launching of the *U.S.S. Jellybean,*" Pipsqueak announces excitedly. "Only fifty seconds till Ensign Pink releases the trigger that will send her down the Ways . . . just forty more seconds until Sparkie smashes the champagne to christen the *U.S.S. Jellybean . . .*"

Sparkie has heard the routine too often to miss the cue. "I christen thee *U.S.S. Jellybean,*" she shouts and

148

smashes the bottle so it splashes all over her. Licking her lips she mumbles happily, "It is champagne."

Pink releases the only trigger in sight, a rope from ship to dock. He hacks it in two with a butcher knife. "Sure it is champagne," he says triumphantly, "do you think we want a jinxed ship?"

The U.S.S. *Jellybean* continues rolling gently, oblivious to her baptism. A makeshift gangway is lowered and we are led aboard. Everything is new and shiny. The deckhouse amidship is adapted as a bar with drinks, sandwiches and cookies. The door of Pink and Pipsqueak's quarters is locked and a sign announces, CLOSED. OUT FOR LAUNCH. The after-deckhouse is fixed up as a guest room with the inscription, FOR ABLE-BODIED SEAMEN AND SEAWOMEN. The hatches are covered and used as dance floors, except number five which is full of sleeping bags, fishing stuff, ping pong tables and whatnot.

Jellybeans are passed around. "Get a mouthful of the yum-yums whose name our boat honors," Pipsqueak offers solemnly. Then he's off on the bridge, the motor gets going, and Pipsqueak steers the boat out into the Bay.

Soon the boat looks like a floating juke joint with guys dashing amidships to grab a sandwich or a drink for their girls and themselves. A cool breeze comes from the Pacific, and the sun slips from its blanket of morning fog on its trip to the Golden Gate Bridge.

A few smaller groups are shooting the breeze, keeping a wary eye on the gyrating limbs of the jitterbugs. Pee-Wee, Bruce and I have escaped into the lifeboat, which is outside the reach of the swingsters, and are looking over the malted milk tablets, biscuits and chocolate stored in tin boxes, when a nice-looking elderly gent joins us.

"In my day, watching youngsters dance was by far not as dangerous as nowadays," he laughs, smoothing his flawless blue suit with both hands. "Now I know how it feels to be saved by a lifeboat." He sits down and

149

relaxes. "You are Bruce, aren't you? And I'll bet that's Joe, and you, of course, are Pee-Wee. I know all about you. I am Gerald's father."

That doesn't wise us up much until it turns out that he's Pipsqueak's old man. He insists on calling Pipsqueak Gerald, and tells us that it has cost quite a bit of dough to get the materials for the *U.S.S. Jellybean* but he considers it a good investment because Gerald and Paul (which is his name for Pink) have learned quite a bit by building the ship. The boys got such a kick out of working in the yard that they decided to build a Liberty ship themselves, and they spent all their time-off working on the boat.

"I'm a believer in doing things the hard way," old man Pipsqueak tells us. "There is no better method than the tried and tested one of trial and error."

Before you know it, he and Bruce are off on a discussion about teaching which comes to an end only when Pee-Wee manages to edge in the question about such things as wartime restrictions on sailing around the Bay. Pipsqueak's old man hints that he stands pretty high with the Coast Guard and besides, he claims, Gerald knows the Bay from the ground up and he probably knows some parts which even the Coast Guard hasn't seen.

Meanwhile the sun has burned off the fog, and the four Richmond yards become visible—a dazzling display of flashes from thousands of day-shift welders and burners. Wherever you go in the Bay Area, the yards are present, twenty-four hours a day, seven days a week. They are present in the lunch-pail and hard-hat parade of the workers, in the stream of share-the-car riders, and the gleam of lights on the night horizon.

The passengers of the *U.S.S. Jellybean* are having the time of their lives. Pipsqueak on the bridge is surrounded by a crowd and everyone takes a turn steering the boat. The bridge also serves as a stage where people pop up with a speech or an imitation which is always greeted with laughter. Suddenly Pink is up on the bridge, waving his hands and shouting till everybody is quiet. He's all flushed and his hair flutters in the breeze.

"Folks!" he yells. "Listen, folks. Sparkie and I...uh... we've just decided... I mean I have made up her mind... I mean I've asked her and she's said yes..."

Sparkie is next to him, her full lips parted in a happy smile and her face as red as her hair. Cookie is jumping up and down, shouting words that are drowned in the general bustle. Hands are shaken, arms squeezed and kisses showered. Only Pipsqueak, who is still steering the boat, stays quiet. Too quiet for my taste. Abruptly he gives the wheel a hard over, swerving the boat around and throwing everybody off their feet. The girls let out Coney Island roller-coaster screams and get hold of the nearest he-arm, and a big wave of whoopee sweeps the boat.

Pipsqueak hands the wheel to Jason and heads for the bar. He grabs a quart and pours himself drink after drink. Pink finally notices his mood and joins him.

"Anything wrong, Pip?" he asks, placing a friendly hand on his shoulder.

Pipsqueak doesn't answer.

"What's the matter?"

No answer.

"Say, Pip, don't be a wet blanket, c'mon now—it's me, Pink, remember?"

Pipsqueak seems to remember. "Why didn't you tell me?" he asks.

"Tell you what?" Then Pink also remembers. "Why, hell, I'm as surprised as you. The dance, the boat, the excitement—you know. It just shot sky-high like the red flares out of the signal pistols we bought for the lifeboat. What diff does it make whether I told you or not?"

"It's all right," Pipsqueak says, "forget it!"

151

"C'mon. No secrets. Cough it up."

"No secrets," scoffs Pipsqueak. "Who has secrets from whom?"

"Oh, don't be an ass. I told you and everybody as soon as I knew it myself."

"But you shouldn't have done it here. Look, Pink, we spent a year together building this tub. And we planned how we would sail it. Even our dads didn't know about it, and they were to shell out the beans for her maiden trip. We had it all planned together—and now you've forgotten."

Pink sits silently. "I see," he says "I'm sorry, Pipsqueak, I didn't think of it that way. Everything was— so different all of a sudden. Y'know what I mean?"

"Oh yeah," says Pipsqueak. "Love. It makes a prize cabbage out of a guy. Well, it's your tough luck, not mine."

"Okay, tumble-bum, if it makes you feel better. And now turn on both batteries, will you?"

But Pipsqueak isn't himself anymore, neither on the way back nor the next few days in the yard. Only when he hangs a sign, QUIET! WAR WORKERS RESTING, on the door of the women's washroom do we know he is his old self again.

The next day we know why. Pink shows up in a flashy red and blue shirt, the kind an usher in a circus might wear, and his face and eyes are flashy too. The big news is that he's quitting to join the merchant marine. Ever since he began building Liberty ships he'd had a hankering to go out on one of those boats we built, only his old man wouldn't let him. He wanted Pink to finish his studies and join the navy. But now, with Pink's mind made up to marry Sparkie his father agreed to let him ship out right away, and Pink isn't the boy to say no to a trip, even if he has to wait a while until he can say yes to his girl. And Pipsqueak is so hopped up over Pink's going overseas that he waltzes around the yard. He'd love to go along but he has his heart set on the air corps and is taking flying lessons. All he has to do is pass the test for color blindness but he thinks he needs more vitamins in

152

his system. That's why he carries a bag of raw carrots with him and nibbles them all day long like peanuts.

And Sparkie? It's hard to tell what she really feels. There's so much backslapping, handshaking and good-lucking, and Pink feels so happy and important, that Sparkie wouldn't be Sparkie if she didn't feel proud, too.

So it's Pink who's the first of our gang to change from the assembly line to the fighting line. There is a drop of sadness in our backslapping, a little pang deep inside us all. You can see it in the way the jeans and overalls crowd around his silk shirt, in the way we look at his quit slip and the way we work that day. Yesterday he was one of us, today he wears a visitor's badge. The gang is beginning to break up, and goddammit, it gets you.

But that's not the last time we see Pink in our yard. Two days later he shows up wearing a white seaman's cap over his left ear.

"I got a job on the *Samuel Snyder*, and we're coming to take her out right from the outfitting dock," he tells us happily.

"The *Snyder*?" shouts Chuck. "Why, that's a Way Five boat!"

"Sure," nods Pink. "I told you I'd sail on one of them. I built 'em, now I sail 'em. And I'm darn glad we've made a habit of putting four-leaf clovers in all of 'em."

"Where did you put it on the *Snyder*?" asks Pip-squeak. "On bulkhead 39, as usual?"

"What d'you mean, where I put it," Pink yells. "You put it there yourself."

"I didn't," says Pipsqueak. "I thought you did."

Pink takes off his cap and slaps it against his palm in a fluster. "Gee, here we're putting clovers in these boats for one year, and just when I go out in one of them we forget!"

There is a second of silence while Pink and Pipsqueak stare at each other. Sparkie watches them both. Sandy

153

takes out a little package which he hands over to Pink. "Well, if you forgot to put the clover into the boat, this one may come in handy." It's a golden four-leaf clover to pin on his shirt, a farewell gift from the gang.

"Gee, that's swell," Pink says, fastening it in place. "Just what I need. Now I feel better."

"Aw, come on, grow up," Alibi scowls. "Those boats are welded so solid that the steel plates would break before the weld would."

"Steel *is* solid, isn't it?" Pink is awkward with the farewell and isn't sure of what he wants to say. "Thanks a lot!" comes out.

"Take it easy now, sonny," says Alibi. "If you see a sub, remember we gave you a couple of guns along. And if you see a babe, remember the hi-signs. Nothing is more satisfying than shooting an enemy or kissing a friend. But gun or kiss, take it easy."

"Alibi, *you* take it easy," warns Sparkie. "I made him promise to keep his fingers off girls. If I ever find out he has broken his promise," she goes on solemnly, "I shall never speak to him again."

"All right, all right," laughs Alibi. "American boys are supposed to make friends all over the world, aren't they? What are we fighting for?"

"For this," says Pink, taking Sparkie into his arms and giving her a good hearty kiss. "That'll have to last me a long time." He shakes hands with us, very fast. "So long folks, be good." He holds Pipsqueak's hand a little longer. The two boys look at each other but neither says a word. Then Pink is gone, a white cap drifting among hard hats.

Three weeks later Sparkie has a cable saying that Pink has arrived safely at—censored. She is showing it around and everybody is happy with her. Another three weeks go by, and we figure he might pop up any day now, for it shouldn't take him more time for the trip back than for the trip over to wherever he was. When he doesn't show up, Alibi tells us that the unloading takes a couple of weeks; they can't just dump the stuff from the hatches on the beach and run home again. So we wait two more weeks, and Chuck says that maybe they didn't go home straight but made a jump to South America to bring home some ore or coffee or something. Another two weeks go by, and guys show up who shipped out after Pink, were in the South Pacific and are back getting ready to load for their next trip. The papers have stories about Japanese submarines, and men drifting around in lifeboats, some picked up weeks later, and I can't help thinking how many don't get picked up at all. Pee-Wee tries her bit by telling Sparkie that there's no reason to get low. You never can tell where the boys are sent to. She didn't hear from her husband for half a year once, Pee-Wee tells her, and then he turned up on the other side of the globe. Maybe Pink went to India or Africa and one day would show up in New York. But Sparkie has the blues looking at the headlines. Pipsqueak tries to cheer her up but he doesn't feel so bright himself.

Then, one day, neither of them shows up for work, and we all feel uneasy about it. Next afternoon Pipsqueak is back to confirm our worst fears. Pink's father got one of those telegrams. The *Samuel Snyder* was sunk and Pink not among those picked up.

This is a sad day for the gang. War has come home to us from those faraway battlefronts we supply just so they will stay far away. When the whistle rings the shift in and we all go about our jobs, Sparkie is with us. We crowd around her, and Cherie impulsively gives her a hug.

"You shouldn't have come to work today," Dimples says softly.

Sparkie shakes her head. "That's no reason to lay off," she says. "That's a reason to work."

She turns on her welding machine like it was a machine gun, and stocks herself with welding rods like they were bullets. Then all of us go to work. Jason's sledge sounds more grim and Swede's chipping gun more deadly. Fewer cigarettes are lit and fewer moments are goofed off. It's as if someone were behind us swinging a whip, and it isn't the Gestapo.

I happen to work with Bruce that day. He's the only one who works that way all the time. But today, from time to time, he looks around, a whimsical expression in his eyes. "See what I mean?" he says. "Today they know what it's all about. Today they see the connection between a little punch mark and a life. Even Cookie sees it today. Watch her work. Watch all of them work. I tried to tell them, but they wouldn't listen. Thousands can die, but it doesn't make a dent if they read it in the papers. Words can't teach them. One of them has to die, someone close to them."

Sparkie moves so fast today that her welding looks like jagged pieces of lightning. When she finally opens her hood her eyes are blurred, and it's not from welding smoke. At break time Pipsqueak tries his best to cheer her up; we all try, but we feel rather helpless about it.

However, you can't count Pipsqueak out so easily. In their time-off he tells Sparkie as much about Pink as she wants to know. He shows her the caves where he and Pink used to hide and live like stone age men. He shows her how they trapped rabbits and how they roasted them on the fire with potatoes they swiped from the nearby fields. To top it all he makes Sparkie ensign on the U.S.S. *Jellybean* and lets her steer the boat around the Bay.

I'd say Pipsqueak makes a great job of it. Not that Sparkie is her jolly old self again, but you simply cannot stay in splinters with Pipsqueak around. He never passes her without pulling her hair or tickling her or writing some pun on her hood, and she takes it the way it's meant, not to annoy, but as some form of attention. She
156

giggles and shrieks, and when a girl giggles and shrieks she can't give herself up entirely to grief.

Cherie, however, tells me (and she has it from Cookie) that Sparkie cries herself to sleep every night and that sometimes she is lower than a flat keel. But every afternoon, Sparkie slips into her jeans with the grim resolution of someone out for revenge.

One day I'm on the far end of the assembly carrying some flat bars when Alibi pokes me in the ribs. I drop the bars on my safety toes.

"Bust my binnacles!" he yells, pointing toward the plate shop. A figure is running toward our assembly, running in big jumps, a white cap on his head and a big visitor's badge on his chest, and I'll be apple-eyed if it isn't Pink! He waves to us and presses his forefinger to his lips. He spots Sparkie through leathers, hood and welding smoke, sneaks up to her, opens her hood and presses his palms against her eyes.

"Oh stop it, Pipsqueak," she says, wiggling and trying to free herself.

He lets go and she turns around. When she sees Pink she goes soft and wobbly. She just manages to hold on to him, her hood drops down, and he keeps her tight in his arms, touching her red mop with his lips. But there's not much time for privacy. The whole gang is around, wanting to have part of Pink. Pipsqueak first, who doesn't even wait till Pink lets Sparkie go, but throws his arms around both of them.

It takes some time till you understand your own words, let alone the others. Yes, he was torpedoed all right. "But they can't get me," he laughs. "Not shrimps like our enemy. The old rust bucket went down, and it's Pipsqueak's fault because he forgot to put in that four-leaf clover. But I had . . ." he proudly flashes the gold leaf pin we gave him. "That thing pulled me through all right."

We want to know all about it but it seems to be a long story, and Pink hasn't even seen his folks yet. He arrived in Alameda and hitchhiked right to the yard. "Let's have a celebration tomorrow, on board the *Jellybean*," he suggests, "and I'll tell you the whole story."

He breezes off again, and Sparkie and Pipsqueak go along. We others have two more hours, then we go home for a quick sleep and a shift of clothes, and around 9:00 in the morning we are aboard Pipsqueak's boat.

The *U.S.S. Jellybean* dances on top of the slight ripples that the breeze from the sea sends toward the shore, and she too seems to be happy with the return of her ensign. The boat is loaded with a cheerful crowd and Pink struts around, every inch a hero. Pipsqueak and Sparkie trail in his wake, complaining all along that he hasn't told them anything. Finally, Pipsqueak grabs Pink's arm, forces him up the bridge, waves his arms and announces, "I herewith promote Ensign Pink to Lieutenant J.G., not meaning Jerky Goof—and get the hell on the ball and tell us what happened!"

"Yeah, tell us, how was the boat?" asks Jason.

"She was a good ship," says Pink proudly, "and it took three torpedoes to finish her. But I don't want to begin with the end. Sailing on her was hot stuff while it lasted. When we left here she was loaded down to the limit. We had more gas aboard than you can get for a truckful of C coupons, and number five hatch was filled with ammunition. If we'd been hit then, we really would've been sunk, in more ways than one. But the sea was calm and nobody thought of subs and tinfish except a handful of guys who had been hit before. The work wasn't particularly thrilling. I was on the twelve-to-four watch and spent most of my time painting bulkheads, doors and whatnot.

"I always suspected that life at sea would be different. You don't even talk the same language anymore. When

158

we build a boat, a crane is a crane. When you sail it, it's a boom. Midships is no longer the place where your stiffeners toe to, but a place where the officers sleep. A bulkhead quits being a unit you assemble and becomes a wall on which you tack your favorite pinup girl. The guy who bosses you around is not the leaderman but the bos'n."

"And he usually is a slave driver like Sandy," Chuck puts in.

"Yes, he made us work," Pink goes on, "but it didn't make much of a diff. What really counts is how you feel. And you feel grand. There's the ocean and it's your ocean, and there's the sky in unbelievable colors, and it's your sky, and you feel like climbing up the mast, shouting. Instead you climb up, paint bucket in hand, and give it the old battleship-gray treatment. And you don't mind either.

"Well, we sailed for seventeen days, and it felt just like a Sunday morning fishing trip. Without the deck cargo, the tanks and the guns, we wouldn't have known there was a war on. No papers, no radio, no newsreel. The war was far away. And still, it could have been right underneath our flat keel. We arrived safely in New Zealand and unloaded our cargo. I better not tell you the name of the town because it's a new army base and it would be a nice fat target for the Japs. Our boat was the first American ship to land there, and the whole town turned out. Even before we went ashore, we saw the girls standing at the pier, waving and shouting and laughing at us."

"I get it," says Alibi, rubbing his palms on his knees. "Don't give us that army base stuff. Naturally the name of that town is a military secret."

"Oh, stop it, will you?" Sparkie says, pouting. "What have those New Zealand girls got that we haven't got?"

Pink throws his arms around her waist and holds her while he goes on. "We had a wonderful time there. We were invited for meals and dances, went swimming at the

159

beach, and they used up their gasoline to show us the sights, and gas rationing is much tighter down there than it is here."

"Just who used up their gas?" Sparkie asks.

"Oh, everybody. They just killed themselves to give us a good time."

"Girls too?"

"Of course, Sparkie, there were girls too. Girls and their brothers and their mothers and fathers. There's nothing to look worried about. I never so much as held hands with them."

"Sailors tell strange yarns," Alibi says in a humming sort of way. Juanita pokes him in the ribs and Alibi, grinning, shuts up. Pink still is holding Sparkie, but she backs up on him.

"Well," Pink gets going again, "naturally we had work too, getting ready for the trip back, painting and cleaning and some loading. One day we got an order to build a special deckhouse aft on the boat deck, and that could mean just one thing: we were getting passengers. Rumors started floating around. One day it was General MacArthur going to Washington for a conference, next day it was a Japanese admiral we had captured, and so it went on right up to the morning when we were set to pull out. We were at our posts when a group of guys came up the gangway. Billy, the A.B. with whom I worked on the same watch, shouts, 'Slap me down, if that isn't Jimmy Jumms,' and everybody's looking down, and sure enough, it's him and his whole band."

"Gee," says Lovella, "I read in the papers that they've just come back from a tour in Australia."

"Say, isn't Lola Ramirez with them?" Sparkie asks suspiciously.

"She sure is," Pink tells her, "and you should've seen the riot when she came aboard."

"We heard her in Chicago," Chuck reminds Miggs, "the hottest canary I ever heard."

160

"They were swell, all of them," Pink assures us, "and they played for us any time we asked them to. And Lola sang her best songs for us and wore a new dress every day. It was a grand trip until—well, there was a war on, after all, even if we'd almost forgotten.

"I had just gotten off watch and gone into the messroom to have a bit of night lunch. Pete had come down from the wheel and told us the old man was up on the bridge. And if the old man is up on the bridge at that time of night, it means trouble. It means subs.

"Well, I can't say we weren't worried, but we decided the best thing we could do was to hit the sack. When I reached my foc's'l, my four-leaf clover was missing. It wasn't such a hot time to lose it, so I went back to the messroom to look for it. Not a soul was around and all I could feel was a quivering, and I wasn't sure if it was the ship or me. For one moment, and for no reason at all, I was scared. Then I saw the clover pin on the floor, under the table. I bent down to pick it up when the first torpedo struck. The lights went out and all the dinnerware came crashing down. The door leading to the pantry buckled like in a dream. I wasn't scared anymore. I could think very clearly and I was surprised that I could. 'Nobody knows where I am,' I thought. 'I've got to get out of here by myself.'

"Just then the second tinfish hit. I was thrown clear across the messroom against a bulkhead and knocked out. Next thing I remember was a tremendous thud. It was the third torpedo but I didn't know it at the time. I still was in a daze and couldn't figure out what it was all about. Everything was dark and full of the weirdest noises. I felt something in my fist. The four-leaf clover. That brought back everything, and I held it tight. Then, through the racket, I heard the whistle. Seven short blasts and one long one. 'Abandon ship.'

"I got on my knees and began crawling along the deck. I remembered the instructions for emergencies. I

161

crawled toward the nearest door. I had to crawl uphill, which meant the ship had a port list. I reached the door, but it was jammed. I tried with all my strength, but it didn't budge. I held tight so I wouldn't slide back, got on my knees again and began feeling around till I found the plywood panel that was put there for the emergency escape. I pushed it out and wriggled through.

"Outside it was hell. Fire all over the place, water and steam pipes busted. I was walking up to my knees in water. Steam came out hissing from nowhere, but I hardly felt the scalding until later. I just had one aim: to get up on the boat deck to the lifeboats. Then, when I finally managed to get up there, the lifeboats were gone. The boat-falls hung empty, their heavy blocks beating against the ship's side, sounding a steady death knell in the lonesome dark."

We sit around Pink quietly while the *Jellybean* dances up and down. Sparkie holds Pink's hand so tightly that her knuckles are white. Cookie nibbles her finger-tips, and Pipsqueak's holding half a carrot which he's forgotten to eat for quite some time.

"Well," Pink goes on, "my only hope was to get a raft, so I tried to go down on the forward deck and get one at number two hatch. But flames were shooting out of the vents at number three, spreading rapidly, blocking my way. So I went aft, passing the deckhouse which was blown to bits. 'There are some more rafts between four and five,' I remembered, hurrying as the ship was slowly settling.

"Just when I was about to climb down the after ladder to the main deck I heard a cry. It came from the little deckhouse we had built for Jimmy Jumms. I tore away a piece of plank—the thing fell apart like tinder—and there was Lola, lying on the floor. I asked her if she was hurt but when she saw me she began to scream like mad. There wasn't much time for conversation, so I grabbed her and
162

dragged her down the ladder. She was screaming and kicking as if I were murdering her and not saving her life. When we reached the main deck I finally understood what she was screaming about. She wanted a little red case on her dressing table. You'd think she would've died without it. So I climbed up again, found the case, and on we went to number four. I kicked the pelican hook and was relieved when the raft plunged into the drink. Lola was trembling and staring at me with frightened eyes. I told her to jump. That threw her into a fit. 'I don't want to die,' she kept yelling. For one split second I wondered what had happened to her Mexican accent, but the next moment the mast came down and a flame as high as a house shot out from number four. I pushed her in and jumped after her.

"She didn't struggle when I helped her on the raft and lashed her down. I took out the oars and pulled away from the sinking ship. The waves carried us high up into the air and deep down again. As we got safely away from the ship, I suddenly felt ill and weak. My head was throbbing and it was then that I realized that I was burned. I must have passed out. When I opened my eyes the sun was out, dancing crazily in a deep blue sky. Sometimes when a wave lifted us high enough, I looked around. Nothing and nobody. I opened the hatch and looked inside. C-type rations, cans with water, biscuits, a set of flares and flags, two hatchets, a signal pistol, a sea anchor, blankets, first aid kit—that was all and we had to make the best of it."

Sparkie lets go Pink's hand and sits up. "You mean to say you spent all that time on the raft alone with Lola Ramirez?" she asks.

"Sure," says Pink. "And she was not such a bad pal, after all. The waves of saltwater washed the makeup off her face. And away went her play-acting. She wasn't the Mexican torch singer anymore but a freckle-faced scared kid from Brooklyn. She told me her story, which was

163

definitely not the one you read in the magazines. Her father was a grounds-keeper at Ebbets Field and seems to have known all the diamond dirt of Brooklyn. For hours she went on telling me baseball stories and we both got a kick out of them. But she would've knocked me cold with our last can of fresh water had I said one word against the Dodgers. She showed me what she had in that red case, which was the only thing she cared to save from the ship. It was a baseball, autographed by the entire Dodger team. So there we sat, lashed down to a raft in the middle of the South Pacific, she with a baseball and me with a four-leaf clover, trying to make ourselves believe that everything would come out all right.

"She told me about the time when she went roller-skating in Prospect Park with her boy friends, and how she saved pennies and nickels to go to the Brooklyn Paramount to see the big bands play. She used to sit through all the shows, and copied the singers, the way they walked and smiled and moved their hands. She didn't tell me much about what happened after she got a break and became a star. All she told me was about her childhood. I guess the ten days on the raft made her homesick, not for the stage, but for Brooklyn."

Sparkie, at this point, removes Pink's hand from her hip, jumps to her feet and runs toward the stern of the boat.

Pink stares after her, dumbfounded. "What's the matter with her?" he asks.

"She was crying," Pee-Wee says.

Pink gets up and goes after her.

"She doesn't go for the idea of Pink's spending ten days alone with Lola Ramirez," Cookie explains. "I wouldn't either if I were in her shoes."

"Look," says Pipsqueak. "It wasn't his fault that she was on the raft with him. He couldn't drown her just to please Sparkie, could he?"

164

"I don't know," Cookie shrugs. "I just don't like the idea. Cherie, how would you like to see Ski spend ten days on an island alone with Betty Grable?"

Pink returns, white as a sail. "I can't find her," he says.

"She can't be far," Pipsqueak shoots a glance toward the shore, a mile away, "unless she's an awfully good swimmer."

"Oh stop it, will you," Pink says, angrily.

We all go looking for Sparkie. Pee-Wee is the one who finds her. "She locked herself into the after-deckhouse and wants to see Pipsqueak," she reports.

Pink has his hand on the doorknob of the after-deckhouse the same time as Pipsqueak. But Sparkie wants Pipsqueak only. Pink stays outside, puzzled.

"I wonder who has more reason to be jealous," Lovella remarks, a shade louder than necessary.

Pink turns sharply toward her. "What d'you mean?"

"Nothing," says Lovella.

"What's going on here?" Pink grimaces. "Here I come back, and the first night she runs off. It doesn't make sense." He interrupts himself and looks at every one of us. A light seems to dawn on him. "It *does* make sense. I was dead, wasn't I? Now I know why she guessed Pipsqueak when I covered her eyes. That's why she has the key to the after-deckhouse and my ensign's cap and why she wants to see him and not me. It does make sense, all right."

The door of the deckhouse opens and under the sign FOR ABLE-BODIED SEAMEN AND SEAWOMEN, Pipsqueak and Sparkie emerge. Pipsqueak is beaming all over, holding Sparkie around her shoulder. "Everything's hotsy-totsy," he announces merrily. But he stops cold when he sees Pink's face. "What's wrong now?"

"You know very well what's wrong," Pink says, sharply.

"What do you mean?" Sparkie says, so cold you'd think she could spit ice cubes. "That woman must have twisted your mind."

165

"Leave Lola out of it, will you?" Pink's face gets red. "You don't have to drag her into this. You changed your mind. It was all a mistake. Okay. It's okay with me. I won't die of it. There are girls all over the world."

Pipsqueak has followed the argument with growing amazement. "Listen, old boy," he says, "get on the beam. I just tried to cheer her up while you were away, that's all."

Sparkie bursts into tears and sinks against Pee-Wee who tries to talk sense into her.

"You see," Pink turns to Pipsqueak, "the lady's in love with *you*, and now you've hurt her feelings. I'll be glad to get out to sea again where I have to face nothing beyond sharks and tinfish."

The next few days give no clue. Sparkie is a bit sulky at times, and Pipsqueak is his old clowning self. Alibi had bought a new pair of mountain boots, studded with hobnails, such as the Alaskans might wear. During the lunch break Alibi dozes off, lying on a steel plate, his legs drawn up so his feet rest on the steel. Pipsqueak takes Sparkie's stinger and carefully welds Alibi's hobnails to the assembly. When the whistle goes, Alibi finds his feet glued to the skid, and his face sends us all into stitches. Sparkie laughs till tears roll down her cheeks. She slaps Pipsqueak on the back and when she's able to talk again she gasps admiringly, "You're quite a card, Pipsqueak—a joker!" Swede has to chip Alibi loose.

One day neither Pipsqueak nor Sparkie show up. Cookie looks worried and Cherie tells me later that Sparkie wasn't home all night. At the end of the shift everybody knows that Pipsqueak has eloped with Sparkie. Lovella's right, Cherie is wrong, and everyone's surprised, except Lovella, of course. "The way she looked at him yesterday you didn't need a seeing-eye dog to know when the launching date was," she says.

166

I don't like it, and neither do Cherie and Pee-Wee. Pink is still in town, getting ready for his next trip, and the whole thing is a holy mess and someone will get hurt. So we decide to see Pink.

Pink lives with his parents in a knockout of a house in the Berkeley hills, overlooking the Bay. Pipsqueak lives nearby in a house which is no shack either. Pink is in exactly the mood we expected him to be, noisy and anxious to show us around, waving the Pipsqueak incident aside with a snap of his fingers. He shows us the view, explaining that on a clear night, without the nasty fog, we could see San Francisco, both bridges, and all the islands in the Bay. He shows us his phonograph records and moving pictures and his baseball outfit, but whatever he shows or tells us, Pipsqueak seems part of it. And so, finally, Pink breaks down and begins to talk about the Sparkie affair. "I don't care what she does," he says, "but that Pip could do this to me . . ."

Pink really lets his hair down. He tells us Pipsqueak was here yesterday and that they had it out. "He tried to sound me out on whether I cared for Sparkie. Well, I was pretty mad and talked a lot of applesauce, but I made it clear that Sparkie was still my girl."

Cherie shakes her head and says she thought she knew everything about *toujours l'amour*, but now she's not so sure. Pee-Wee sighs, "Yes, it takes a girl to make a man out of a boy," and Pink adds scornfully, "You mean, it takes a cat to make a rat out of a man," when the door opens and Pipsqueak's father comes into the room.

He stops for breath, nods vaguely in our direction. "We just found out the boat's gone, too," he says. "The Coast Guard tells me they can't have passed the Golden Gate. They must be cruising in the Bay."

Pink is beginning to simmer again. He walks around kicking the furniture as he passes.

"Listen, Paul," Old Pipsqueak tries to follow him. "A gale is coming up. And that miserable fog makes it hard to

167

find them. You know these inlets and hiding places where you used to hole up. Where do you think they are?"

"Oh, leave me alone," Pink yells. "A cold bath is just what they need. Maybe it'll bring them to their senses."

Papa Pipsqueak tries his hardest to get something out of Pink, but the more he nags, the less he gets. Finally he gives up. "Something has to be done," he shouts, "and if you won't help me, I'll have to manage this myself." He slams the door behind him. Cherie, Pee-Wee and I stay on. Maybe Pink will give us a clue.

It's very dark outside and the storm keeps the window panes clattering. They would have clattered anyway from the way Pink is pacing the room. First he just rages, then he swears, and in the course of it all, he uncorks quite a list of names for Pipsqueak and Sparkie. Then he sits down and tells us bits about his friendship with Pipsqueak and his romance with Sparkie. It doesn't always make sense, but it relieves the pressure.

Outside it's as black as in an inner bottom and the gale is whistling around the corners, tousling the treetops. "It makes me sick to think of all the guys who are at sea on a night like this," Pee-Wee says, staring out of the window. "My husband is one of them. Sometimes I have nightmares. I see him in a lifeboat no bigger than the room I'm living in, tossed up and down by waves higher than a house. I try to guess what he's thinking."

The telephone rings and Pink leaps to it. We keep silent while he listens. Pee-Wee touches the corners of her eyes with a handkerchief, and Cherie catches her around her waist. Pink's face is white and tired, and suddenly a drop appears on his forehead and rolls down his brow. Then he begins to talk very loud and fast. "All right," he says, "all right, now listen. Try Suisun Bay, right off Seal Island, maybe as far out as Preston Point. Oh no. No, no, no. Not there. Much farther out than the Martinez Ferry.

168

Oh, I can't explain it. I'll be out there right away. Meet you at the Martinez Coast Guard station."

"I'll go with you," I say. "Maybe I better drive."

"I'll drive all right." In a moment we're all down in Pink's garage taking out his two-seater. "I know all the shortcuts."

The two girls mumble something which is supposed to be encouraging, and Pink and I take off. The wind shakes the little car, but Pink's hands are firm on the wheel. He goes down the Bayshore Highway. There are not many cars out tonight and, thank God, no cops around.

"Joe," says Pink, keeping the needle well over seventy miles, "I'm a skunk. If we can't find those two I don't want to live. Pipsqueak means more to me than a brother, and I can't imagine life without him. Sparkie—well, Sparkie's something new, and sometimes I think she means more to me than even Pipsqueak. I don't like the idea, it's mean for me to have someone who is more to me than Pipsqueak. It shouldn't be, but I can't help it. When I was at sea, I often wondered whom I would pick if I had to choose. I don't know. I just hoped I wouldn't have to choose. I wanted them to be my friends, to have them both." He is silent for a while, then he adds, "Now they're friends and I have neither of them."

We are well beyond San Pablo when he goes on, "It must have happened to Pipsqueak just as it happened to me. Just like that. We've liked the same things all our lives: boats, butterflies, machines, caves, potatoes baked in an open fire. Why should it be different with a girl? He was bound to fall for Sparkie. The only way not to fall for her is to keep away from her. If you talk to her, take her to a dance, sit next to her—you can't help liking her. And if you like her, the whole world is fenced off. It's just the two of you. The rest of the world is beyond the fence, in a fog."

He drives a couple of miles before he goes on. "Pipsqueak knew all that and he kept away from her. But

169

then—I went to sea. He talked to her. He didn't mean to fall in love with her. It just happened naturally. I can understand it now, but it still makes me mad. You can have a boat together with a guy and can share a baked mickey, but with a girl it's different. A girl you have to have for yourself. I feel like saving those two and throwing them in the Bay again the minute after."

And a moment later, "No, Joe, don't believe it. I just want to save them. I'm going away again and I'll never come back to the Bay."

The gale still is gaining force. Once in a while we can see a couple of bright stars, but the next moment it looks like we are sewed in a sack. Pink knows his way around; he needs neither stars nor road signs, and it's after midnight when we arrive in Martinez. Old Pipsqueak is there and some Coast Guardsmen. Nobody wants to say any more than necessary. Pink goes with the motorboat crew. Old Pipsqueak and I stay behind.

We go over to a gas station where they serve coffee and doughnuts. It's a miserable place with a lame man shuffling about to prepare the coffee, and a parrot in the back room which, from time to time, breaks out in hysterical laughter.

"They must find him," Old Pipsqueak says, staring at the shore line. "It can't, it mustn't happen this way. Look what I got this morning. A letter from the air corps. They have accepted him. That's what he wanted. Be a flier now, and an engineer later. If he could've seen that letter he wouldn't have gone with that girl. He never cared for girls. It doesn't make sense."

The parrot laughs itself sick. It gives Old Pipsqueak the shivers. "All right, all right," he says. "It's my mistake, I guess. I still see Gerald as a kid. When I was his age I was almost married. But why didn't he tell me? I would have arranged things. I've always arranged things for him. I like to arrange things for him. But maybe he didn't like it any longer. Nowadays when the young bird gets fledged he flies off—in a bomber."

We go back to the Coast Guard Station for news. Time crawls along. "I can't understand what's taking them so long," Old Pipsqueak says over and over again. "The storm is calming down and the moon is out. It shouldn't be hard to spot a ship like the *Jellybean*. The Bay isn't so wide here. But," he adds under his breath, "it's still plenty rough."

He goes outside and stands on the beach, a lonely figure, his coat waving in the wind. The water is still wild, and you think you're seeing a boat moving, then you realize it's the reflection on a wave.

Now we do see a boat. Old Pipsqueak runs along the shore, unable to stand still. The gale is still blowing, but for one moment it dies down and all is quiet.

"If he isn't in that boat, I may never see him again," the old man murmurs. Then the wind breaks loose again.

The boat draws nearer. I try to count the figures in it, but long before I can make anything out, Old Pip shouts, "He's in it, Joe, he's in it!" A couple of minutes later I see him, too. He's standing on the bow, waving.

The motorboat comes in, leaving a white streak behind. Pipsqueak jumps out first, dripping wet, and heads straight for his father's arms. Pink is in last, carrying Sparkie who clings to his neck, her head resting on his chest.

"Come on, " says the old man, "change clothes. I brought dry stuff along. Here." He opens his car and drags out a shirt and a suit and some frilly stuff. "I brought some for the girl, too," he explains shyly.

Ten minutes later we all have hot grog which Old Pipsqueak brought along in a couple of thermos bottles. Sparkie is curled up against Pink, smiling happily, and Pipsqueak is bubbling with joy. I can't figure it out. And I see Old Pip can't either.

171

"What happened to the *Jellybean*?" he asks.

"It's sunk," Pipsqueak reports cheerfully.

Sparkie wiggles loose from Pink's grip and points a menacing finger at Pipsqueak. "He did it on purpose," she cries.

Old Man Pipsqueak sits back and laughs. "Oh no, not him. The *Jellybean* was his prize possession."

"Yes, he did," Sparkie insists. "Before I knew what happened, I found myself in that horrible lifeboat of his. He strapped me down and gave me nothing but dog biscuits. Oh, I hate him! I shall never speak to him again!"

"I'm leaving in a couple of days anyhow," says Pipsqueak, waving his letter from the air corps. "And as to our lifeboat experience, Sparkie, I'm sorry it wasn't more comfortable. Next time we build a ship, Pink, please remind me to put in a shower and central heating for the lifeboats."

"Oh stop it," says Pink, drawing Sparkie toward him. "That's how life is in lifeboats, Sparkie. Now just imagine the same thing, but miles out in the Pacific, with no land around."

"She imagined that," Pipsqueak says. "She imagined that for twenty-four hours."

"Did you strap down that Lola woman too?" Sparkie asks.

"I sure did," Pink says.

"And feed her dog biscuits?"

"You bet."

"And her hair hung down like an old sock?"

"Exactly."

"And you kept shouting at her every time she began to cry?"

"Certainly."

"Oh, darling," Sparkie sighs happily, nestling closer.

Pink takes Sparkie home in his car, and I go with the Pipsqueaks. "Just drop me at Richmond," I tell them. "I want to catch some sleep before I go to work."

172

The old man drives and I sit with young Pipsqueak in the back seat. The boy leans back comfortably, his legs stretched out. "Girls are a sack of ants in the pants," he says sleepily. "I wonder what they've got for brains. I told her and told her that a boy and a girl on a raft have other worries than making love, but I might just as well have told it to a horse. I was plain lucky to have gotten that weather report, I guess. It was a perfect night."

He stretches out some more and soon is sound asleep, the kind of sleep only the deserving deserve.

Burning Money

Happy is our Negro hand-burner. Every afternoon before whistle time he can be seen underneath the hullway feeding a dozen or so shipyard cats, throwing them hunks of sandwiches and grinning from ear to ear in his delight at watching them eat. No one minds except Okie Red, our machine-burner.

Okie Red is on the employee committee to keep the yard clean and he keeps telling Happy that the cats are in the yard to eat rats, not sandwiches.

"De Lawd make de cats an' de Lawd make de rats," Happy says.

"Yeah," replies Red sulkily, "but he made the rats for the cats to eat."

"He make de stuff in de san'widges," says Happy simply. "Mebbe he want de cats to eat dem too."

Okie Red turns to me. "We're having a hard time

getting people to throw their junk into the garbage cans, then that screwball comes along and fishes it out again."

"You mean to say he actually takes stuff out of rubbish cans?" gasps Cookie.

"Yeah. And I wouldn't put it past him if he eats it himself, too. He's the gol'darnedest skinflint I ever saw."

"How do you know?"

"He never joins a raffle and he never gives a nickel when we pass the hat for someone that got hurt. He's the only burner in the yard who's not on the payroll bond deduction plan. He says he can't sign his name, but anybody can make a cross on a dotted line. But that's the way they are. Those niggers, they don't give a damn about anybody."

It's not the cats or the garbage. It's that Happy is a "nigger" and that he's tight. Red is in charge of the war bond collection, and he wants the burners to come out on top.

One day I'm surprised not to find Happy under the hull feeding the cats. The cats are not the only ones to miss him. We on the skids miss him too. When we need a hand-burner all we have to do is spot the red safety hat, holler and wave, and on he comes, dragging his line after him, disentangling it patiently whenever it gets caught on a beam. He always smiles while we explain to him what we want and smiles as he goes about his job. When he has nothing to do he burns scrap, and when that is done he looks for a bucket of red paint to give his hat and shoes a new coat. But today he isn't there. No red hat, no white, grinning teeth.

Slim, the black burner from Six, takes his place for the day. Happy's absence is a mystery to Slim too. Happy hasn't missed a day, and he's been in the yard for a year.

Next morning Slim has found out what happened and it's a sad story. Happy's daughter was killed in an auto accident.

So Happy had a daughter? "Oh sure," Slim says, and rolls his eyes. Haven't we heard of Penelope, the Bluebird of the Trocadero? No? Well, that was Happy's daughter. A lanky, long-legged, light-skinned beauty. Slim sighs, "I wish she'd listened to me and stayed away from the singing racket. She had brains, Penny had. She could've gone to college with me. We Negroes need brains like her. But she wouldn't do it. Her heart was in the night club business. I didn't want her to go singing. Swing music is a curse. It fills you with rhythm, every corner of you, and leaves no room for thinking. She should've gone to college with me."

"Didn't Happy want her to go to college?" Lovella asks.

Slim slaps the air with both palms in disgust. "What does that doggone Uncle Tom know about college? When he saw Penny in her red evening gown with a lot of junk gems all over, he beamed like the moon. He sneaked into the Trocadero more than once just to get a peek at her. Oh boy, was he a proud dad! He collected her pictures from programs and newspapers, together with clippings he couldn't even read. Two of them weren't even about her singing but he didn't know. They were about her speeding when she knocked down an old lady and was kept in the jug until someone bailed her out. She was his only kid."

"It must be an awful shock to him," Okie Red remarks, looking thoughtful all of a sudden.

"Yeah, it's a shock, all right," Slim agrees. "But what gets him down most is the question of the funeral. He wants her to have the best burial money can buy, with music and singers and flowers. He's selling everything he has, and that isn't much."

"I wonder what he did with the money he made," says Red. "Spend it on the kid?"

"Oh, I don't know. Penny did pretty well herself. She was very popular, Penny was. But Happy—he doesn't care where or how he lives. He bunks in a garage, and shares it with guys who can't get a room. He cooks his meals from nothing at all. He used to be a railroad cook, y'know, before he came out to the Coast."

Okie Red pulls out a piece of paper and a pencil. "We'll get him the dough for the funeral," he says firmly and goes about collecting. When our shift is over, he has a pile of coins and bills. Okie Red and I decide to take it all to Happy the next day.

When Slim told us Happy lived in a garage, he had put it rosily. Maybe the place was a garage when Model T's first came out, but now it looks more like a target for army practice. The furniture is made of parts dragged in from the car junkyard. Remains of back seats are made up as beds; steering wheels, covered with planks, are used as chairs; a bumper holds up a rag dividing the "room" in two; an apple box with a rearview mirror and a bucket of water make the bathroom.

Happy sits on one of the steering wheel chairs, a cat on his lap. He doesn't see the cat and he doesn't see us. He's staring holes into the air. It's hard to talk to him because we can't be sure that he hears us. Okie Red takes out the money and places it before Happy.

"Here," Red says."From the guys in the yard."

Happy comes to life. He sees us and something like the old grin comes back to his lips. He doesn't mean to grin, it's just an automatic reaction of a jaw that has been grinning for fifty years.

"Ah don' need dat money," he says.

"It's for the funeral," Okie Red explains. "You can have a great funeral for your daughter."

"Ain' goin' have no fun'al fo' her," Happy mumbles.

"What do you mean, no funeral," Red says. "A person must have a funeral."

Happy shakes his head. "Good person wanna nice big fun'al fo' keep de debbil away," he explains. "Wid an evil person it ain' make no dif'runs."

178

Red looks at me, I look at Red, and we don't know what to say. "Don't you want Penny to go to heaven, Happy?" I ask finally. "Take that money and get her the grandest funeral you can buy."

Happy pushes my hand away, slowly but firmly. "No, no. Ah ain' need dat. Got mo' money den Ah knows what to do wid." Suddenly tears flow down his cheeks.

"Listen," says Okie Red, "there's nothing wrong with having too much money. That's nothing to cry about."

"Dey ain' nuttin' wrong wid good money," he says, "but dat's debbil money. If yo' touch it he sho'll git ya." He puts the cat down on the ground and looks up at us. "Ah tell you what happened. Ah goes to her room in de city an' Sam an' his fren' dat buys ol' clothes come 'long. Dey look 'round an' look 'round an' take out from de closets and drawers what dey like to buy and gimme twen'y bucks for it. Den dey look 'round some mo' an' Ah reckon mebbe dey might could find somep'n else to buy. An' fust thing ya know, dey find dem stones."

Happy lets out a deep sigh. "Penny's stones," he repeats sadly. "Penny's pretty, pretty stones. Somep'n's burnin' in 'em. Like a fire. Sometimes dey look red, den when yo' look agin dey'll turn green on ya. Deys always somep'n movin' 'round in 'em. Me and ma chil' sho was crazy 'bout 'em. Every time she go an' buys anudder she come an' show me. She dance 'round me an' kiss me an' say, 'Pa,' she say, 'Ain' dem pretty? Ain' dem look like a tousan' dollars, an' Ah ain' pay no mo' den five bucks fo' dem. Dey make dem look so good yo'll think deys real dahmons. But dey ain' nuttin' but coal. Dat's what's burnin' in 'em. Jus' coal like in de kitchen stove.' Den she kiss me agin an' hol' dem stones 'gainst her pretty dress jus' to please me an' dance 'round like she dance over dere in de city. Me an' her sho like de looks o' dem stones.

"Now Sam an' his fren' wants to buy dem. Ah tell 'em O.K. Ah sell dem. Ah figger Ah kin git twen'y bucks fo'

179

dem, mebbe. Sam look dem over and his fren' look dem over, an' dey fool 'round an' fool 'round an' ain' say nuttin' no mo'. Den dey says let's go an' show dem to anudder feller. So we goes downtown to de hock shop an' de man look dem over too. He be very unfren'ly an' ask where we git dem stones from, an' Sam he tol' him dat dey belong to ma chil' dat was a singer. De man do's a lot o' fonin' an' den he get nicer an' says O.K. dem stones was bo't all right in a sto' uptown. He tell me he gimme two tousan' dollars fo' dem. He says dem stones ain' no coals, dem are real dahmons."

Happy's hands hang down sadly, at half-mast. "Only rich folks kin buy dahmons," he says, "or wicked folks. Penny ain' never been rich."

"Maybe she earned a lot," Okie Red says swiftly. "Maybe you gave her money and she saved it up to buy those stones."

Happy shakes his head. "Ah never give her no money. Ah ain' never got no money. She gave me. She was a good chil' till de debbil got 'er. Dat's de debbil movin' 'round in dem stones. Ain' coal dat's burnin' in 'em, it's hellfire. Dat's what it is."

A rat is running across the floor and the cat is right after it.

"Why don't you move into a decent place," says Okie Red. "This here is no place for a man to live. Now you have two thousand bucks . . ."

"Ah ain' goin' to take dat money," Happy says. "Oh no. Ain' want no part of it."

"What did you do with it?" I ask.

"Ain' touch it. It's right where it was."

"In the hock shop? And the jewels too?"

"Dey sho is." Happy gets up, shuffles along to an old orange crate and begins to rummage in it. "Ah don' want no hellfire in ma room here." He fishes out a battered pot. "Ah's goin' make some nice hot coffee fo' ya."

180

"No, no," says Okie Red quickly, tossing an eye at the brown stuff Happy is pouring into the pot. "I really couldn't."

"Well," I say, "we might as well run along. If there's anything we can do for you, Happy . . ."

"No," says Happy, "nuttin'. I don' need nuttin'."

There is heavy fog covering the midday sun, but after having been in the dark garage, it blinds you.

"Those niggers," says Okie Red, "make me sick to my stomach."

"They don't all live that way," I throw in.

"It makes no difference how they live," he insists. "They just make me sick to my stomach. I could stand a cup of good, strong coffee. How about it, Joe?"

So we go and have some coffee in a little joint nearby. A juke box fills the room with a whacky tune. All the booths are taken, one of them by a black girl and a white man.

"See," Okie Red nods his head in their direction. "That's how the trouble starts. You give them rights and they think they have the right to do everything. They go and mix with white folks, their girls ankle up to white men. That ain't right. They're meant to be niggers and should stay where they belong. Know what my grandfather used to say? If the Lord would've wanted them the way we are, he would've saved the black paint. I bet that guy who gave the diamonds to Happy's daughter was a white man. Things like that make my blood boil."

"I can't figure you out, Red," I say. "If you don't like the Negroes, why did you go through all that trouble to get him money?"

"That's different." Okie Red signals the waitress for more coffee. "I don't mind Negroes as long as they stick to each other. Happy has lost his kid. That's different."

His voice gets soft, and Okie Red isn't a guy whose voice gets soft very often.

"You have kids?" I ask.

He shakes his head. "I'm not married," he says. "But I have my brother's kid living with me." He fishes out a photo of a ten-year-old girl, lanky, with two braids dangling down her shoulders.

"Nice kid," I say, giving the picture back to him.

"You bet. Nicest kid you ever saw. Full of life. Yeah . . ." He puts the picture back in his billfold. "Full of life. My brother and his wife died when she was a baby. TB, both of them. I took Tessie and brought her up. I used to run a laundry down in Oklahoma. Wasn't easy, at first, I mean with the kid. But it was worth it. You bet your life, it is worth it. I'm afraid, sometimes, that I don't give her the proper care. Have her lungs checked regularly. Now she's getting to an age when she can use more attention. What she really needs is a mother. That's one thing I never did give her."

"Just take your pick," I say, winking at him. "There are plenty of girls in the yard."

Okie Red stays serious. "You're not kidding, Joe," he says. "I never had much use for women, and I could manage all right without them. But now . . ." He leans back, his fingers knotted together and looks straight at me. "What do you think of Lovella?"

This one catches me off guard. Lovella and Okie Red? That doesn't make sense. But you never know. Alibi and Juanita didn't make sense either, and they turned out to be all right.

"Isn't she married?" I say, lamely.

"Divorced," he says. "She's got a boy of eight. Maybe it would work."

"What does she think of it?"

"I don't know. Never asked her. I just wondered, toyed with the idea. How would it be to have a gal like Lovella all for myself? She's so—different."

Now, when a guy says a girl is different, then it's got him. And when a man like Red starts doodling with spilled coffee, it's got him bad.

182

"I've worked out a plan," Okie Red goes on, concentrating on his finger drawing oddly shaped coffee lines. "They're fixing on giving me a leaderman's rating soon, and they want me to break in a new machine-burner. Well, I know Lovella is sick of welding—maybe she likes burning better. It takes a while to break in a new burner for the machine, and I'd have to stick around her to show her the ropes— and then, y'know, I'd have more of a chance to talk to her, to find out how she feels."

If Okie Red hadn't told me I wouldn't have guessed. He and Lovella hardly talk to each other. At lunch they don't sit on the same beam. I don't think Lovella even knows Red exists. Every day she shows up in a knee duster, her golden hair swinging on her shoulders, and she gets a kick out of the men whistling as she walks by. Then she changes into her leathers, and at break she wears slacks and a hug-me-tight. When she picks up her time card at 11:30 she shows her pretty legs again under the knee duster. And at work she often takes off her hood, shakes her hair, and waves her hand at truck drivers or men carrying templates. She waves so much that Alibi asks her how she happens to know so many guys.

"I don't know them," Lovella says cheerfully, "I just wave at them and they wave back at me."

During the next few days something new has been added, a straw in the wind. Lovella wears a rose on her leathers—every new day a new rose. The roses look fresh and dewy in the afternoon and tired at the end of the shift, just like Lovella herself used to be. But now her eyes shine eight hours in one stretch. I look at Okie Red and I look at her, and I put one and one together. It still doesn't make sense, though. They hardly speak to one another. Red acts shy when she's around, and little Miss Itchy-Ears sure can keep a secret when it's her own.

She hasn't switched over to burning. Okie Red still runs the machine, and Slim handles the hand torch, taking

183

Happy's place. Old Happy has not shown up at all.

"He hasn't gotten over it yet," Slim tells me. "Neither have I. Sometimes I feel it's all my fault. What happened to Penny, I mean. Y'see, I was sweet on her once. I told her a lot about discrimination. My mind was full of the things they say against us, and I wanted to find out why it is that way. Maybe there is something wrong with us. Maybe something can be done about it. I told her what I thought about it. You want to know?"

"Sure," I say, "go ahead."

"Well, this is the way I see it." He's full of it all, and his words bubble out like water from a steaming kettle. "There's that 'Negro problem.' It's no problem, really. We have a different color, that's all. We are people, aren't we? When we get hit, it hurts, and when we get shot, we die, like anyone else. We die for America right now because we're thankful to be here and not over in Africa anymore. It's a funny thing if you think of it. They brought us over to be slaves, and now we are freer than lots of other people all over the world. But that's not what I was talking about. I say, the whole trouble is our color. The darker we are the less they like us. The lighter we are the more we are accepted. We simply have to become lighter. I'll marry the lightest girl I can get, and I hope my children will be lighter than I am. Then, maybe, they'll get a break. All we want is a break, and we'll be as good as a white man."

He has set his circle torch and starts burning lifting holes in a hatch-end beam which I've marked for him. "You see," he goes on as he sends a fountain of sparks into the hatch, "I told Penny all that. She wanted to get a break. That's one reason she went in for singing. As a blues singer or a dancer you're accepted. You make contacts with white people. They like your dancing and singing. I don't like that way of mixing with white folks. I think you should mix with them intellectually, go to

184

school with them, learn languages, travel around, learn from them and teach them what you know. You can become a scientist, a doctor, a businessman. But Penny didn't think she could do that. She wanted to sing for them, become famous—and a famous Negro always can do good for the other Negroes. That was her angle. I'm sorry she didn't want to do it my way. She had brains, Penny had."

He goes on burning lifting holes, and I'm still thinking about what he told me when the lunch whistle cuts swing shift in two. There we sit again, unpacking our sandwiches and unscrewing our thermoses and chewing the rag when Okie Red shows up, all steaming hot.

"That dadburned son of a biscuit eater!" he rages, throwing himself on a centerline column. "Sure enough she was cheating."

You can see it's a strain on him not to use the words he would use with no girls around.

"What's up?" Alibi asks.

Our gang has a weekly pool. Everybody chips in four bits and the one whose paycheck number shows the best poker hand wins a twenty-five dollar bond. For the past few months many bonds went to Cindy, our tacker from Oklahoma. It takes quite a hand to beat her. If you have a full house she has got four of a kind. And if you've got four of a kind, she's got higher ones. She's had too darned much luck, and Okie Red has done some sleuthing about her.

"Her whole family works out here in Richmond," Red reports. "Father, mother, brothers, sisters, in-laws, maybe a dozen of them, and all with the same name. Y'know how they fixed it? They always showed us the stub with the best poker hand, sometimes the father's and sometimes a brother's—and collected the dough from us all. They always had twelve chances to our one. And that's not all. They played in eight different pools, and collected the dough there too."

"Why, of all the dirty skunks!" Jason explodes. "I hope they kick them all out."

"That dame won't stay in our gang," Okie Red promises grimly. "I'll see to that."

"She better not," Alibi hollers, "and we ought to kick them hard enough to toss them right back to Oklahoma where they belong."

"That's how they all are, those damn Okies," Jason says. "Dirty and dumb. But smart enough to cheat."

Okie Red's face gets hard. "Say, listen," he counters. "Take it easy now. We've been bamboozled, but that's got nothing to do with Oklahoma."

"It has too," Jason gets all steamed up. "Those Okies just swamp us. You can't get a room to live in, and you can't get a seat in an eat joint because they're all over the place. American history is wrong. General Grant didn't take Richmond, the Okies did."

"Why don't they go and fight Japan—they took California without losing a man," Alibi hums the battle hymn of the anti-Okies.

"I wouldn't mind," Cookie speaks up, "if they weren't so messy. Those squirts of tobacco drive me crazy. Why, the other day I picked up a wedge, and my hands were full of it. Two shipwrights stood there, plugs in their cheeks as big as apples. They had 'Okie' written on their hats like it was something to brag about."

"They must raise them in barns," Dimples chips in, "and they don't know how to live in decent apartments. They muck up everything. Their kids break the furniture, and what the kids miss, their old man busts up when he comes home drunk on payday."

Everybody has a story. "Just wait till after the war," Alibi says. "*Then* you'll see a mess. Those prune pickers will work for a nickel an hour, and we all will be lucky if we can sleep on the sidewalks."

Okie Red hasn't said a word, but his face has grown grim. "Cindy was a crook, all right," he breaks out finally.

186

"Okay, so what? There are crooks and messpots in every state. If I hadn't found out about Cindy you would've gone on feeding her four bits a week till cows give beer. And I'm an Okie, too."

"You're all right, Okie Red," Alibi laughs out and pats Red's knee. "If all Okies were like you, I wouldn't mind them."

"You aren't an Okie, Red," Dimples says. "You just have their drawl."

Okie Red eases up and peeks over toward Lovella. She hasn't said a word. She smiles and her purple-edged fingertips caress the rose on her hug-me-tight. She hasn't heard a word we said, and Lovella isn't one who misses many words.

There's something about Lovella that needs a little surface-scratching. I know that. I can feel it nibbling inside me. Curiosity spills the catsup, y'know. So I go and ask Pee-Wee because she often works with Lovella.

Pee-Wee knows Lovella's life story inside out and upside-down. Lovella hasn't exactly told her, but Pee-Wee can jigsaw it together. Lovella started out as a hash slinger in Salt Lake City. She knew she was good-looking and the truck drivers who wanted to date her told her so, too, but Lovella didn't want dates with truck drivers. She wanted to become someone Lady Teazle writes about, so she got herself a job as a waitress in an uptown restaurant. That's where she met Bill. Bill wasn't exactly a top-hatter but he had connections, and ambitions too. They married, had a baby, and Bill went up the ladder until he wound up as assistant manager of the department store where he'd begun as a salesclerk. But the more he earned the more he spent on horse-racing. He promised a dozen times not to look at a horse again, but he always broke his promise. The marriage finally blew up when she discovered five hundred bucks in his wallet all prepared for the day's races, after he had refused to buy some garments the baby needed.

"I guess she felt pretty lonesome," Pee-Wee says. "You get used to a husband, even to a bad one. The boy is eight now and needs a father."

"Any prospects?" I ask.

"Yup. She doesn't talk much about him, and that in itself is a good sign. He's a cheese manufacturer."

"A cheese manufacturer!"

"Yes," says Pee-Wee, surprised at my outburst. "What's wrong with a cheese manufacturer?"

"Nothing," I admit. "I just didn't expect it."

"She met him through friends of her first husband," Pee-Wee explains. "And he sends her plenty of roses. But that's all I know."

Next day Happy is here again. He isn't wearing his faded overalls or his red shoes and hard hat. He is in an old suit and his square face looks strange under a cap.

"Ah's come here fo' quit," he says.

"Why?" asks Pee-Wee. "Don't you like working with us anymore?"

Happy squirms in embarrassment. "Yo' was mighty fine t'me," he says. "Jus' as nice as kin be. But Ah've gotta git a real job now."

"What do you mean, a real job?" Alibi's eyebrows rise with his temperature. "You think building those ships is a game?"

"And burning sure is important," Okie Red stresses.

"Ah knows, Ah knows," Happy tries to defend himself. "But Ah jus' have to make a livin'."

"Make a living!" Red repeats. "Why, you will never get a better paid job than this one."

"Ma chil' she give me twen'y dollars a month," Happy explains, using both hands to make himself clear. "Ah kin take care o' m'self on twen'y bucks all right. But now she's gone an' Ah gotta git 'long widout her help."

"What, for goodness sake, do you do with your own money?" asks Okie Red. "That's what I want to know."

188

Ah ain' had no money," Happy insists, looking about him unhappily.

"No money, eh?" Alibi sneers. "You don't get a paycheck every Thursday, do you?"

"Sho Ah git a check all right," Happy says. "But what Ah need now is real money."

"Now wait a minute," Alibi spreads out both hands and flutters with his fingers to keep the others quiet. "What did you come out here for, all the way from South Carolina?"

"Well," says Happy, "it was dis way. Dey tell me we fight fo' liberty. We ain' need no cooks no mo'. We need men fo' fight an' men fo' build ships. Ah ain' no good no mo' fo' fight, so Ah come out here fo' build ships fo' liberty."

Nobody says a word for quite a while, then Alibi comes out with an "I'll be damned." And a moment later he repeats it over and over. Red shakes his head and murmurs, "Ships for liberty," and the girls look at Happy, and Happy looks at all of us and seems to be plenty scared.

"Ah ain' mean no harm," he says. "But Ah jus' cain't go on dat way. Dem little papers o' 'preciation is all right but now Ah need real money and have to look fo' a job wid pay."

"What did you do with those little papers of appreciation?" Pee-Wee asks.

"Ah give dem to Penny. She like fo' show dem 'round to her fren's an' tell dem her pa been build ships fo' liberty. She sho was glad fo' git dem every week."

"Say, listen," Alibi decides to explain to Happy what a paycheck is. But Happy looks and looks at him and can't get it. Then Pee-Wee takes over the explaining and Happy looks even more puzzled, so they call the burner foreman to see what he can do about it.

The foreman listens, shakes his head and wants to know if Happy signed the checks before he gave them to Penny.

189

"He can't even write his name," Pee-Wee answers for Happy.

"I tell you what I can do," says the foreman. "If the checks haven't been cashed, I'll get our cashier to make out duplicates for them."

He does some telephoning and in the end he turns to Happy and says, "I'm sorry, Happy. I can't do a thing for you. Your daughter must have cashed them all in."

"Penny got the money," Pee-Wee explains to Happy. "That's a tough break, all right."

But Happy lights up into the brightest grin saved up for holidays. He throws up his hands and shouts, "Praise de Lawd an' tanky! So dat's how yo' give her dat money fo' buy dem stones! Ain' been no sin nor debbil. It sho take a load off ma mind."

"I am glad you feel that way about it, Happy," says the foreman. "And now, how about staying in the yard and getting some pay for yourself?"

"Sho," says Happy. "Ah like burnin'. Ah always want to catch one of dem golden sparks. But if yo' catch 'em dey jus' burn ya, dem little debbils. Sho Ah'll stay. Ah'll toil even mo' harder an' fix dem holes where yo' want 'em. Not dat Ah needs all dat money, but Ah is happy dat ma chil' ain' done nuttin' wrong. She might could tol' me an' explain what she want wid it. Ah would ha' given her, but it's jus' as well."

"That's the spirit," nods the foreman. "We've got a more responsible job for you, Happy. You've been a darn good hand-burner and I'd like to put you on a machine now. Okie Red'll fix you up."

But when Okie Red hears about it he gets all hot under the collar and does quite a bit of cussing. "How can he do this to me? It's bad enough to have a stupid nigger in my gang, but on the same machine! I'd rather quit!" He walks into the foreman's office all steamed up, but when he comes out, he seems off the boil. He even smiles under

190

his breath as he goes up to Lovella and tells her the burner foreman wants to talk to her.

Lovella slips off her hood and her bandana, dabs her curls, takes a sniff of her rose and steps off the skid. Okie Red, meanwhile, takes the tip off his machine, shines it up with sandpaper, cleans the channels with a fine wire, oils the joints and keeps his eye on the craneway. Finally Lovella comes back and he jumps up to meet her. But she tells him she would appreciate it if he'd keep his nose out of her business.

Okie Red draws back as though he'd been punched in the nose. "But you told me you're sick and tired of welding."

"I've other plans now," she says.

"But listen," Red urges. "It's a very easy job if you know how. You'll like it and I'll show you the ropes. You'll work with me . . ."

"I don't want to." Lovella pulls her welding line. It gets caught on a beam and she yanks it furiously. "I just don't want to, that's all."

Okie Red takes her line, swings it around the beam, and pulls it for her. "Why not?" he asks. "It don't make sense."

Lovella tears the line out of his hands and flings it onto the skid. "Didn't it ever enter your Okie brain that I don't *want* to work with you?"

Okie Red's reply gets stuck in his throat, he gulps and stares at Lovella. She is busy fumbling with her stinger. "I am sorry I said that, Okie Red," she mumbles. "You see, I'm used to a different kind of life."

"Okay," Red says. "I'm an Okie. You're too damn good for me. Okay."

He turns around and bends over his machine. He strikes his lighter and, with a pop, gets his torches burning.

I knew that Okie Red would take it hard, but still I didn't expect him not to show up the next day. Happy is

191

on the hand torch again and Slim handles the machine. Lovella isn't here either, and Alibi, who's got more work to do than his crew can handle, barks that Lovella is getting too darn stuckuppity. Who does she think she is, anyway, a goddamn duchess?

Next day both are here again. No rose is dangling on Lovella's blouse, and both she and Okie Red look gray like the overcast days.

"It's happened, Joe," Red tells me as soon as he gets hold of me. "What I was scared of for years, it's happened. They've found a spot in Tessie's lungs."

He sinks down on his toolbox, exhausted. "From now on it's not a matter of care and love," he says slowly. "It's a matter of hard cash. That's why I was so scared. I never could save much on this kind of a job, with those X rays and checkups for Tessie. If you miss one day your next paycheck has a big cut. I've got to send Tessie away. Those places are expensive. But I've got to do it. If I don't, those bugs will eat her up as sure as my torch eats up those steel plates. I've seen what they did to my brother and his wife. If you don't do it right from the start, there's no way of stopping them."

It's a long day today, the kind of day you look at your watch every ten minutes, thinking an hour has gone by. The kind of day when you go for a drink of water because of that dry feeling inside, and you keep lighting cigarette after cigarette. After the lunch break I help Pee-Wee put up deck beams, and she seems to be as gloomy as the rest of us.

"Heard about Okie Red?" I say. She hasn't, and I tell her.

"Think we can get the money for him?" she asks, wrinkling her forehead.

"I don't know," I tell her. "What we can get together isn't more than a drop in the bucket. He really needs a hatful this time."

192

"Well, every dollar helps," Pee-Wee says. "What money can fix isn't so hopeless. Look at Lovella. Have you heard about her?"

Pee-Wee puts her beam in place and marks it up for the tacker. "Her deal's off," she says, leaning heavily on her sledge. "She spilled the whole story. Her man was one of those—gentlemen, you know. He was so much of a gentleman that Lovella didn't dare tell him she worked in the yard. She was ashamed of her job. But of course he found out. Why, a woman shipyard worker! Never in the history of cheese manufacturers did one of them stoop so low. He just turned up his nose at her. Shipyard dirt! Phooey! He went back to his cheese. And this, my friend, is the end of a beautiful romance."

She takes up her sledge and bang! it goes in the best Jason manner. "I wonder why everybody has to turn up his nose at everybody else," she says, as mad as I have ever seen her. "If you say 'shipyard worker' they see lowdown creatures rolling in dirt. They don't see the people breaking up their homes and traveling all over the continent to get a job done that just has to be done. Someone has to get his hands dirty."

The next day Pee-Wee is taking up a collection for Okie Red. "Red has passed the hat for so many of us, we have to help him now," she explains. Two bits and four bits are coming in, and Pee-Wee has got about forty bucks when she comes up to Happy. He is busy emptying his toolbox.

"Do you want to chip in for Okie Red?" Pee-Wee asks.

Happy tips over the toolbox and shakes it hard to make sure that it's clean inside. Then, carefully, he folds his torn overalls, puts them in the empty box together with scraps of old rags, stuffs it with newspaper, and pats the whole thing lovingly.

"What in heaven's name are you doing?" Pee-Wee asks, looking at the rags in his toolbox.

193

"Ah's makin' a bed fo' Pussyfoot," Happy explains.

"Who is Pussyfoot?"

"Yo' dunno?" Happy asks, surprised. "Pussyfoot is dat nice white cat an' a big fren' o' mine. She's goin' have babies mighty soon. That rubbish 'round here is no comfo'ble place for God's critters fo' have de chillun."

"If you care so much for little kittens," says Pee-Wee, "you will want to give something for Red's kid too."

"Red's kid?"

"She's very sick. If we can get Red a lot of money, we can save her. But everybody will have to chip in, or she'll die."

"Oh, yeah," says Happy. "Ah see. Ah jus' ain' got ma money on me today. Ah'll bring it tomorrow."

So the next afternoon when I go to get my tools, Happy waves toward me excitedly. "C'mon Joe, c'mon. Look. She got four of 'em." He giggles and lifts the cover of his toolbox. There is the big white cat and close to her, nearly under her, four kittens, two white ones and two black ones. "Ah always reckon yo' makin' goo-goo eyes at the black tomcat," he snickers. The girls come and stand around Happy's toolbox: Cherie, Dimples, Cookie and Sparkie, Lovella and Pee-Wee, and they look at the kittens.

"Ah brought dat money fo' ya, Miss Pee-Wee," Happy says, and takes a wad of bills out of his pocket.

I can hear Pee-Wee sucking in her breath. "Why, Happy, these are hundreds of dollars."

"Two tousan'," Happy says. "An' it's *good* money, Miss Pee-Wee, never yo' fear."

The girls call Okie Red while Pee-Wee turns the bills helplessly in her hands.

"Red, just think, Happy brought you two thousand dollars for Tessie," Cherie cries, hopping from one foot to the other. "Now you can send her away. Isn't that *magnifique*?"

Okie Red stands still and stares first at the bills and then at Happy.

194

"Is good money," the Negro repeats. "Good money. Dem stones were no debbil's stuff. Y'know, Ah earned it m'self."

Something breaks loose in Okie Red's face, a little muscle at the jaw. "Why do you give it to me?" he asks.

"Ah don' want it," Happy answers quickly, "an' Ah don' need it. Ah is perfectly happy as Ah is. Chillun need money an' stones an' such-like to be happy. Ma chil' is in heaven an' need no money no mo'. An' I don' need it either. De Lawd give me dat money an' He know Ah don' need it. An' Ah knows de Lawd ain' doin' such foolish things. When Ah hears dat yo' chil' need money Ah says to m'self, 'Dat's what de Lawd gave ya dat money fo'.' "

Pee-Wee presses the bills into Okie Red's hand. "It really sounds like a miracle," she says, and her voice isn't too steady right now.

"And He sure chooses strange ways," Okie Red adds, closing his fingers around the bills and getting the feel of them. "I can't put it in words, Happy. This here money means so much, and I . . ."

But Happy isn't even listening. He watches the cat licking her kittens and laughs his hoarse, happy laugh. "Look at dem," he shouts. "Look at dem little wigglies. Pussyfoot ain' bother wid nuttin' but her chillun. Dey love one anudder an' git pleasure from one anudder an' dat's how de Lawd want it."

"I love that little black one," Cookie says. "Sparkie, do you think Dad will throw us out if we bring it home?"

"I don't know," Sparkie squats down next to the toolbox, touching the kittens with the tips of her fingers. "I'd rather have the white one."

"Oh, no," says Happy. "Yo' ain' take dem away from de Ma. Dey belong to her, an' it ain' make a bit of dif' runs to her what color dey be."

He pushes the box carefully under the shipway so they are protected and goes about to hook up his line to

195

the acetylene pipe. We others go for our tools too, for it's close to whistle time.

Okie Red and Lovella stay behind. Red still has that amazed expression as he stares at the bills in his hands.

"Sometimes I wonder if those niggers are as dumb as we think they are. My grandfather always said . . ."

"Never mind your grandfather," Lovella snaps. "Can't you ever think for yourself? That guy Happy certainly made me think."

"Gee," Okie Red says, "I feel like—well, like two thousand dollars. You don't know what that money means to me."

"I know," Lovella nods. "I have a kid myself."

"Yes," Okie Red murmurs, creasing his forehead. "You have a little one too." Then, abruptly, "How about switching over to burning?"

"No," says Lovella.

"Why not?"

"Because," explains Lovella, "if I did, you'd think I did it because of the two thousand bucks you've got now."

"Oh you—" Red says, searching for words. "Woman!"

"Okie!" she retorts. Then suddenly she smiles and lets her long eyelashes flutter. "A funny thought just came to me," she says. " Bill used to spend hours figuring out which horse was better than all the others and in the end he lost money on all of them. He never could tell a winner by looking at them from the outside."

"I get you," Okie Red nods. "But it's different with people. With people, it doesn't matter how fast they run but how well they love." He stops, embarrassed, and murmurs, "If y'know what I mean."

"I know what you mean," says Lovella.

"Gee, I feel good today," he repeats, stretching. "Everything'll come out all right."

He looks down at the money in his fist. "This is just a loan. I'll save up and pay it back to Happy." Then turning

196

to Lovella he says, "How about switching over to burning?"

Lovella stands there, biting her upper lip. "Okay," she says. "Let's try burning."

They both avoid each other's eyes and look at Pussyfoot. The cat purrs happily, licking the blind, helpless faces of her black and white kittens.

There She Goes, My Wonderboat

Summer has slipped by as quietly as can be in a shipyard filled with deafening noise and in a world filled with war. Ships have grown from nothing, slid down the Ways, others have taken their places and taken the graceful plunge too. Our gang works so smoothly now that it is no longer an effort to knock off those steel units faster and faster. The farmers, housewives, salesmen and schoolgirls have learned how to assemble a ship.

"Remember when it took us a whole shift to put together that unit?" Pee-Wee looks over a row of beams, all straight and square. "Now, with good tackers, we can do it in an hour and a half."

Bulgy, her tacker, grins. "I get a kick out of doing them fast," she says.

"I don't know." Pee-Wee frowns. "It's fun, all right, to know how to do things, but it's more of a thrill doing them

199

before they become routine. Remember, Joe, how I used to dare Jason to beat me putting in beams? Every wedge I used was an invention. Every new beam was a challenge! Now, it's old stuff. Our pioneer spirit is gone. It's plain humdrum.''

"And how!" Lovella sighs. "That's why I switched from welding to burning, just to change."

"We're quite a gang of old-timers here," Pee-Wee muses. "Sandy, Chuck, Jason, Alibi, Lovella, Dimples. Of course, life isn't the same without Pink and Pip-squeak. And whatever happened to Tiny?"

"He's the ace welder on the deep tanks," I tell her. "And now we are going to lose two more men to the army. Alibi and Chuck got their reclassification. I guess we'll get some more women."

"Pretty soon we'll have more women than men," Pee-Wee giggles. "I'm looking forward to the day when we'll be able to treat the men the way they treated me when I first came to the yard. They certainly turned the heat on me, didn't they, Joe? Well, Bulgy, our time'll come—and we'll make it tough on them, too."

"How can you make it tough on 4-F'ers and grand-dads?" scoffs Bulgy. "We'll have to feed 'em vitamin pills to keep 'em alive."

"Oh, I wish the war were over and we could all go home again," sighs Pee-Wee, "even if it means dusting and dishwashing."

"Housework will be heavenly," Lovella says. "Even ten kids would sound like a Christmas carol after the chippers and riveters."

Chuck comes balancing over the rails. "Hey you!" he hollers, jumping on the unit we've just finished. "Come over a minute. Sandy wants to talk to you."

"This is no time to give us a new job," Lovella complains. "It's five minutes to the whistle."

"What does he want?" I ask.

200

"I don't know," Chuck throws a piece of soapstone into the air and catches it. "He looks excited. Maybe we messed up something."

"Or he got a promotion," Pee-Wee guesses. "I saw him palavering with a bunch of big shots this afternoon."

"Then we'd lose him as leaderman," Chuck adds. "That'd be worse than a bawling out."

Sandy does look pale. "You all have heard the rumors about a record boat," he says, and a quick smile flits over his face. "Our yard held the world's record all summer with that 24-day boat, but now Oregon has knocked off a ship in ten days. That was a blow to us, but we refuse to call it quits. Lots of the fellows in the yard have offered suggestions, and now we've worked out a scheme to beat that ten-day boat—and beat it for keeps. We're going to build a ship in five days! And when I say 'we' I really mean we. Our gang was picked to do the assembling. I accepted for all of you."

After a moment of speechlessness everybody talks at once. Cookie jumps up and down. Chuck slaps Sandy's shoulder. "Fine work, old boy," he shouts. "They couldn't have picked a better man."

"It's your success, not mine." Sandy speaks to all of us. "Our gang has the best record in the yard. I never could have gotten that record without you."

"Neither could we without you," says Cherie.

"That shows what can be done by teamwork," Sandy replies. "None of us is a topnotch shipbuilder. In fact, none of us has been in the yard for more than a year. But together we're the pick of the bunch."

The whistle blows, but for the first time none of us pays attention.

"We'll do things never done before in the history of shipbuilding," Sandy promises solemnly. "But I don't want you to be under a strain. Don't get nervous. It's our old boat, we'll just build it a little different. We'll work it as we've always worked it. If you're a hundred percent sure of a job, go ahead and do it. If not, come and ask me. If I'm

201

not sure, I'll go and ask my foreman. If he doesn't know, he'll ask his quarterman. And so on, until someone knows how. Well, I guess that's all the news for today. See you tomorrow."

Next day I feel like a rooster at dawn. Driving to the yard is usually a dull business, but today the outlook is as bright as the sun reflection on the cars moving on the highway toward the yard. A stream of cars, a stream of workers. An artery that feeds a heart, a heart that pumps a machine: America's War Production. A melody is in the air. My motor hums it, and something in me hums it too.

> *I'm goin' to build a wonderboat,*
> *A five-day boat, a wonderboat,*
> *I'm goin' to build a wonderboat,*
> *A wonderboat, all by myself.*

Am I really singing it? I haven't been singing silly ditties for a long time. Not since I drove about the country selling prewar vacuum cleaners, a lifetime ago.

Here I am again, walking through that gate under the REMEMBER PEARL HARBOR sign, together with thousands of tin hats, lunch pails and overalls. But are they going to build a wonderboat? No. I am. We are. Pee-Wee, Jason, Bruce, Sandy, and the others of the gang on Five.

Alibi looks more than ever like Superman ready to fly off to save a lady in distress. Cherie merrily waves her bandana at me before she tucks her hair into it. Chuck stuffs his pockets full of tools, and Lovella is busy getting her machine ready although it's still ten minutes to the whistle. Swede sharpens his chisels and the sparks fly from the grindstone. Jason arrives, out of breath. He opens a box full of cigars and starts passing them around.

"What's that?" Chuck asks.

"A boy," Jason explains. "And boy, what a boy! Ten pounds three ounces. He just arrived in time, so I could make the train."

Congratulations and backslapping overwhelm him from all sides. "A guy who can build 10,000 tons in five days ought to be able to launch a measly ten pounds in nine months," Alibi says.

"Saves an alarm clock, anyway," Okie Red grins, lighting his cigar. "And alarm clocks are harder to get nowadays than babies."

"How about it, Pee-Wee?" Jason holds his box in front of her. "Won't you smoke one to my little one, old flanger girl?"

"Sure," says Pee-Wee and, without a moment's hesitation, she begins to puff.

"You'd better take it easy there," Jason tells her. "We might need you around here today."

Sandy looks at his cigar thoughtfully. "I'll be the next one to bring cigars, I guess," he says.

"Wahoo!" Alibi yells. "Knock them off fast, that's our motto!"

The whistle blows and the music blares from the loudspeakers. Instead of the usual march tunes, it's the Star-Spangled Banner. Coincidence, but it fits our mood. While the day shift rushes toward the gate, we stand quietly.

But only for a moment. Then Red says, "If we are to build that boat in five days we better not lose another minute."

We jump up the assembly, itching to build those units faster, bigger, more efficiently. Somehow, we expect Sandy to pull rabbits out of his hard hat. But Sandy pulls no rabbits. He behaves as always, moving around fast, organizing, explaining, seeing that everybody keeps busy. We keep busy all right, but with our old units, and we're assembling them the old way. The ship we built during the last thirty days went off this morning, and the keel is being laid for the next one, the five-day boat.

"How the hell can we do it?" Jason barks disgustedly. "It takes more'n five days to build the double bottoms."

"I don't get it either," Pee-Wee says. "Where are the miracles? Where are the mirrors and false bottoms?"

The shift that started with all of us on tiptoe begins to drag. We can hardly wait for the lunch break. We grab our pails and flock around Sandy. Every one of us is here today, even Cherie who always eats in the craneway with Ski, and Dimples who uses her lunch hour to study Chinese with Tiny. All of us are here to ask the question, "How come we're building so slowly?"

Sandy laughs while he unwraps his sandwich. "Slowly! Why, in the last war it took them a year to build a boat of that size."

"Never mind the last war," Jason blows off. "We're here to build a boat in five days, and now we've wasted the whole afternoon!"

"Oh, that's not the record boat," Sandy says, pointing at the ship the day shift began this morning. "That's an ordinary thirty-day boat, and we'll do what we always do. Next week our platform will be cleared and we'll start assembling the wonderboat. The keel for it will be laid thirty days from now, November 8th."

"A five-day boat assembled in three weeks!" Alibi moans. "That's cheating!"

"I knew it was eyewash," Jason states, stretching his legs.

"You can't start out with nothing at all and have a finished boat after five days," Sandy says. "That's impossible."

"Then what the hell are we talking about?"

"We're talking about what we're going to do. And this is it: we'll assemble the double bottoms. Other skids will do the decks and still others the bulkheads."

"This is getting better and better," Alibi scoffs. "We'll take three weeks for the five-day boat, and the whole yard will help us."

"Yeah, that's about it," Sandy admits. "It's an experiment, like everything around here. You have to look

204

at it this way—we've got twelve shipways here in our yard. We can only build twelve boats at a time, right?"

"Right."

"Okay. Roughly 250,000 pieces go into each boat. When you take each piece to the hull separately, as they did in the last war, it takes more than a year to build the boat. That means you have to wait one full year until your next keel can be laid, because your valuable space on the shipway is blocked. On the other hand, we have lots of space in the yard, miles of it. So why not preassemble units for the boat all over the yard and take them to the hull in one big piece? Then the ship will be on the shipways only as long as it takes to weld those units together. The fewer units we need, the bigger the preassembled hunks are, the faster the ships can be finished. When we tried that method first, a year ago, the cranes lifted about 1,000 units up to the hull, instead of 250,000 separate pieces, and it took us about a hundred days to build the boat. We cut the number of units to 500, to 300, and now to 200. The time to weld them together into a ship went down to sixty, forty, and now to thirty days. But we want to come down to an average of fifteen days, and that means new ideas, new organization, new planning. Our record boat will show what can be done. If it's successful it will revolutionize shipbuilding. Lots of experts say it can't be done. It's our job to show them they're wrong."

"Gosh!" says Gosh. "Old Nick, goshen gosh!"

That's how we all feel, only we express it in a torrent of words.

"We'll try to make it with less than 100 units," Sandy explains, and some will weigh more than 100 tons. We'll have four Whirley cranes instead of two, and they'll be fed with units from all over the yard. Our assembly will be the focal point. We'll be in charge."

The rest of our lunch tastes better. Shipbuilding is an adventure again. "If this keeps up," Sparkie says, "we'll preassemble two halves of a ship and weld them together

205

in twelve hours. I wonder what Noah would say if he could see us building ships?'' She winks at Bruce.

"He'd become a hull foreman and send his menagerie to welding school." Alibi decides.

"By the way," Sandy says, "I have to ask you for a sacrifice."

"Do we work three shifts instead of one?" asks Pee-Wee.

"You almost got it," Sandy nods. "The big boys in the office picked the best three assembly gangs to work on Way Five for the wonderboat. One from each shift. The most important shift will be the day shift, and they want the best crew to work on it. It so happens that our gang has been chosen to be the best. So we are asked, beginning next week, to work days, just until the launching. Is that okay?"

"Sure is," says Jason proudly, and he expresses the feeling for all of us. And so, next Monday, we get up with the roosters, and know again what it feels to have an evening for ourselves. But, on the whole, we miss swing shift, the spectacular sunsets behind Mount Tamalpais, the cooling evening breezes after a hot day, the lighting up of the San Francisco Bay to match our welders and burners. But there is too much work to do to wonder and compare. The work is the same, only more so.

The first sign of things to come is the appearance of little Chinese Tiny, our long lost son. We old-timers give him an enthusiastic welcome. Chuck tells the newcomers how Tiny saved a launching single-handedly and got his picture into the papers together with the President.

"Hey, sonny," Alibi shouts, "let's dig in once more and get some footage!"

Tiny cracks his happiest grin. "No wonderboat without wonder welder." He taps a forefinger on his chest in case someone has missed the point. Then he spots Dimples and gargles something in Chinese, and she, with

206

some effort, gargles something back, then Tiny gargles lots more and shakes her hands excitedly.

"What's the big news?" Alibi asks.

"It's wonderful," Tiny beams. "You don't know? Miss Dimples' boy friend comes home Christmas and he know everything how we fixed up Mr. Magi and everything is all right so they can get married."

Dimples gets red and dimpled all over her face and turns away quickly. Tiny is introduced to Cherie, Cookie, Sparkie and the other girls who are new in our crew. Tiny isn't a bit shy and his English isn't gluey anymore. He is the world's best welder, and he knows it.

"Look at the crane coming!" he shouts, pointing toward the plate shop. "He go by himself."

We look in that direction. A huge Whirley is coming toward us, laying its own rails. It travels on a piece of rail about a hundred feet long, holding in its grip another piece of rail, the ties fixed to it, looking like a huge ladder. The Whirley stoops, lays rail number two down where number one ends. Two shipwrights connect the two pieces and the Whirley travels on to piece number two. Before it reaches the end, it turns around, picks up piece number one from behind and puts it down in front. And so the gigantic crane travels, on its own two pieces of rail, wherever it wants to go. And it wants to go to our assembly, to help build the wonderboat.

"The giraffe is loose!" yells Alibi. "With Tiny in our crew again and Whirleys wandering about the yard, it's a cinch we'll build that boat in a jiffy!"

The crane reaches our assembly and connects with the permanent rail which runs alongside the assembly and the hull up to the edge of the water.

"What now?" Cookie asks, watching the newly arrived crane stooping down and getting hold of our shed that has protected our assembly from sun and rain. One yank—our shed dangles in midair, and there we are, roofless.

"Upsy-daisy!" cries Sparkie. "Never a dull moment."

"Yep, we're really going to build giant units," Chuck says proudly. "The shed would only be in the way."

The units we build are our old friends, the inner bottoms. They are assembled in three parts, joined together later on the shipways. But today we build them in one super unit. Sandy, even more excited than usual, spans a string across the whole length of the assembly and is very particular about every sixteenth of an inch. He hums to himself as always when he works on a problem. Engineers buzz around, measuring and looking through their transits. A couple of shipfitter bosses stick their heads together, watching Sandy. "He's a whiz in figuring things out," they say. "He used to be an architect. These boats are built more like a house than a ship anyway."

The more of mystery, the more we like it. Cherie hops over to us, fleeing from a heavy steel plate swinging in midair over Sandy's carefully placed line. "Do you realize," she cries, "that we are witnessing something sensational? A keel of a ship is laid on the assembly!"

"D'you mean to say," asks Cookie, "we are going to launch that boat from the ground?"

"Poppycock!" says Chuck. "That's just a mock keel, to line up the units the same way they'll be lined up later on the real keel."

The assembly begins to look like a real ship, or rather like the bottom slice of one. The five units, each about sixty feet long, are fitted so closely to one another that they are practically one piece. We lustily climb "aboard" and down, all day long, and only after shift do we feel how tired we are.

"Hey you up there, what's the big idea?" It's Pop, our time-checker, who comes to the assembly every day to check our attendance. He's a fat old man with a stiff leg. He hobbles around in the craneway, helplessly. "How do I get up there?"

"There'll be ladders tomorrow, Pop," Sandy promises. "Then you can check us again. Today you have to take our say-so."

By that time our assembly looks like a scrap heap. The crane brings valves, brackets, parts of machinery, bundles of winding pipes. "Like a forkful of spaghetti," says Pee-Wee. All that gets dropped "just about where it'll go." Then special crews come along and put everything in place. They breeze in, do their job, breeze out again.

"Look what our assembly's come to," Okie Red sighs, moving his machine through a mess of lines. "So many people are working here you couldn't stir them with a stick!"

Alibi's crew has multiplied. It's Dimples' idea to paint one stripe on a helper's sleeve, two stripes for a trainee, and three stripes for a journeyman. Tiny wears his sergeant stripes with pride. He couldn't get them in the army because of his size, but in the army of production he made the grade.

Our gang is now far outnumbered by special crews. In fact, you have a hard time finding anyone. You see a pair of feet sticking out of a manhole, while the rest of the guy is underneath the plate you're standing on. Suddenly you jump because your feet are burning, and out of the manhole comes Tiny with a smoking stinger. Or you're balancing over a tangle of welders' and burners' lines which try to ensnare your foot like hungry snakes. You have to quickly grab a girder, and chances are it's red-hot. Or you see a piece of pipe where you've never seen one before, and you look into it to see where it comes from and get a fountain of sparks right into your face, and there's Happy with his torch burning out the other end.

Then there are the big shots, in shiny silver hats and clean shirts, squinting and checking on things. They bend down to a stiffener, take out a two-foot ruler, and measure. Then, with an air of importance, they chalk a cross on the stiff. It's been approved. Half an hour later the spot is swamped with guys who drill holes, counter-sink, bolt and screw, and your bet is as good as mine what it's all about.

"I thought I knew something about shipfitting," Pee-Wee groans, "but now I see I don't know a thing."

Sandy seems to be the only one who knows. He moves swiftly, spots mistakes faster than you can make them, checks, supervises, and hums little tunes to himself.

He approaches us like a rocket. "Hey, Chuck, will you and Joe get those little platforms on that bulkhead?" Sandy asks, unfolding a blueprint. "There are two ladders on both sides of the shaft tunnel, see, and here is a platform so people can get across. Storage hasn't sent it out yet, so you have to burn it from scrap. You'll find the measurements right on that detail."

"But where does it say how it rests on the shaft tunnel?" Chuck asks. "The tunnel is curved."

Sandy looks the print over. "Doesn't seem to give any information on that," he finally says. "Go up on a finished ship and see how it works."

So we climb up the boat on Ten which is just about ready for the launching, but there's no platform on that bulkhead. "We have nothing to do with it," a foreman in the belly of the boat tells us. "That's done at the outfitting dock."

We go out to the outfitting dock and have a look at a boat which is about to be delivered. No platform. "That's done by a special crew," a shipfitter boss tells us. "I don't know anything about it."

"We can't spend all day on that silly platform," Chuck decides. "We just have to figure it out ourselves."

Back on our assembly Chuck and Sandy put their heads together to find out how they can shape the platform so it'll rest on the tunnel. Happy is ready to cut with his torch, but every time they decide how to go about it, they hit a snag. Sandy makes little sketches, humming to himself, while Gosh stands by, goggle-eyed as usual.

"Why don't ya make yerself a template?" he suddenly pops out. Everybody looks at him because no one has ever gotten anything out of him but a "Gosh" in one form or another. "Just take a piece of cardboard, hold it against the end of the tunnel . . ." and he goes on explaining how he would do the job.

"Holy smokes, that's right," Sandy admits, more goggle-eyed now than Gosh. Why didn't I think of that? It's so simple. Good for you, Gosh!"

"That's the way we did it up in Maine," says Gosh.

"You worked in a shipyard before?"

"Sure," says Gosh, "for thirty-five years."

"For heaven's sake, man, then you know more about ships than all of us put together. Why haven't you ever told us?"

"Nobody asked me," says Gosh. "And I never knew what you were doing here. I still don't know how you get them ships done."

"No wonder he was speechless," Pee-Wee giggles at lunch break, "seeing us housewives build those ships twenty times as fast as he used to with his crackerjack shipbuilders. What else could he say but 'gosh'?"

"Our yard is really something to say 'gosh' about," Sandy admits. "Especially this record boat. Everything is done in prefabrication. I wonder if we'll ever be able to build a house that way. Some architect friends I went to school with think it's impossible. But that's what the old-time shipbuilders said too."

"You know what it would mean to build a house like building Hull 440?" Sandy says thoughtfully. "It would mean building the dining room, kitchen and bathroom in one piece, the bedrooms and the parlor in another. You put in the piping and wiring, hang up the curtains, cover the floor with hardwood and a carpet, build in the furniture, paint and varnish the doors, paper the walls, hang pictures on them, place the refrigerator and the stove in your kitchen and the telephone next to your bed. Then you load the whole piece on a trailer and take it a mile downtown where the foundation of your house was laid.

You drop it in place, join it with the other pieces preassembled somewhere else, put on a ready-made roof with a chimney on it, and next day you can move in."

"We could build towns that way," Cherie warms up to the idea. "Europe will be a shambles and they'll want to build it up in a hurry. We could preassemble the houses right here and ship them over. Why, we could build Rome in one day!"

More and more the whole yard swings into the spirit of the "wonderboat." Everywhere are units, preassembled and just waiting to be taken aboard. All of these units are fitted out in every detail, have their final coat of paint and big signs warning FOR HULL 440 - DON'T TOUCH or RED HOT, HULL 440. The number 440 is all over the place. Cookie would have lots to look at if she took time off to go sightseeing. But she doesn't even think of it. We all work as hard as the day we thought Pink was killed. Only this time there is a lot more of the old pepper in our work. That ship is our baby and we don't even know her name. She is still just a number to us.

Sparkie is the one who finds out her name. It's no military secret, it's painted right on the forepeak where the name of the ship always is painted. Only the forepeak of our wonderboat is still half a mile away at the peak assembly, near the East Gate. There it sits, resting on the ground like a hedgehog, fitted out with everything down to the alarm for the gunners, waiting for the day when it'll become the bow of a boat. It is painted gray and in big white letters it says: *Robert E. Peary.*

"That's the pay-off," Sparkie squeaks, "the name in place, but the keel not yet laid!"

"We sure build everything backwards," Cookie says. "Laying the keel is the last thing we're doing."

The big day is drawing closer. The old ship on our Way is finished and the scaffolds around it are chalked up with graffiti like FIVE-DAY BOAT NEXT! or BRING ON THE WONDERBOAT. On our assembly the bulkheads are fitted to the decks, and if a deck has a buckle, the bulkhead is burned to fit that buckle so there won't be any delay "when the race starts." That day we're having lunch thirty feet high on a staging on top of a main bulkhead. Not that it is comfortable up there, but you simply can't eat lunch on an ordinary beam if you are building a wonderboat and everything is bigger, higher, faster. So we climb up the bulkhead for lunch. Way down is our boat. Machinery, valves, pipes, brackets—the open belly of the boat. Stored in the craneway are pieces of shell and slices of decks, waiting to cover that belly.

Tiny is tickled to pieces with the red tags we're wearing in addition to our badges. Only guys with those tags are allowed on our assembly. "Only the best workers get tags," he says. "Friend in the city wants to buy my tag. Give me two dollars. But not me. Not sell. Want to keep it, show to friends."

"Yes," says Pee-Wee, "this'll be something to remember. Never in my life will I forget the way I followed Sandy up a bulkhead, down a manhole, across a scaffold, through a shaft tunnel. It's been a challenge, but it's been fun."

"You know you're living," says Lovella. "It's exciting, every minute of it."

"Well, tonight the real thing begins," Chuck adds thoughtfully, "and in five days the whole show's over."

"I won't make it," says Alibi. "I have a date with Uncle Sam on Thursday."

"Can't you be here for the launching?" Dimples asks. "You still get a couple of weeks after induction to get your things in order."

"I'm having the two weeks right now," Alibi grins. "What else do I have to get in order but that record boat?"

"Still, I hope you can make the launching," Sparkie says. "It's our family affair. Too bad Pink can't be here.

But Pipsqueak will make it. He's trying for a furlough. He didn't build that boat, but he is one of us."

"Sure," says Cherie, "how can we launch a crazy boat without Pipsqueak? It wouldn't be right."

"It'll be quite a celebration," says Pee-Wee. "You know Bruce wrote a launching song?"

"No," cries Cookie. "Did you really, Bruce?"

Bruce nods. "Tried to."

"I hope it isn't as cockeyed as the brackets you put in," Jason grumbles. But nobody pays much attention to him. Cookie is all hopped up like in the good old days. "Who's going to play it?" she wants to know. "Couldn't we sing it ourselves?"

"Say, that's not a bad idea," Chuck says. "What do you say, Bruce?"

"Singing, me?" a question mark from Jason.

"I think it's a great idea." Bruce's face brightens up. "It's just what a song like that needs. How about it, gang?"

There's cheering from all sides. "Sure we'll sing it," shouts Cookie. "It's our boat, isn't it?"

"All right," says Okie Red, "we're all set for the launching of the *Robert E. Peary.* All we have to do is lay her keel."

Next morning, the H-for-Holiday feeling is here again. This is the day! Now, let's go, fellows, and show what we can do! Up in Oregon they don't believe that we can beat their ten-day boat, but we know, every one of us, that we can.

It's dark and cold and everything is wrapped in a wet fog. The lights of the yard are striped with slanted streaks of fine raindrops. But we don't call it rain. It's just a typical San Francisco heavy morning fog. The steel is wet with dew, but we don't feel it. We're burning inside, and that makes us feel warm and dry. Where's our baby? Her keel was laid at 12:01 a.m., she's close to seven hours old. But when we see her we can't believe our eyes. She's no

214

baby anymore. She weighs more than 700 tons. The inner bottoms are in, the shell is on. Much of what we've built these last three weeks the cranes have taken to the hull in three hours. A big sign announces: RICHMOND NO. 2 PREFABRICATED SHIP. Two clocks are underneath. One is showing the days from the start, 0 to 5, the other the hours of the day, 0 to 24. The race against time is on!

Units are streaming from all over the yard to our assembly, and last-minute jobs have to be done. Sandy is up on the boat directing the battle. From time to time he sends us out on a mission and we feel like a crack battalion rushed to a spot where the going is toughest. At ten o'clock the drizzle turns into rain.

"Sunny California," Jason sighs, looking up at the gray sky. "Just a heavy fog, my foot!"

Pee-Wee is helping him with strongbacks. "We haven't had a drop of rain since March," she says, "but it *would* rain today!" She carries a roof of her own, made of cardboard, over her head. "The first rain of the rainy season."

"C'mon," Chuck shouts. "Get goin'! The schedule's slipping."

That's what everybody is worrying about. The schedule! The guys in England and the South Pacific are waiting. The Russians are waiting. The Chinese are waiting. The whole world is waiting for us to prove that it can be done. For if a ship can be built in five days, the battle of supply is won.

But the cranes have to be more careful, and if the cranes slow down, production slows down. We have to move fast to make up for lost time.

"My grandmother always told us how they cleared the forest to build our house," Alibi says, dragging dozens of lines off the place where a bulkhead is going to be put. "Now I know how she felt."

Four cranes move along holding up one of the super-units. Slowly, cautiously, they approach the hull, ringing

215

their warning bells without let-up, with the 100-ton unit dangling up there right between them. "Heads up!" the rigger hollers to us, and we shout it to one another. We step down into the craneway and let the unit pass. Then the wave of workers flows back to work. Safety crews are around, watching everything that might cause an accident.

So it goes, hour after hour, the rain comes down in a steady pour, and the cranes bring up one unit after another from the shell assembly, the prefab, the warehouse. They bring the boilers assembled in Los Angeles, the ventilators from Chicago, the compass from Boston, the anchor from New York City, the propeller from Eddystone, Pennsylvania, and the lifeboats from Kokomo, Indiana. When our shift comes to a close, the *Robert E. Peary* weighs 1500 tons, twelve times as much as a good daily average.

"Why, it's one-sixth of the boat," says Pee-Wee, taking off her soaked cardboard roof and shaking herself like a poodle. "A sixth of a boat in fifteen and a half hours! We'll make it!"

"Take it easy, now," Alibi cautions her. "The parts have to be welded together."

"Shu' we make it," Tiny says, pouring water off his hood. "We make wonderboat, all right."

"Wonderboat is right," Al, the leaderman of the temporary swing shift nods in amazement. "Can you beat that! Last night, when we went home there was nothing at all on that shipway. And now a sixth of the boat is finished. If that's not a miracle, I'd like to know what is."

The rain keeps coming down all afternoon. At night I hear it tap against the window every time I wake up. I cannot help but worry if we can for sure make it. Everything was figured out in advance but the weather. The weather can't be prefabricated yet. I feel pretty low staring into the darkness of the night, and then I wonder

216

how all those guys on graveyard feel who are going ahead with our record boat while the water pours down on them from the black mist above.

First thing I do when I wake up in the morning is listen. No tapping on the windowpanes! It's cold and foggy but the rain has stopped. Wahoo! We got a break! We have another chance! But by the time I get to the yard it has become obvious that this is not the regular kind of San Francisco morning fog. It is more the London type, as Miggs tells us. Everything is wrapped up in it. The hulls are just gray outlines you can guess rather than see. The lights on top of the cranes shine from high up like dim moons behind clouds. The humming and clattering and the ringing bells warn you from nowhere against dangers you can't see. Even the chippers' noise comes muffled and strange.

Nobody is in the mood to talk. "We have to make the best of it," Sandy says tersely. "We've got to fight the weather as well as time. We have to go ahead, and that's that."

The cranes move so slowly that you want to go and push them. You have to look twice before taking a step. Only the welders can work full speed, squatting on one spot, their hoods over their eyes, not caring whether the whole world is wrapped in mist or not. The hull crackles with melting welding rods. The fog around Hull 440 glows orange, red, and yellow like a beautiful sunrise.

Then, at noon, the fog suddenly clears up. The ships, cranes, waiting units show up like magic. The air is good and clear. Shipfitters, riggers and flangers swarm about busily like bugs after a rain. Sandy steps in to reorganize the battle. "We're five hours behind," he says. "We have to make up for it."

The rest of the day I only remember in fragments, like the preview of a movie: Cherie and Cookie high on a bulkhead fixing clips . . . a rigger saving precious minutes by swinging like Tarzan on a rope from assembly to hull . . . Jason carrying a 100-pound fan up a ladder twenty feet high . . . Bruce, limping with a broken toe and refusing to quit . . . and above all, Sandy here, Sandy there, Sandy all over the place.

When we leave at 3:30 Sandy stays on, and he's still there when we show up the next morning. That third day brings the masterpiece of prefabrication, the 190-ton deckhouse. It comes in four parts, cut straight through like a stage setting, in trailers with twenty-four mammoth tires. It has three floors and you see rooms and stairs, looking like a house with the front wall ripped off by a bomb but the interior untouched. The galley is so fully equipped you could go right in and cook a meal for the whole gang. The captain's room is complete up to the inkpot on the desk. There are officers' quarters, toilets and showers, and the wheelhouse with a confusing number of switchboards. All of that is picked up by the Whirleys and dropped pat onto the upper deck. Four lifts—the whole house is set up in an hour and twenty minutes. It's Sandy's dream of architecture come true.

Sandy doesn't think of going home that night either. The general doesn't leave the battle before victory is won. And victory is within reach. We've caught up with those five hours lost through rain and fog, and on the fourth day we are ahead of schedule.

"Well," says Alibi at the end of this day. "I have to leave the rest to you now. Take good care of the wonder-boat—and of the yard." He shakes hands with every one of us.

"My turn comes up in two weeks," says Chuck. "See you in Tokyo."

"Okay," says Alibi. "Good luck. Good luck to all of you." He turns swiftly and leaves the assembly.

"Did you see that?" asks Chuck.

"Well, in two weeks when you have to leave," says Pee-Wee, "you'll have tears in your eyes, too."

218

"Maybe I will," Chuck admits. "It's not so much the yard. It's the folks you work with."

"When I first came out here," Cookie remarks, "I thought you were a bunch of bums. But you sure have improved."

"Same here," Dimples nods. "It's a good lesson. If at first you don't like someone, don't give up. Take three steps aside and look again. There's always some angle from which he'll look worthwhile."

"Our gang's breaking up," Cherie says, "but we have something to remember. We didn't do so bad there," she points to the *Robert E. Peary*. "She still looks kind of unfinished. Think we'll make it?"

"No trouble," says Chuck. "I only wish Sandy would go home tonight. He's been on the job for three days and nights straight."

"I've tried to talk sense to him," says Pee-Wee, "but he insists on staying."

"We can't relax now," Jason warns. "There's still plenty of work ahead."

"Maybe we should stay too?" Pee-Wee ventures.

"If you want to be Superwoman," Jason jests, "go give me a hand moving that plate down the craneway." He points to a thirty-foot steel plate.

The wrinkle is on Pee-Wee's forehead again. "Get me two pipes, Joe," she says, "will you?"

"Want to blow at the plate?" Jason sneers.

Pee-Wee takes the pipes and slips them under the plate, one pipe on each end. Then she rolls the plate down the craneway, easy, like on wheels.

"I'll be busted!" Jason exclaims. "Archimedes did it again!"

Sandy comes by, his eyes deep in circles, glancing at his timetable. "We could cut down some time at the outfitting dock if we had an additional gun crew."

"What d'you want to shoot at?" Jason queries. "Sea gulls?"

Sandy smiles as only a very tired man can smile. "I mean a gang to install a gun, not to fire it."

"We'll do it," Chuck says. "Give us a blueprint and we'll do it."

"Sure," Pee-Wee pipes in. "We'll put in that gun for you."

"If you don't get a crane," Jason says, "Pee-Wee will roll it up the hull on a couple of pipes."

"You really would stay overnight?" Sandy asks.

"I'd love to put teeth in our wonderboat," says Cookie, "so it can take a bite off a Zero."

Tiny's button eyes light up. "I'll weld gun," he says, and he keeps repeating grimly, "I'll weld gun."

This is our part in the war. We couldn't have found a better job that night. The crane brings the gun, pointing straight toward the sky that goes yellow in the west. And in the west, there's Japan.

We put in that gun.

It's the shortest of all nights I have ever spent awake. Crackling with welders, sparkling with burners, droning with chippers, the wonderboat races toward completion. It's a night cold with frost and hot with gumption. At 3 a.m. we have a bit of night lunch. Okie Red makes some coffee in the burner shack for us before we start the second half of the night. When the sun comes back again, Hull 440 has become the *Robert E. Peary*. At noon she is ready to join her sisters on the seven seas.

After a hectic hundred hours, the spirit of work gives way to that of celebration. The decks are cleaned, hoses rolled up, welding machines taken off, scaffolding knocked down. A sign is fixed to the deckhouse saying: COMPLIMENTS OF MEN AT PREFAB PLANT. LOTS OF LUCK!

A string of flags is hoisted from stem to stern. A launching platform is set up, five times as big as any we ever had in our yard. A large board is hoisted to the bow of the ship announcing:

"Eight and a half hours ahead of schedule!" Sparkie shouts. "I feel like singing 'Happy birthday to you.'"

"Bruce's song will do just as well," says Cherie.

"Where will we stand when we sing it?"

"Right up there, next to the microphone," Chuck tells her.

"Gee, and look at us," says Lovella. "We ought to be dressed up for it."

"Overalls and hard hats are just the thing," Jason says. "We'll launch it the way we built it."

"This is really a workers' launching," Pee-Wee adds. "Bulgy's husband will offer the benediction. He's a minister working as a welder on the hulls."

The guests begin coming on, many of them in uniform. One of them sneaks up behind Sparkie and covers her eyes.

"Pipsqueak!" she shouts. "You made it!"

"Couldn't let you down on a day like this," he laughs. "I had to hitchhike in planes."

"How can you?"

"That's easy," Pipsqueak tells her. "Just tie your thumb to a kite." He shakes hands, swapping cracks. "Where's Sandy?"

Just then the loudspeaker calls Sandy's name three times in a row. "Very urgent," it says.

"What's wrong now?" Chuck frowns, looking around for Sandy. "For heaven's sake, I hope nothing went wrong."

221

"I fix it," Tiny assures us. "Just find out what it is."

"Here comes the Chief," Pipsqueak points to the shipfitter superintendent, "and with him always comes trouble."

The fitter boss seems worried, the way he looked when the bulkhead was burned upside down. "We just got a call," he says. "Sandy's wife was brought to the hospital this morning. It's a boy."

"Whoopee!" Cherie shouts. "His boat and his baby launched the same day!"

"For goodness sake, man," Chuck sighs with relief. "A baby's no reason to look so grim."

The boss doesn't cheer up a bit. "Don't you know that Sandy was taken to the hospital too?"

"Anything serious?" Bruce asks.

"He'll have to take it easy. They'll keep him in the hospital for a couple of weeks."

"Gee, that's tough on his wife," Pee-Wee says.

"That's what I'm thinking," the boss says. "Sandy and his wife both come from New York and they don't have a darn soul out here. All their folks are in the East. Sandy often told me how homesick his wife feels. He promised her they'd go back East after the war."

"And now she has the baby—and not even Sandy's with her," Cherie says.

"We'll look after her," Pee-Wee decides. "I'm going to see her right after work."

"I know how to knit a baby sweater," Cookie says. "I did one before."

"I'll stay with her when she comes home," volunteers Ma Hopkins. "I raised dozens of kids."

"If it comes to changing diapers," Jason grins, "I've got four weeks' experience."

"We'll adopt the baby as our godchild," Dimples says, "and if they haven't got a name yet for the baby, why not name it after its big twin brother!" And she points at the *Robert E. Peary.*

222

The fitter boss relaxes. "It sure takes a load off my mind the way you folks step in. I don't know too much about babies myself. Do what you can for Sandy. And maybe they really might want to name the child after the boat. I know Sandy would like it. But I better run along. She's about ready to go."

The crowd is studded with cops. Juanita is among them. Alibi, she tells us, left for camp this morning. We are led to the launching platform and have a good view over the yard. The Whirleys stand still, the assemblies are empty. Twenty thousand workers, the entire day and swing shifts, are flocking around the record boat. Photographer and newsreel reporters are ready to shoot, the microphones are set, the speaker leafs through his manuscript, the sponsor fidgets with her bouquet, the minister, Bulgy's husband, keeps clearing his throat, and from deep down below comes the hollow sound of the knocking out of the keel blocks.

Here we are, the gang on Assembly Way Five. Bruce in front, all set for his song; Cookie, Sparkie and Pip-squeak next to him, their safety valves popping; Tiny, pushing Dimples into the front row; Pee-Wee, her etched line between her sea-blue eyes; Jason, towering next to her, looking at the song in his hands sheepishly; Chuck, his eyes wandering over the crowd to spot Miggs; Lovella, patting her blonde hair and waving to friends; Okie Red, watching her proudly; Swede, trying to hide his shaking hand; Happy, humming a tune, swinging his head and tapping his foot; and Gosh, goggle-eyed, his whole person one big forceful 'Gosh.' Sandy, Alibi and Pink are missing, but in spirit they, too, are with us. The speaker steps in front of the mike. He praises the *Robert E. Peary* as a wonder in more than one respect. A wonder of team work, of free collaboration, a triumph of the democratic system.

Then our turn has come. Bruce's hand goes up and we start out, a unity of voices.

The flashlight is flashed,
And the bottle is smashed,
While the streamers fly high on the ship,
And the girl with the flowers
Gives her blessing—and ours,
And we know she's off on her trip.

There was a time when Jason thought he couldn't work together with girls. There was a time when Okie Red would rather have quit than handle the same machine with a black man. When Red was an 'Okie' and Tiny a 'Chink.' When Chuck would ruin a unit because he didn't get a raise. But we forgot our squabbles and joined forces for the wonderboat. And now we have joined in singing our song, a tune catchy and proud.

There she goes!
A boat a day
Down the Way,
There she goes.
    She'll sail the ocean
    To keep in motion
    The boys who hit our foes on the nose.

Hit them hard
While we play
Every day
Our part.
    For the guns that killed them
    Came on boats—WE built them,
    We, the gang of the Richmond yard!

A thousandfold cry joins us. "There she goes!" It is more than the routine phrase shouted at every launching. We are part of it, every one of us. The weld around the hatches is Tiny's. The platform across the shaft tunnel is

224

Chuck's. The gun on the forepeak is Jason's and Pee-Wee's. And so, while the *Robert E. Peary* glides down the Way, the red, white and blue streamer and broken bottle trailing behind her, something in every one of us shouts proudly, "There she goes—MY wonderboat!"

A stream of workers. An artery that feeds a heart, a heart that pumps a machine: America's War Production.

Wherever you go . . . the yards are present, twenty-four hours a day, seven days a week . . . in the lunch-pail and hard-hat parade of the workers, in the stream of share-the-car riders, and the gleam of lights on the night horizon. . . . they are people breaking up their homes and traveling all over the continent to get a job done that just has to be done.

S. AGENCY UPHOLDS WOMEN'S RIGHT TO SHIPYARD JOBS

'We're Proud of You . . . and You Will Go to Work'

Women seeking employment as welders and burners in Bay Region shipyards receive assurance the Government upholds them in their dispute with unions from William Hopkins, regional director of the War Manpower Commission (seated at left), and JA W assistant director (standing). "We're proud of you," Hopkins assured the women, "and I can definitely assure you that you don't have to worry."

C PLEDGES LP IN ROW

You'll Go to Work,' Director Promises

(Continued From Page 1)
and secretary, respectively, of San Francisco CIO Council.

nother union entered the work for women picture today when cials of Marinship announced they had been notified by the tfitters Union the yard will not permitted to hire women ship-

"You will go to work," promised men's Bryant, assistant regional rector of the War Manpower mmission, to a group of 14 women welders and burners who appeared before him to air their tale of the controversy this morning.

WMC Official Receives Protest
The group of women appeared before James V. Bryant, assistant regional WMC director at his request allowing yesterday's disclosure by The News that several hundred women trainees have been denied and are being denied union clearance for shipyard work.

"We're going to insist that women be employed in the shipyards," he said.

Regional Director William Hopkins spoke to the women's group briefly after its meeting with Bryant.

"We're proud of you," he said, "and I can definitely assure you that as jobs are concerned—you don't have to worry."

Thousands, probably millions of you, will soon be working as you want to work. You will work."

Mr. Bryant said, "Labor and management must co-operate in order to obtain the most efficient response of labor."

and union hiring halls, they said, on the grounds that facilities and conditions at the yards were not adequate.

But they told the ... contention that their training is incomplete, charging that they put in the training hours required while many who with as little as eight hours training are taken out of the classes and cleared by the ship...

"MISS VICTORY"
THE TYPICAL AMERICAN GIRL WAR WORKER

(A contest sponsored by the SAN FRANCISCO EXAMINER to find the more typical American girl war worker among the war industries in the Northern California area. The winner will receive a $1,000 War Bond and a trip to Chicago for the final selection of a 'NATIONAL MISS VICTORY').

APPLICATION BLANK

.... (name of company) .... makes the following nomination for "MISS VICTORY OF NORTHERN CALIFORNIA".

Name ....
Address ....
Type of work performed .... Age ....
Date when regular employment began .... Phone ....
Work attendance record ....
Special training for this work ....

Previous work experience ....

General recommendations from fellow employes ....

OUTSIDE PATRIOTIC ACTIVITIES (such as Red Cross, USO, AWVS, civilian defense, canteen work, etc.) ....

Sacrifices made in giving up normal life for war work ....

Single ....
If married, number of children .... Married ....
Husband's work ....

Women in the yards? . . .
Steel and skirts. The idea is too
big. Powder puffs and iron . . .
Can it work?

We want to come down to
an average of fifteen days,
and that means new ideas,
new organization, and
new planning.

*…o why not
reassemble
…nits for the boat
…ll over the yard
…nd take them
…o the hull in
…ne big piece?
…he fewer units
…e need, the bigger
…ne preassembled
…unks are, the
…ster the ships
…an be finished . . .*

*Our record
…oat will show
what can be
done. If it's
successful
. . . it will
revolutionize
shipbuilding.
…ots of experts
…ay it can't be
done. It's our
job to show
them they're
wrong.*

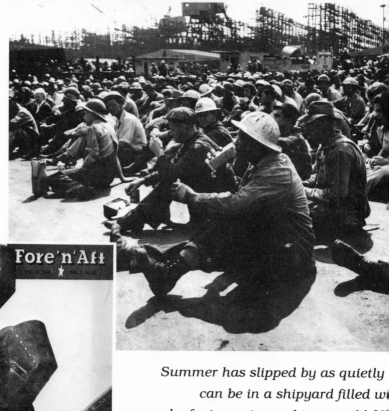

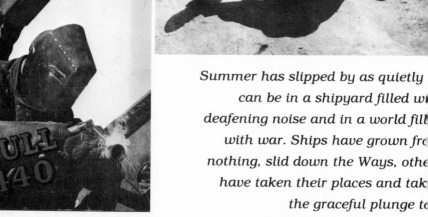

Fore 'n' Aft

HULL 440

Summer has slipped by as quietly
can be in a shipyard filled wi
deafening noise and in a world fill
with war. Ships have grown fr
nothing, slid down the Ways, othe
have taken their places and tak
the graceful plunge t

THROUGH THESE GATES
GO THE
WORLDS BEST
SHIPBUILDERS

THE PERMANENTE METALS CORPORATION
Richmond, California

TO THE MEN AND WOMEN OF SHIPYARD NUMBER TWO:

When the Benjamin Warner, Hull 2700, left our
on July 14, 1944, we finished our last ship. The James Otis, w
with the delivery of our first ship the James Otis, w
required 160 days to construct and a total of 486,0
from keel laying to delivery, while our last ship it
31 days and 295,000 manhours. I personally would li
employee for the wonderful job done in making this
in time, and also in establishing some of the reco
in Liberty Ship construction.

Yard Two achieved national recognition in
fully familiar. You all remember the well-a
Liberty Ship Program. You all remember the well-a
Robert E. Peary which was launched in four days s
days, setting an all-time speed record for ship c
the hull that has brought national recognition to Yar
many crafts in this yard into a first-class ship

One record of which we are very proud, w
fully familiar, is the fact that The Permanente
lower failure than any other shipyard building
to the Truman Committee Report) and this in its
the quality of production which we have achieve

I know that every employee of Yard Two
present Victory Ship Program, and I know that
of what he accomplished when building Liberty
to make every effort to keep our banner flying
Production. Our yard is so well known through
cannot afford to have our reputation tarnishe
of working with you, that we will come out or

Sincerel
J. C.

THE PERMANENTE METALS CORPORATION
Richmond, California

Dear Fellow Workers:

I would like to shake the hand of every man and woman in these
yards and in so doing pay my respects and appreciation for a job
well done. That gesture of warmth and friendship would be most
easily understood in a world full of words.

But since such is impossible, may I translate this desire into
heartfelt congratulations for your successful completion of one of
the world's greatest shipbuilding programs. In the construction and
delivery of our 519 Liberty Ships you men and women established many
enviable records and accomplished many feats of construction. Because
of that we can all look back with pride at your outstanding achievements
and look forward with confidence and anticipation to the new Victory
Program which lies ahead.

It goes without saying that your heart rides with every ship turned
over to the government; that you take personal satisfaction in providing
our fighting men with tangible evidence of your faithful support. I
know that you are as jealous of our reputation and performance as the
most eager soldier in the uniform of his country, and I feel certain that
you will spare neither hourn nor talents in building and delivering these
ships for actual service.

Your loyalty and attention to duty has made possible the building of
a great organization. You and your fellow workers have shown the world
what can be done, and we know we can count on you. All of America knows
you can be depended on, and it is this confidence coupled with your continued fine work that will make possible greater records of achievement
in the future and eventual post war security.

Sincerely,

C. P. Bedford.
General Manager

THE PERMANENTE METALS CORPORATION
Richmond, California
September 27, 1944

ellow Employée:

er the last of the "Bridge of Ships" was complete, the
NJAMIN WARNER" steamed out the channel to the sea. Just
518 sister ships before her

e was no ceremony, no fanfare as she left. Just a lone
her on the shore who recorded in color one of history's
nts.

arting moment was typical of the Yard Two spirit
t time for a backward look at a parting ship, because
busy building newer and bigger ships critically
Pacific War Zone.

We members of a great team. Together we have
y storics in our brief shipbuilding history but we
me through with flying colors, and the many flags
ur Yard Masthead have been a symbol of your prow-
through" when the going is tough.

ight months of our Liberty Ship program were the
st period ever experienced then or since by any
e topped the country's last great Liberty
We settled an eight months' record for
ram by the most difficult conversion ever faced by a
honors that will probably stand forever. Right
d — from Libertys to transports and we face
le ever — the launching of 16 and delivery of
oris from Yard Two by November 1, 1944

"come through"... again. Good luck!

Sincerely,
THE PERMANENTE METALS CORPORATION
(Shipbuilding Division)

T. A. Bedford, Jr.
Assistant General Manager

There she goes . . .
— our Wonderboat!

U.S. SHIPYARDS FOR
CONSTRUCTION OF LIBERTY SHIPS

Alabama Drydock and Shipbuilding	Mobile, Alabama
Bethlehem Fairfield Shipyard, Inc.	Baltimore, Maryland
California Shipbuilding Corp.	Los Angeles, California
Delta Shipbuilding Co.	New Orleans, Louisiana
J. A. Jones Construction Co.	Brunswick, Georgia
J. A. Jones Construction Co.	Panama City, Florida
Kaiser Company	Vancouver, Washington
Marinship Corporation	Sausalito, California
New England Shipbuilding	South Portland, Maine
South Portland Shipbuilding Corp.	South Portland, Maine
North Carolina Shipbuilding Co.	Wilmington, North Carolina
Oregon Shipbuilding Corporation	Portland, Oregon
Permanente Metals Corporation Yards No. 1 and 2	Richmond, California
St. John's River Shipbuilding Co.	Jacksonville, Florida
Southeastern Shipbuilding Corp.	Savannah, Georgia
Todd Houston Shipbuilding Corp.	Houston, Texas
Walsh-Kaiser Co.	Providence, Rhode Island

I wrote these stories in 1943 and 1944 with the exhilaration of a Columbus. I had discovered America! In a California shipyard I had found what I had hoped my new country would be: future-oriented, alive with activities and ideas, determined to do the impossible. The shipyard was all that, and more—a melting pot within the melting pot America, where it did not matter what you *were* but only what you *did*. I was grateful to the people who built ships faster than German submarines could sink them.

Here was life, and I had escaped death. I had come through the lowest point of my life, a refugee from the Hitler nightmare that had robbed me of country, family, friends, career. Here was a new beginning.

As a writer, I did have an advantage over most of my fellow refugees. Behind every situation, were it ever so distressing, was a story I could write. Whatever I went through, there were two of us: the victim who got kicked around, and the observer who would write about it.

The shipyard was a writer's dream. The workers came from all parts of the country, from all ways of life, and everybody had a story to tell. I was no reporter, I never "interviewed" anyone. I just listened. The stories trickled in, during lunch breaks, while we waited for new work orders, during work as a team. I did not take notes, just tucked away bits and pieces, and reassembled them. I was a spinner of tales based on real people talking about real life. This was the raw material of America as I saw it then. Today I can no longer tell with certainty what was "fact" and what was "fiction," but I do know that I did not have to invent much. I was inclined to tie up loose ends that life had left dangling, and to tack on happy endings where pain had remained. Perhaps I had the unconscious desire for order while my life was in chaos, and a longing for happiness while I felt sorrow. Most of my family, including my parents, had been taken to concentration camps; the whole world was threatened; and my own future—which now included a wife and a baby—was in question. I was a writer in a language that had become the language of the enemy.

To write these stories in the language of my adopted country was a slow and painful process. In my head I knew what I wanted to say, but what came out seemed so much paler than these colorful tales deserved to be. My wife, a native New Yorker, was untiring in helping me, and my foreman Johnny Volkoff, a talented and frustrated writer himself, went over my manuscript as it emerged, chapter by chapter, and lent me his ear for the nuances of the American vernacular I had not yet mastered. He even got some Kaiser executives interested in my manuscript, and there was talk about publishing it as part of a shipyard promotion. I want to thank Johnny, wherever he is. But by the time the book was completed, the war had ended, the yards had closed, and the manuscript wandered into my drawer.

I had almost forgotten the manuscript when I read, in the spring of 1980, that the last unaltered Liberty ship still in existence was being towed to Fisherman's Wharf in San Francisco, to be exhibited as a museum piece. I went to my drawer and reread my stories. They sounded remarkably fresh. The whole world of those shipyard days during World War II came alive. I wrote an article, based on the last chapter, for a local paper. The result was astonishing. People called who had worked in shipyards. Young people, too, expressed interest in a time which for them was history. And finally, Strawberry Hill Press wanted to publish the book.

Looking over the stories, after a lifetime of other interests, one question disturbs me: Where am I in these stories? Why did I choose as a narrator a pallid vacuum cleaner salesman from Nebraska who is the only character not based on a real person? In 1980, writing the story for the local paper, I assumed the role of the narrator as a matter of course.

With the wisdom of hindsight, I can now guess an answer. We go through life like persons driving a car with the headlights in back—we can only see where we have been, never where we are going. Yet, we drive courageously forward.

My guess is that I had a badly damaged self-esteem. I was a piece of flotsam, hardly a person. I was like an ant that had been buried by a sandstorm and was beginning to dig itself out. Dr. Joseph Fabry, the middle-class Viennese, had ceased to exist. What was left was Joe, the observer, the chronicler. So I observed the medley of Americans about me but never noticed myself. Perhaps I did not want to identify myself—a foreigner, a refugee, a nobody. This was not my story, it was the story of a working crew. My publisher advised against changing this perspective, and I think he is right.

Yet, a change was beginning to happen. The shipyard was my first foothold. It gave me the feeling that, again, I was Someone, I was Useful, I Belonged. This was the priceless gift the workers on Assembly Way Five presented me with, they put me back again into the flow of life.

Once you build a 10,000-ton ship in 4½ days you can't be all that bad. When you are accepted, in spite of your accent, you can't be a

236

complete outsider. I was a greenhorn, a stranger in a strange land, but we all were greenhorns in the land of shipbuilding as it had never been done before. I found the courage to write in English, and although the stories were not published then, they gave me the confidence to find work again as a writer and editor, first for the Voice of America, later for the University of California. In the early sixties, I became acquainted with the Viennese psychiatrist, Dr. Viktor Frankl, who had gone through three years of concentration camps and had come out with the conviction that life has meaning under all circumstances. I have become his student and his friend, and am devoting my "retirement" years to promoting his "logotherapy" (therapy through meaning) in a world which increasingly suffers from a sense of meaninglessness.

Looking back as a logotherapist upon my shipyard days, I see a lesson of general validity. We can endure hardships and overcome differences, if we have a task to fulfill. Six days a week of strenuous labor seemed like an exciting adventure because we clearly saw a purpose. The meaningless little jobs in which assembling a ship was broken down became meaningful because we saw the complete ship rise on its keel, and we knew that our bits of work had a place in the whole. And we knew how vital these ships were in getting our troops across and in keeping them well supplied with what they needed to win the war.

In the beginning there was friction within the crew. But by the time we built our wonderboat, the differences seemed minute. It was perhaps the first time in American labor history that women and minorities were accepted as equals, oldster and youngster were welcomed, and the emphasis was on what united rather than on what separated us.

Looking back on my shipyard days through these stories, I wonder how much I had romanticized the gang on Assembly Way Five. They may have been the result of my wishful thinking for a world in which people would be like those I had portrayed. But the 4½-day ship is a reality. The string of ships that rolled down the ways, each built within three weeks instead of a year, is a fact. The cohesiveness of the gang, made up of a most unlikely combination of people, is no dream.

As I look at the headlines of today's papers, the reports on the television news, and I see skepticism, mistrust and despair, I wonder: Am I still a hopeless romantic who sees something good come out of even such tragic events as war and Hitlerism? Logotherapy has taught me a valuable lesson. The meaning of a situation is sometimes hidden in conditions which, in themselves, are meaningless. The meaning of my shipyard days, with their background of tragedy, was to help me find new trust in people. Perhaps I did describe the people in the shipyard, not as they were, but as I hoped they would be—as I hoped people in general would be. When these doubts come I remember the words of the German poet Goethe who said: "If we take people as they are, we make them worse; if we take them as they ought to be, we help them become it."

I hope my grandchildren will live in a world full of people as they were during the shipyard days in World War II and as I described them in these stories.

Joseph Fabry
Berkeley, California
April, 1981

238